DARK FIRE: YESTERDAY'S TEARS

David M Benson

ISBN 13: 978-0-9885815-6-2
ISBN: 0988581566
Library of Congress Control Number: 2015905511
David Benson, Miami Beach, FL

FOR LAURA, AGAIN (AND AGAIN)

Prologue

THE ODDS SUGGESTED that there would be a day like this, but they did not give any hint of what the mortar shell would sound like as it screamed toward you or what would go through your mind as it did.

Their unit had been at it for over a year, since her twenty-third birthday, cleaning up after failed missions or taking on the ones that could not be allowed to fail. The kind of missions you could never talk about afterwards and that, if you died performing them your loved ones would never have the comfort of knowing how much evil you had prevented.

Most of Jane Garrison's days were not the sort that a former high school valedictorian, cheerleader and Fulbright scholar typically graduated to. But Garrison was not typical, and even compared with the average

American soldier who found herself there, her days in Afghanistan were anything but routine.

Hers was officially a non-combat unit, which would explain why women could be part of the team. But it did not explain the M4 carbine that was slung across her chest, or the Glock 19 holstered at her waist. Or, for that matter, their very specialized computer and communications gear or the MK47 grenade launchers carried by several of their number, let alone their DARPA-developed tools, most still in beta, tools that Defense Advanced Research Projects Agency leadership entrusted only to them.

The insignia on her faded camouflage uniform suggested she was a captain, but then again so did the uniforms of each of her comrades. And instead of their actual names, the name patch on each of their jackets simply read **Death,** written in the abjad farsi lettering understandable to most Afghanis.

Their very specialized orders were developed in a darkened room deep inside the Pentagon and delivered by encrypted e-mail, and the individual assignments were then fleshed out among themselves. No one could recall the last time they had had received a live briefing and an outsider would be challenged to figure out who among them was the team leader. And while Jane was not the youngest of them, she was not far from the oldest.

They rarely interacted with other units but when they did it was only to request support of one kind or another, requests that were never denied. They were likewise seldom asked to explain their role or at whose behest they were acting. When suppositions were made that they might somehow be aligned with Delta Force or the Rangers or Special Operations Command, perhaps even the CIA or a private defense contractor, they neither confirmed nor denied the possibility.

They were all savants of one kind or another and bringing them together had been a stroke of genius not often demonstrated by our military. They had received highly specialized training and their mission planning was unparalleled. The attention to detail was reflected in the team's unusually high success and low casualty rates. They kept to themselves when not on a mission and traveled to their target zones in two stealth helicopters, the noise suppression aspects of which were much more highly valued than their radar evading capabilities, and their arrival was always a surprise. They were all patriots, of course, but they were committed less to what they were doing than to the manner in which they were doing it.

But despite how strongly the odds might have been stacked in their favor, how thoroughly they parsed the details, how many satellite images they and their handlers in DC studied, there were an enormous number of variables to be accounted for in each of their missions. Every member of the team knew that variables were just that, and that for any given assignment on any given day there was always one or two that could not be anticipated and accounted for, aberrations of some sort.

Such was the case early one morning as Garrison and five of her colleagues crouched outside a small, once brightly colored stucco house with peeling paint and crumbling walls while six more of their brethren entered the house and quietly took the lives of two Taliban government ministers and their security guards. Garrison should have been piloting one of the helos but it had been too long in her view since she had gotten dirty and this seemed like as good a time as any to correct that. So she had traded places with another of their half dozen pilots.

Their first step on any foray was the deployment of highly sophisticated airborne jamming equipment, capable of shutting down all forms of cell and internet services in a target area, while they were still on their approach. But today their quarry had apparently managed to get off some sort of SOS and scant minutes after their arrival a barrage of mortar fire rained down on the dusty front yard where Garrison and her comrades watched and waited while the assassins were still inside.

It was the usual imprecise, scattershot affair, but the bad guys got lucky that morning. As Garrison raced to reach cover, a round exploded directly in front of her and wreaked outrageous violence on her young, fit body.

Please let me die quickly was the last thought that went through her mind as her brethren hauled what they thought was her corpse to the helo and the pain mercifully shut down the agony.

1

EDAN DUFF KNEW that calamity was a possibility, but there were so many things that could go wrong that it hardly paid to contemplate each of them individually. Nothing at all might happen, at least nothing bad, but it was not outside the realm of possibility that the world would end, or worse.

And all for a single nail.

Not even to remove it, actually, but just to hammer away at its awkwardly protruding point until that tiny dagger was flush with the edge of the bathroom door from which it had protruded since the house was built. It was something he could do right now. He already held the hammer in his hand.

Edan looked down at it now.

After the house had been completed the punch list had been long, though not so long as the size of the house and the complexity of its design might lead you to imagine. In any case, much blue tape had been expended, inch-square bit by inch-square bit, delineating the things that needed further attention. Somehow the protruding nail had eluded all the inspections. And Edan had not felt compelled to call the builder back to make it right, or felt the need to take care of it himself, until now.

Besides, Sim liked that nail. He had no idea why and she had never signaled a desire to explain, so he had accepted it and moved on.

But it was the perfect test, or at least *a* perfect test and he had considered a great many, since computer modeling was not an option. Hammering in the nail had the advantage of simplicity and its accomplishment would be immediately apparent upon his return. It also provided an excuse to bring along something inanimate other than his clothing, something that would not fit in his pocket, as his phone did. The hammer he now held in his hand. And because the task was so banal, should the world around him vanish as a result of the manner in which he proposed to complete it, there would at least be irony.

On the other hand, there might be no one around to appreciate it.

He had set up the laptop computer and recording equipment, in this case a high resolution camera mounted on the laptop, the previous afternoon. The computer sat open on the marble counter, next to the sink, positioned so that an image of the edge of the door, the errant nail in the center, filled the screen. Edan leaned over, made a few keystrokes, ending the recording session, named the file, saved it, and started a new recording session. Once he had checked that everything was again functioning as it should, he stood upright and took a deep breath.

"All right then," he said, as he turned his back on the Southern California sunlight that cascaded through the wall of glass bricks that formed one side of the bathroom and marched out.

The walk from master bathroom threshold to laboratory door consumed three full minutes and Edan willed himself to think only of pointless trivia during the journey. It seemed senseless to expend more energy thinking about the potential ramifications now, so close to the brink. The aggregate of thought he had already expended on the possible fallout from the test had not brought him any closer to something resembling an answer. There was no good reason to think that any more would do so now.

Edan's house was built into a hillside above the Pacific, not far from Monarch Beach, one side facing the pounding ocean and the other side hard against the alluvial matter and heavier sub-soils of the excavated slope. It was through a narrow tunnel bored deep into the hill that he now strode, and as he did the only sounds were the occasional screeches of his rubber soles against polished linoleum. Fluorescent lighting blinked on in segments as he moved through the long, windowless white hallway toward his goal, which was a wide, gray steel door at the very end. To the right of the door was a keypad and there was a final screech as he stopped before it. He entered a five-digit code, then pressed his left index finger against a biometric finger-print reader and leaned in to bring his left eye close to an iris scanner. After a moment he backed slightly away and entered yet another five-digit code into the keypad. The sound of bolts unlocking echoed down the hallway and Edan pushed the heavy door open and entered his lab.

More lights blinked on. The facility was impres-sive by almost any standard, tantamount to something you might find in a major corporation's R&D facilities. In fact, it was an only slightly scaled down version of the facility that Edan's company had on its corporate campus. But it was really not overly surprising given the wealth and accomplishments of its owner. And it was not merely the size of the lab that impressed. Equally, it was the amount and quality of very specialized equip-ment that it contained.

The device sat on the floor to the right of the entry door and not far inside it. That was by design, as it would ultimately have to leave the lab. Edan walked up to it and undid the Velcro fasteners that secured a soft, quilted cotton cover that hid the device from nonexistent prying eyes.

Covered, it could have been a large piece of furniture waiting to be carried away by moving men. Uncovered, it resembled an overgrown glass building block more than anything else. An extremely clean glass block that was actually difficult to see from certain angles. If you walked right up to it and stared for long enough you could just make out the slender tubes that suffused the glass. These ran vertically around the entire periphery of the device and continued horizontally across its top. At its bottom they appeared to vanish into the block's floor, a translucent slab that gave off a soft pink glow. The underside, out of sight, contained an array of balls and rollers not unlike the cargo handling decks that allow pallets and containers to be easily loaded into and moved around inside the belly of commercial aircraft. Hydraulically actuated titanium rods hidden in the corners of the device allowed it to lift itself as much as three feet off the ground. And clear as the glass appeared, it was somehow impossible to see what, if anything, was inside the block.

The device was made primarily of a substance that could accurately be called *glass* in the sense that it was hard, brittle, non-crystalline and transparent, as the dictionary said it should be. But there the similarities with other types of glass ended. The block stood six feet high, two inches taller than Edan. Its long sides measured six feet, as well, while its shorter ends were four feet wide. There was no perceptible way to tell what it was for or what made it work, if indeed it could be said to work in any manner.

Roughly half of the thick floor was actually an enormously advanced computer, the most particularized ever built, using technologies of Edan's conception, some of which would slowly make their way into the vanguard and then the mainstream in the years to come, much as other things of his imagining had. The remainder of the floor housed several hundred lithium polymer battery packs and a dozen more lithium metal-to-air batteries to which the makers of electric automobiles and other consumer products might eventually gain access. The glass floor itself was suffused with tens of thousands of nearly microscopic holes through which the computer and batteries could breathe.

Reality suggested that the twenty-odd square feet of floor space inside the device was barely large enough for six people to comfortably occupy, standing upright. But reality, a fleeting concept at best to Edan, who had been described at various times as something of a cross between Stephen Hawking and Steve Jobs, had little to do with the functionality of the glass cube.

He had already carried into it two dozen blow-up dolls and myriad Styrofoam and high-density foam cut-outs, along with suitcases and bunches of balloons and had not found it the least bit cramped. The interior space always appeared brightly lit and seemed to expand as more things, or presumably more people, entered, and thus far he had not discovered its capacity. And there was no sense of being trapped in a tight space, nor was there any other discomfort. Edan expected that if he was ever called upon to explain the phenomenon, the listener would make it through less than two minutes before deciding to forego the rest and simply suspend disbelief.

Getting inside required a comparable mindset. There was a narrow open slat that ran from floor to ceiling at one of the long ends of the cube that, if you got close enough to see it, appeared to be about eight inches wide. But when someone tried to walk through it he simply did and found himself standing inside the glass cube. Objects of any size and shape passed through just as easily. The first time he had entered the device, Edan turned sideways as he approached the slat, but he confirmed soon enough that presenting a narrower profile had no impact on the slat's function.

Once inside there was still no perceptible way to tell what the device was for or what made it work. There were no obvious buttons, dials or other controls anywhere inside, although a small, unlabeled circle was etched about five feet up one of the narrower vertical surfaces of its interior, not far from the entrance. When it was touched, a holographic QWERTY keyboard appeared on the surface nearby.

Computer modeling had been useful for certain things, though. It had shown the glass block to be as strong as if it was entirely solid, but its weight was considerably lower than you would expect, again for extremely technical reasons that would challenge even Edan's ability to explain them rationally. And while it had taken two years and the better part of a billion dollars to design and construct, its cost was essentially meaningless. It was arguably the most valuable man-made object ever built.

After a moment's hesitation, Edan, dressed in beige chinos and a dark blue golf shirt that had his company logo stitched into the left breast, his iPhone and wallet in his pockets and the hammer in his hand, stepped through the slat and into the device. He put the hammer down on the floor and reached out to touch the etched circle. The keyboard appeared, he entered a series of letters and numbers and the device came to life.

As a final thought about the possibility of calamity crossed his mind, Edan took a deep breath and pressed *Enter.*

2

"I THINK A more serious test is in order," Edan, standing at the bathroom sink, a towel cinched around his waist, shaving, said on the morning following the nail test.

Sim, already dressed, had crouched down next to the door frame. She was running her right index finger back and forth over the smooth spot from which the nail had formerly protruded and seemed not to hear him.

"Did you say something?" she asked after a moment's hesitation.

"Just that I think we need a more serious test," he repeated.

"I'm still trying to process *this* one," she said when she stood up a moment later. "Can I see the video again? Maybe that'll help."

Edan smiled.

"I kind of doubt it will," he said, "but sure, why not. After I shower, okay?"

"Fine, but make it quick."

The shower stall was large, lined with polished onyx and equipped with overhead and wall-mounted nozzles on two sides. On its outside perimeter, a wall of floor to ceiling windows allowed a panoramic view of the Pacific. But the slope of the hill ensured that no one on land could see in, making only those on boats having powerful binoculars or telescopes potential peeping Toms, at least at times when the sun's reflection did not impede their labors. There were those who kept that sort of eye on the house, some as employees of the owner, some not. But what might be seen through the shower glass was not their principal aim, nor Edan's principal concern, and they very likely would have put on a show for the watchers, he mused, if Sim had joined him and if Sim not been Sim.

Edan and a cadre of colleagues from a small but rapidly growing subsidiary of his company had been at the military hospital in Landstuhl, Germany, demonstrating their very special wares, when the plane carrying Captain Jane Garrison had arrived from Afghanistan. A practical demonstration of what the group claimed they could accomplish was hastily arranged. Captain Garrison had been unconscious for much of the time since sustaining her wounds and undergoing emergency field surgery, and when she briefly awoke and was told of the nature and extent of her injuries, she requested that she not be treated any further and be allowed to die. Such a request would have been problematic even in a civilian hospital, but the military was certainly not about to accede to wishes such as that.

New legs were the easy part. They rendered her an inch taller, a side effect of the paucity of samples the team had been able to bring along for the planned demonstration. They were much stronger than those they replaced, yet equally as shapely, and upped her shoe size, as well. The essentially permanent interface with what remained of Garrison's own thighs would, with time, be largely masked, thanks to the nature of the artificial skin used to sheath the legs and to the compounds used to enhance the healing of her own skin. Still-secret neural connection techniques, including sensors on the bottom of the feet, created a feedback loop almost akin to natural feeling, although somewhat more limited, and assured a short learning curve to master the new limbs.

Her abdomen and chest had been severely damaged, as well, and her left lung had been destroyed. An artificial lung, roughly the size of a soda can, was implanted to replace it. Her partially-injured right lung would recover and expand a bit in time and the artificial lung would assure her survival until then and provide additional capacity thereafter. One kidney had been damaged badly enough to have been removed, but living with only one would likely not be a problem. Although it was not crucial to her survival, implanting an artificial spleen completed the abdominal and thoracic surgeons' work.

Plastic surgeons then took over. Garrison's eyes had been uninjured and her face had mostly been spared the brutality inflicted on the rest of her body. But her features had seemed somehow altered afterwards. The doctors muttered something about the effects of the blast concussion on the underlying tissue and bone structure and left it at that, as did she. Her nose, however, required several procedures to restore both function and a normal appearance. Garrison thought the changes to her face were something of a blessing. People who knew her from before often failed to recognize her, at least at first. Breast implants were next and the grafting of a good deal of lab-grown artificial skin, as natural and functional than that used for her new legs, completed the doctors' work on her abdomen and chest.

Miraculously, her heart had been largely undamaged, although she refused to think of it as a miracle. Death would have qualified as one, though, and she rued the fact that the Taliban's mortar round had not struck her directly.

She tried to take care of that mistake as soon as she was allowed home on leave. Her Kel-Tec P-32 semi-automatic pistol had not been used for nearly a year, so she poured a glass of wine and cleaned it, sitting at the dining room table of her condominium in McLean, Virginia. The clip was full but she emptied it and put in fresh ammo, filling it with seven rounds of .32 ACP cartridges and slapping it back into the small gun. She pulled back the slide, took a last sip of wine, stood in the center of the living room and held the gun to her head and pulled the trigger.

The bullet entered an inch or so above and in front of her right ear, exiting at nearly the same point on the other side. The shock and pain caused her to immediately crumple to the floor but the shot had not killed her. It had, however, taken with it portions of her frontal and temporal lobes. She had dialed 9-1-1 herself and the looks on the EMTs' faces when they saw her and the gun had been priceless. At the hospital, a great deal of testing, along with an MRI, took place, but there was nothing the doctors could do for her but take steps to prevent infection and ensure that the external wounds healed as well and as quickly as possible.

The long-term effects were another matter. There were the occasional headaches and bouts of fatigue, as well as some memory loss, although it seemed to be the wrong memories that were lost. More important were an erosion of empathy and her sense of humor, and she had trouble processing certain things as quickly as before. But a much more serious impact of the brain trauma was that she was left with no sexual desire or ability to become aroused, and no sexual function.

None whatsoever.

Together with her man-made parts, it was why she had re-Christened herself Sim, for simulated girl.

And somehow Edan Duff had formed an attachment to her. At first she thought it might simply be the pride of seeing the things that had come out of his labs function so well, but later she realized there might be something more. He had visited her during her recovery from the gunshot wound and offered her a job as his head of security. He had left the details of the job sketchy but had made a convincing case for taking the opportunity for a fresh start on another coast, and it had been too much for her to pass up.

Her hair was still wet from her earlier shower and when Edan stepped out of his, he stood there for a moment watching as she used a brush and small electric dryer on her voluminous, auburn hair. As was often the case, she wore cut-off jean shorts and a racer back tee shirt that revealed parts of the tattoo that covered her entire back and much of her arms. Japanese in style and consisting mainly of slender black lines with small areas of bright color, mainly reds and oranges, here and there, the artwork was masterfully crafted and sufficiently momentous to justify the name Sim had given it, as well as having been named at all.

She called it *Dark Fire,* and while no actual flame was depicted it was a blazing portrayal of the experience of war and once viewed it was not easily forgotten. The fact that *Dark Fire* was also the translation from Gaelic of Edan Duff's name, albeit in reverse order, had not been lost on her.

"What are you looking at?" she shouted above the noise of the dryer, the hint of confusion on her face. "I know it can't be my nipples poking through the cotton fabric. Even you couldn't make a new set of those for me, apparently."

"You've shown me the tattooed-on ones, though, and they look pretty real," he said. "It looked like the guy did a great job."

"As long as you don't get too close," she said, moderating her voice as she turned off the dryer. "Anyway, that's why I let him do my back. So, tell me the truth. You wish we could fuck, don't you?"

It was not the first time she had asked.

"And you hate me for saving you, don't you?" was his reply, also not for the first time, as he picked up his towel and began drying himself.

As soon as the words came out, he knew what her reply would be.

"Ah," she said, running her hands down her shorts and racer-back tee shirt clad body, "but you didn't save *me*, you created *this*."

He shook his head slowly.

"You are so fucking gorgeous," he told her.

"I should do something about that," she said, glancing at his erect penis, "since I seem to elicit that reaction a lot from you and can't follow through."

"What do you mean, *do something* about it?" he asked.

She shrugged.

"I don't know, cut off all my hair, have my breast implants removed," she said.

He appeared to be giving it serious consideration.

"Of course," he finally said, "you could just go and get a Maori tattoo on your face. That would probably do it."

She almost laughed.

"Maybe all three," she said.

"I'd probably lust you anyway," he said, but his erection began to fade.

"We'll see," Sim said, pretending not to notice. "Or maybe you should just get dressed and we should talk about a more serious test for the device."

3

"OKAY, HERE ARE the new rules," Edan announced.

They were sitting outside on the huge terrace behind Edan's house that fronted the Pacific, straddling the corner of a glass-topped table that could seat eight or ten, set under a huge umbrella that blocked the mid-day sun. A wooden salad bowl filled to the rim with various greens, cucumbers, green and red peppers, several varieties of tomatoes and olives, as well as a few scallions, sat on the table top more or less between them. Sim used salad tongs to pile the mélange onto glass plates while Edan poured sparkling mineral water.

"I thought there was only one rule," Sim said. "Change nothing."

"That was before," he said. "Now that we know the world doesn't end if you do change something...."

"We can move on?" she suggested.

Edan nodded.

"Besides, just by going back, arguably you're changing something," he told her, "or at least that's one view of things."

"There's another view?" she asked.

He nodded again, this time more enthusiastically.

"Yeah, well, if you can actually go back in the first place," he said, "which it now appears that you can--"

"Too bad you can't get some kind of recognition for that, by the way," she interrupted to say. "I mean, it's like the biggest thing ever, right?"

"Maybe later," he said. "Anyway, since you can actually go back, arguably what you do when you go back has already happened anyway, at least on some level, so you're not really changing anything, although you've got to get into some serious quantum shit to show--"

"Spare me," she said. "So what are the rules now?"

"Now that I think of it," he replied, "it's entirely possible there actually aren't any rules."

"Hang on," she said, putting down the tongs and scooping up some kale and a cucumber between thumb and forefinger and popping them into her mouth, "You started off this discussion by saying there were new rules, now you're saying there are no rules. I'm the girl with the slightly defective brain, remember? I need things a little more straightforward than that."

"Sorry," he said. "When you get right down to it, it occurs to me that there's really no rulebook, you know. I mean, how could there be?"

Sim finished chewing and was about to pick up some more salad with her fingers, but Edan stared at her hand and she hastily picked up her fork instead.

"So, are you saying you could go back and do absolutely anything and it would still be okay?" she asked.

"I don't know about *anything*," he replied. "There should still be self-imposed limits, at least. So, for example, it would probably be a good idea not to go back to a time after the birth date of anyone traveling."

"Hang on," she said, holding a forkful of salad in midair, "you were already obviously born when you went back to fix that nail."

Edan smiled.

"Do as I say, not as I do," he said, spearing a forkful of salad of his own.

Sim's response was to give him the finger.

"You're going to have to do better than that," she said.

Out in the Pacific, a handful of sailboats plied the deep blue waters, halfway between horizon and shore. Closer in, no more than a hundred yards away, there were two power boats, nice ones, sitting at anchor, and Edan let his gaze hover on them for a moment. Sim sat with her back to the ocean, but she seemed to know what he was focused on.

"Don't worry," she said, taking advantage of Edan's distraction to pick up more salad with her fingers, "the sons of bitches can't hear a thing."

"I know that," he said, his eyes still locked on the two fifty-odd footers. "That's why you're still my chief of security. I was just thinking about what else they could do with all the taxpayers' money they're wasting here, not to mention what else I could do with what I have to spend on countermeasures."

"It's not just the government out there," she said. "It's also the nice folks at Teknodyne."

"True," Edan told her, "but my competitors should know better than waste their money that way. They know they're not going to get anything."

Sim shrugged.

"The price of success," she said.

Edan turned his attention back to his lunch.

"I kind of miss the drones," he told her between bites. "I haven't seen or heard one in at least a day or two."

Sim finished chewing her salad and drank some water before replying.

"Remember when I said I was going to put the laser gun through a battery of tests?" she asked.

"Yes, of course I remember," he replied, his eyes turning to her. "I thought that was still a work in process."

She smiled, an infrequent occurrence.

"Let's just say that I was able to move the process along very quickly and *very* successfully," she told him, "Now, getting back to the new rules or no rules or whatever...."

"Wait, so no more drones?" he asked.

"No more drones," she replied. "I don't think even the government wants to keep throwing away money that way."

Edan cleared his throat.

"Okay, back to the rules, then," he said. "Obviously, I've learned that the world doesn't end if you do go back during your lifetime, but I knew I wouldn't be around here at the time I visited. I don't know what would happen if you were to come in contact with yourself, but I've given it a lot of thought and I'm pretty sure I don't want to find out."

"Okay," Sim said, "so rule number one, change nothing, is toast, and the first new rule, if there are going to be any new rules, is kind of half-assed."

"Given the magnitude of the scientific and technological discovery we're talking about," Edan deadpanned, "the least you could do is use more impressive terminology to criticize things relating to it."

Her middle finger came out again before she picked up her fork and ate more salad.

"And rule number one isn't actually toast," he went on. "For all we know there is a kind of tipping point at which you might start to create problems."

"So, going back to fix a nail is okay but going further back and killing Hitler might be a problem, is that it?" she said.

"Something like that," he replied, "although, as I kind of alluded to a few minutes ago, if the universe has a mechanism for dealing with the nail scenario, maybe it could handle killing Hitler, too, who knows?"

Sim actually began to laugh.

"What?" he asked.

Her laugh progressed into a coughing fit and she had to drink some water before she could answer.

"Oh, nothing," she finally said. "It's just that if you don't know, who would? I mean, Jesus, Edan, you fucking invented the thing so you need to know this stuff, or at least sound like you do."

"First of all," he said, "that's why we're going to ramp it up, step by step. And second of all, there's no way of knowing that it's never been done before, assuming the universe does have a mechanism for dealing with it."

She stared at him, wide-eyed, for a moment, but when she finally spoke, what she said was not what he was expecting, which was pressing him further on the part about not knowing that it had not been done before.

"*We're* going to ramp it up?" she asked. "As in, *I'm* going to get inside that thing and go with you?"

"You are," was his reply. "I have a feeling I'm going to need some help from someone I can trust, not to mention a bodyguard."

"And are *we* going to break any rules?" Sim asked.

"Now that I think about it," Edan replied, "maybe we should refer to them as guidelines, rather than rules. I mean, as you so astutely pointed out, no one, including me, really knows how the hell any of this works. Besides, if they're only guidelines it might sound more like I knew what I was talking about."

"So, out with the rules, in with the guidelines," Sim said, holding up her glass.

"There is one rule, though," Edan said, "although *law* might actually be a better term, as in law of physics."

"Do tell."

"You can't go forward, into the future," he said. "I tried. It's a dead end, so to speak."

Sim took a forkful of salad and chewed thoughtfully.

"Hang on," she said when she finished chewing, "you went back to yesterday and came back, I mean forward, to today. That was going into the future, wasn't it?"

Edan smiled.

"Apparently," he replied, "you can go forward to a future that's already occurred, but not to one that hasn't, which might mean we're actually living at the leading edge of time, which is a pretty fucking amazing discovery when you think about it. What?"

"I'm supposed to be the one here with the impaired brain," Sim, who was staring at him as if he were an idiot, said, "and even I see the fallacy in what you just said."

"What?" Edan repeated.

Sim let out a breath.

"You said yourself," she told him, "that even if you don't affirmatively change something when you go back, you've probably changed something just by going back."

"And?"

"And that means there can't be any such thing as a future that's already occurred, that's what!" Sim told him. "By going back and pounding in that nail, you created a today in which you had gone back to the day you pounded it in, but when you left there wasn't a today in which the nail had been pounded in!"

For an instant Edan's facial expression seemed to be saying that he had not thought about it and that Sim had a good point, but it was fleeting and Sim had difficulty hiding her disappointment.

"I also said that the universe probably has a mechanism for dealing with the nail scenario, maybe even the killing of Hitler," he said, "so it apparently also has a mechanism for dealing with changes to the past that don't entirely eliminate the future from which those changes came. I'll be the first to admit that I can't fully explain it and probably never will be able to, but I'm pretty damn sure that the universe allowed me to come back after I pounded in the nail but that right now it would not allow me to travel to tomorrow."

Sim let out another sigh, lay down her fork, put her elbows on the table and rested her chin on her hands.

"What's wrong?" Edan asked.

"Nothing really," she replied. "It's just that what you said makes sense, at least to the extent any of this can, anyway."

"Yeah, there is that," he said.

4

ON SATURDAY AFTERNOON, two catering vans backed into the carport outside the auxiliary kitchen at Edan Duff's house and began discharging their cargos of shrimp, lobsters, Cornish game hens, smoked Coho salmon, white asparagus and other delights, along with cases of champagne and wine and carefully boxed cakes and pies.

Edan's personal chef supervised the unloading of the clunky-looking white Ford Transit vans and the temporary storage of the boxes and crates that came out of them, either in the pantry or walk-in refrigerator of the catering kitchen. While all this was going on, Edan and Sim went to Edan's lab and wheeled the device out to the temporarily deserted carport, loading it into the back of one of the vans. They worked quickly even though Edan was sure that his chef would linger over the placement of the items and then triple check the order sheets against what had been delivered.

After the device was secured in the back of the van Sim, her hair pulled back and a Giants ball cap pulled low to shade her face, slid into the driver's seat. Edan sat down on the cargo deck floor in the back of the van, his back against the closed rear doors. By the time the chef was satisfied that everything ordered was there and in its proper place, had signed the multipage receipt and sent the purveyor's weary staff on their way, Sim had adjusted the seat, made herself comfortable and changed the previous driver's choice of radio station.

When the four-man delivery crew re-appeared, they piled into the other van. With Edan in the back playing lookout, Sim followed them up the twisting drive and out onto the Pacific Coast Highway. At the intersection, the same black Chevy Suburban that had been there for months was parked on the shoulder at the side of the road, three passengers barely visible behind its tinted windows. The big SUV did not follow as the lead van turned left and Sim turned and remained close behind it, heading north.

"Do they really have to be so obvious?" she asked without turning around.

"Hey, it's the government," Edan replied. "Tek, on the other hand, won't be so obvious, so keep an eye out."

"I know how to do this, you know," came Sim's testy retort.

She stayed within a few car lengths of the other van for several minutes, but peeled away and turned right at Laguna Canyon Road while the other driver remained on the Coast Highway.

"No one on our tail that I can see," Edan told her a moment later.

"We're good," is all Sim said as she accelerated hard to make sure that was really the case.

"I'll keep an eye out just the same," Edan told her, working his way slowly toward the passenger compartment, around the device, but keeping a sightline past it, out the van's darkly tinted back windows.

"So, where are we going?" Sim asked.

"Just take this to the 5 and head north," Edan replied.

"Jesus, Edan, we're going to fucking LA?"

"We are."

"Okay," Sim said, letting out a breath, "what's in LA?"

"If you must know," he replied, "I've got two tickets to see the Doors at the Whisky A Go Go on the Strip tonight, although it won't really be tonight."

There was a moment of silence during which the only sound was the van's diesel engine and the whine of their tires on the pavement.

"The Doors as in Jim Morrison?" she asked incredulously.

"Yeah, him plus Ray Manzarek, John Densmore and Robby Krieger," Edan said. "I heard you've always wanted to see them, especially in their early days. And I wouldn't exactly mind seeing them myself."

"Holy shit," was all Sim could manage.

"Hey," he said, "as we do these tests, as far as I know there's no rule, sorry, guideline, against having a little fun."

5

RIP CARVER HAD gotten orders to join the small team monitoring Edan Duff's activities within twenty-four hours of the shoot-down of the second drone. That had been the previous night and he had been booked on the first flight out of Dulles Airport the following morning. His wife had not been pleased, especially since it had ruined their weekend plans, but then again she rarely was.

You're an analyst for heaven's sake, not a field agent, she had told him, her blond pageboy flipping around in lockstep with her annoyance. *Why couldn't it have been you who was hired away by that defense contractor instead of your stupid boss?* she had then asked. *There's no future at the CIA.*

Whether or not that was true, they did not need the money. Both of their families were rich and despite the fact that all four of their parents were still alive, enough of it had come to them already through ongoing family trusts that his income was not an issue. The truth was that even after eight years of marriage she did not like having to tell her friends and acquaintances only that he *worked for the government*, only hinting at which agency, rather than flaunting an impressive title at State or Treasury or Defense.

She had no idea what it was that he really did these days, although she was not far off the mark in a general sense by using the term analyst. And to the extent she had said he was not a field agent any more she was correct. He was the head of Special Activities in the Science & Technology division and expected to keep going up the organization chart from there. But he had let her rant and merely shrugged at her comments, then told her that he went where they told him to go and packed a suitcase.

I'll bet you can't even tell me where you're going! were her parting words.

His only rejoinder had been a wan smile and a weak hug before he went outside into a light, late season snowfall to meet the taxi. As the driver pulled away from the big house in Great Falls, Virginia, Rip realized that the cold and snow were not the only things he was happy to be getting away from for a while.

When his flight landed at LAX at noon local time he was met by a young FBI agent called March and transported to a windowless conference room at the bureau's Los Angeles field office. There the agenda consisted of a lengthy briefing on Edan Duff. March had taken charge of Carver's rolling suitcase at the airport and never surrendered it, leaving it in the corner of the conference room. He was pleasant enough but had little to say, either on the drive in from LAX or since. His reticence was made up for by the head of the field office, the special agent in charge in FBI parlance, a lean, gray-haired fellow named Roscoe Kemp who dressed in equally gray trousers and a blue blazer and looked like he had been around the block during a long career.

There was also a woman from the Defense Advanced Research Projects Agency, the government's high technology R&D center, named Mary McKinney. She was in her early thirties and sported a brunette pixie haircut and rectangular glasses in black plastic. Those ostensible shortcomings to female sexuality seemed to have the opposite effect on Carver. He thought they suited her angular face and graceful neck well and he found her most appealing. But it was her outsized breasts that Carver could barely keep his eyes off, and he could not help but wonder what a garment other than the shapeless green shift she wore might do to show off her wondrous form.

Carver shook hands and gave each of them a business card, and once they had read the name *Ripley*

Wallace Carver III spelled out across its center, explained that people generally called him Rip. After a modicum of small talk, Kemp opened the meeting by explaining that keeping tabs on the reclusive billionaire entrepreneur had been a purely domestic matter until the shoot down of the drones.

"The first one never made it out of his airspace but the second one flew halfway back and we were able to recover it," Mary McKinney, taking over, told Carver, "so we were able to determine that he was using a laser. Once we'd inspected the damage to the drone, calculated the distance it was from the source when it was hit and scrutinized the source itself from images the drone had been sending back, we realized that Duff had developed a sidearm-sized laser weapon which he'd deployed on his roof."

"And you guys are still years away from developing a weapon like that," Carver said.

The woman frowned.

"Everyone is," she said. "It's a power source problem. Conventional sources are still far too big and chemical and nuclear have their own problems."

Carver nodded.

"I've done the reading," he said. "Whatever your reasons were for watching him, I'm guessing the shoot down raised a concern that Duff's laser technology could potentially be obtained by a foreign power, either from Duff himself or, ah, by being appropriated, and that's why you called the CIA."

"Since we've worked with him extensively in the past and he hasn't gotten in touch with us about it," the shapely DARPA woman said, "or any other government agency...."

She shrugged and let her voice trail off.

"Maybe it's not ready for prime time," Carver suggested. "The word on Duff, right from the beginning, was that he wouldn't release a product until he's sure it works as advertised, starting from his college days, which weren't all that long ago of course."

"It sure as shit worked well enough on our drones," Kemp said sourly.

"It's possible it might not be ready yet," McKinney said, her eyes remaining on Carver, "but according to our experts the technology has tremendous value in its current state, even if the weapon isn't in its final form yet."

"Look, for all we know," Kemp, the FBI special agent in charge, cut in to say, "he only plans to develop and use it for target practice in his basement. On the other hand, he could already have a deal with the Iranians or the Chinese. Either way, we need to know where things are headed."

"But the drones were only shot down in the past few days," Carver said. "You were already keeping an eye on him before that."

"For the better part of a year," Kemp replied, and Carver turned in his chair to face the man. "Ever since March over there realized that one of Duff's companies was buying a lot of unusual chemical compounds and other materials and equipment."

Carver looked over at March but the young man's facial expression did not change.

"And now you think he's been using those things to build the laser weapon?" Carver asked.

The FBI man looked over at McKinney, who cleared her throat and answered Carver's question.

"Actually," she said, "my colleagues at DARPA are certain that only a portion of what he acquired would be useful, or necessary, in developing a laser gun. Now we're concerned about what he might be doing with the rest."

"So," Carver said, leaning back in his chair, "he's been buying, ah, suspicious, stuff, some of which could've been going into the laser weapon but the rest of which couldn't, which makes it look like he's also working on something else and the government is worried that this something else could be even worse, for want of a better term, than the laser weapon."

"That's pretty much the case," the woman said.

Carver thought about it for moment.

"Let's see," he said. "I don't do any work directly involving the Iranians, the Chinese or any other foreign power that spies on us or tries to get a hold of our weapons or other technology, and my field skills have gotten a little rusty...."

"Langley's assembling a team to deal with those aspects of it," McKinney said, "or so we're told."

"Okay, so why am I here, exactly?" Carver asked.

McKinney smiled.

"We hear you're very good with puzzles, Mr. Carver," she replied.

6

THE DRIVE FROM the Monarch Beach area to Los Angles took ninety minutes, with Sim able to better the speed limit on the freeway for only ten minutes of that time. For his part, Edan lounged for the last hour of the drive in the passenger seat of the van, having moved from his spotter's post in the back as soon as he was certain they were not being followed.

"They're going to think you're developing laser weapons that can be carried into combat, you know," Sim said, keeping her eyes on the road as she negotiated the merge onto Route 101.

Edan smiled.

"I hope so," he said.

They fell back into silence again as she exited the freeway at Sunset Boulevard, following Sunset west through Hollywood and on into West Hollywood. They coasted past the Whisky A Go Go and Sim, following Edan's directions, turned right onto Hilldale Avenue, made an almost immediate left onto Shoreham Drive and then a right onto Ozeta Terrace. There was a break in the tall hedges that lined the right side of the quiet residential street and Edan pointed at it. Sim steered the van into the gap and continued slowly up a short driveway.

There was a modest old house to their left and a garage straight ahead, both with A-frame roofs and wood siding in need of fresh paint. More tall hedges lined the other side of the driveway, hiding them from the house next door. Sim stopped the van a yard or so short of the garage. Edan hopped out and opened the rickety accordion doors and Sim drove the van inside, stopping inches from the back wall. As she shut off the engine and took off her ball cap, Edan hauled the garage doors closed.

"Whose house is this?" Sim asked as she climbed out of the van and stretched.

"Mine," Edan replied, "as of a week or so ago."

Sim struck a pose, hands on her hips, chin held high, and shook back her hair.

"Bastard!" she said. "You and your fucking tests and rules and guidelines! You already had the Doors tickets before we talked about any of that shit, and now this! You knew all along that we'd be going--"

Edan held out his palm.

"Let's just say I've always been a planner, and an optimist," he said. "And as I already told you, I know you've always wanted to see the Doors perform at the Whisky. And as far as the tests and the guidelines go, this really is a test, a pretty big one in fact, and the guidelines really are still a work in process. And I told you there were none against having fun. Now, even though you look great standing there like that, let's get the device out of the van."

Sim calmed down quickly but not before landing a closed fist punch to Edan's upper arm that was sure to yield a good sized black and blue mark the next day.

"Good thing these garages were designed to hold those big old Caddies and Buick station wagons," Edan said as Sim unlocked the rear doors of the van.

The tall van had just made it through the garage doors but there was more than enough space between the back of it and the doors to make unloading the device relatively easy. And thanks to its ball and roller underside and hydraulic lifting rods, which Edan controlled via a nearly invisible panel near the entrance slat, the device was out and resting on the cracked, concrete floor minutes later. Edan pushed it around to the side of the van, where there was room to park another car. Then he undid the Velcro fasteners that secured the soft, quilted cotton cover and removed it, folding it and tossing it into the back of the van.

"Holy shit, you can barely see it in here," Sim said softly.

Little of the fading daylight made it into the garage through a dirty skylight in the A-frame roof and small, equally dirty windows running along the upper portion of the back wall. She reached out and very slowly brought her fingertips up to the glass block, then began running her hand lovingly along the side of the device. As she did, Edan leaned into the back of the van and retrieved the black nylon duffle bag he had carried with him from the lab.

"Time to go and change," he said, hitching a thumb toward the side door of the garage and slinging the bag over his shoulder.

They went outside and followed a dirt path that led directly to the back door of the house. Edan used two keys to open it and Sim stood behind him in a small mud room while he entered a code in an alarm keypad on the wall, locking the door once the alarm's incessant beeping stopped. She followed Edan through a narrow kitchen with modern appliances and into a dining room that was empty but for an ornate, gold-tone chandelier that hung from the center of the ceiling, which they both had to duck under as they passed.

The dining room opened into a small foyer where the dining room, living room and a stairway came together. Edan took the stairs two at a time and he had already dropped the duffle bag on the hardwood floor of what appeared to be the master bedroom and was crouched down next to it when Sim entered the room.

"I'm not quite as fast as I used to be," she deadpanned when she joined him.

"What they lack in speed, they make up for with power," he said, smiling up at her and reaching out and tapping the leg of her jeans. "Besides, we're working on an upgrade. Now give me a hand with this stuff."

There was no furniture in the room but Edan had dropped the bag not far from the cushioned window seat of a broad bay window. Narrow blinds covered the window and Edan adjusted them so that the little bit of daylight that remained illuminated the window seat. Despite his request for assistance, he began to remove items of clothing and various artifacts from the bag himself, and Sim watched as he laid them out on the wide, flat surface.

There were two pairs of weathered bell bottomed jeans and Sim could not be sure whether the bells of Edan's or hers were wider. On top of hers, Edan placed an off white floral lace-accented blouse with gold trim. It had three quarter length sleeves, a rounded neckline, double darted bust and scalloped hemline. Edan tossed a simple black turtleneck sweater on top of his jeans.

"Can't have any tattoos showing," he said, "so it had to be long sleeves for both of us. Wait 'til you see the shoes."

His turned out to be a pair of black leather ankle length boots with zippers on the sides. Hers were brown leather low-heeled loafers with large metal buckles, making them look something like Pilgrim shoes.

"I think I may want to keep those," Sim said, picking one up to examine it more closely.

Edan next laid out two weathered black leather belts and two vintage watches on wide leather straps, along with a classic ID bracelet with silver links and a brown leather bracelet. Then he took a zip-lock freezer bag out of the duffle. It containing a wad of cash, which had fanned out in the bag and looked to Sim to be mainly ones and fives, a set of keys on a Ford key ring, a pictureless California driver's license and two cardboard Whisky A Go Go tickets. Last out was a vintage handbag and he handed it to Sim before feeling around the inside of the duffle to make sure that he had left nothing behind.

"Check it out," he told her, gesturing at the handbag.

It was burgundy leather, about a foot square and three or four inches thick, and had rigid brown leather handles.

"They called it a Bohemian Mexican hippie leather bag back in the day," Edan said, as he stood up and started emptying the contents from the zip-lock bag. "It's, like, brand new, cost a small fortune on eBay. Take a look inside."

Sim opened the bag. Inside was a red leather change purse that contained twenty-five dollars in folded bills, four fives and five ones, and some change, aa well as a California license in the name of Rachel Sims. There was also a hair brush, a small spray can of what the label said was hair spray and a tube of Coty lipstick in pale pink.

"I like the lipstick color, but hair spray?" Sim asked, turning to him.

"It's actually pepper spray," Edan replied. "I couldn't picture you without a weapon and I was afraid they might take Mack away at the door of the club."

Mack was the very slender three-inch switchblade that Sim always carried when a gun was not permitted or advisable, and sometimes carried even when it was.

"Very thoughtful," she said, absently applying some of the lipstick.

"I'm going to go and kind of muss up my hair, get the product out of it," he said, walking toward a doorway that Sim assumed led to a bathroom. "Why don't you just part yours in the middle and let it hang, like all the cool girls did back then. And it'll cover your gauged ears. People didn't exactly have inch-wide stretched holes in their earlobes back then."

"Hey, if my body was going to be modified," Sim said, "I wanted to do at least *some* of the modifying myself."

Edan smiled.

"I know," he said, "but we're probably screwed if anyone sees those."

"Or we'll be sent away to the nut house," Sim said, taking the hairbrush out of the hippie bag. She followed Edan into the small bathroom and stood behind him at the mirror, center parting and then brushing her hair.

"Hang on," she said, pausing. "So that's why you've been letting your hair grow. How long have you been planning this for?"

Edan smiled again and stared off into the distance for a moment.

"A very long time," he finally said, softly. "Good thing the dingus actually works."

"Dingus?" she asked.

"Ever see *The Maltese Falcon* with Humphrey Bogart?"

Sim shook her head.

"When we get back we should watch it," he said. "Now, let's get dressed and get out of here."

Back in the bedroom, he switched on the overhead light and they changed clothes. Then they put on their shoes, swapped theirs for the new old watches and bracelets and Edan stuffed the license, cash and tickets into the right front pocket of his jeans. They checked themselves in the mirror and then gave each other a final appraisal.

"Yup, I'd've gone bat shit crazy for you back then, too," Edan said.

"I like your hair better the way you usually wear it," is all Sim said, taking a last glance at the sandy hair flopping straight down toward his eyes and over his ears.

The area between the back door of the house and the side door of the garage was hidden from view by a fence and the hedges, but Edan took a look around as he stood at the open back doorway before motioning for Sim to go ahead. By the time he had set the alarm and locked the door, Sim was already inside the garage. He joined her, closed and locked the door behind him and left the keys to the house on the garage floor, next to the door.

"Ready?" he asked as they stepped over to the device and stood in front of the entry slat.

"Do I have a choice?" was her reply.

"There's always a choice," Edan said.

"Obviously, you've never been in the military," she said.

Edan smiled, stepped forward and disappeared into the device. Sim stood stock still for a moment, not quite believing what she had just seen, then hiked the handbag higher onto her shoulder and marched toward the barely discernable opening, determined not to turn sideways as she approached it. The next thing she knew she was standing inside the device next to Edan, who had begun making entries on the holographic keyboard.

"It's quiet in here," she said, looking around, "and lighter than I expected."

"Whatever you see, hear or feel," Edan said, making his last entry and turning to her, "assume it's normal."

"Says the man with extensive experience at this," Sim said.

Edan ignored the comment and hit *Enter*.

Almost immediately Sim had the sense of a slight ringing in her ears. A subtle vibration emanated from below her feet and steadily grew and the floor's already pinkish hue darkened. There were no sparks, no flashes of light, no puffs of smoke, no other noises, but the sides and roof of the device, never more apparent than dusky, polished glass, seemed to disappear entirely, although Sim could not see what lay beyond them. There were ever-changing snatches of lines, forms and color, but nothing you could lock your eyes onto.

She began to feel dizzy, too, as if she were standing on a tiny, rolling platform that required her to concentrate in order to keep her balance. All of this continued to build for some impossible to discern amount of time. But just as the dizziness, the ringing in her ears and the vibration were becoming unbearable, it all stopped, suddenly and totally. The buildup of sensations had been gradual, but there was nothing gradual about their cessation. Saying that it had been *abrupt* was understating things in an enormous way. The sounds and vibration and images that had been there were just not there anymore, and it was impossible to tell when they had actually gone away, in much the same way that it had been impossible to pinpoint exactly when on the video the errant nail had disappeared. And at the same moment or instant, if you could even call it that, the walls came back into view, giving off the same dusky cast as when they had first entered the device, and it was just as massively quiet as it had been then.

"Jesus," Sim said softly, "that was...*different*. Although I suppose there was no reason to think it would be like anything else."

She glanced at her watch. It was analog, of course, so it was difficult to tell with certainty, but it appeared that no time had passed since they had entered the device.

Edan made a dozen more keystrokes and then stepped past her and out through the slat. After a moment, Sim followed. They were still in the garage but something seemed different. The van was gone but it was more than that. It smelled different. And while, before, the garage had been empty of everything but the van and the device, now there were a handful of rakes and brooms leaning against the wall in one corner. It was dark outside but the light inside the garage seemed different, too, harsher. The paint looked fresher, as well, although it could have been an effect of the light.

"Welcome to Saturday, June 18, 1966," Edan said, "eight PM, if you want to set your watch."

"If you ignore the fact that the van's gone and those are here," Sim said, pointing at the rakes and brooms, "it seems a lot like 2015."

"For now, maybe, but that's all about to change," Edan told her, taking her hand.

"You know," Sim said, as they walked to the side door, "you never told me how you could be sure that this place would be empty in 1966."

Edan smiled.

"Come on, I'll tell you all about it on the way to the Whisky," he said, holding the side door open for her. "After all, the Door are the opening act and given everything we've done to get here, we don't want to be late for the show."

7

RIP CARVER'S MEETING at the FBI field office in Los Angeles dragged on through an early dinner of supermarket sushi and Pellegrino water, and by the time it finally concluded at about eight o'clock, he was exhausted. It was not until he was back in the same black Chevy Tahoe SUV in which March had met him at LAX that Carver was made aware that there was still a ninety-minute-plus drive to be tolerated before he could settle down for the night.

And another surprise awaited him at their destination, the town of Dana Point. Instead of navigating to the expected Hampton Inn or Courtyard hotel, March instead drove to the Dana West Marina, where he parked the Tahoe.

"I take it this isn't our final destination," Carver said, as March got his suitcase and began walking toward one of the piers.

"No, sir, it's not," March replied, "not yours, anyway."

Wordlessly, Carver followed him across the wooden docks to a small Boston Whaler yacht tender, where March handed Carver's suitcase off to another man. He was older than March and was dressed in tan cargo shorts and a black tee shirt. He stowed Carver's suitcase and helped him aboard the boat.

"It was a pleasure meeting you, sir," March said as he turned to leave.

"Don't let the get-up fool you," the tee-shirted man in the boat said as Carver's eyes lingered on the receding figure of the young agent. "I'm FBI Special Agent Joe Perricone."

Carver turned to Perricone and took his outstretched hand.

"Rip Carver," he said softly as he took a seat. "Mind if I ask where the hell it is we're going?"

Perricone smiled.

"A few miles up the road," he said, hitting the electric starter button for the small Mercury outboard, "to a somewhat bigger boat anchored just offshore from Edan Duff's compound, our command post. I don't suppose spooks get seasick, do they?"

Carver smiled.

"I'm only spook support," he replied, "but no, I don't."

Perricone reached out and untied the single line that held the small craft to the dock and set off at trolling speed through the enormous, crowded marina. Once they were past the breakwater, Perricone opened the throttle wide, which at first seemed to accomplish little more than substantially raising the noise level. But the wind had died out and the water was surprisingly flat and they managed to accelerate to what Carver guessed was perhaps fifteen knots. The evening air was cool and by the time they reached their destination twenty minutes later, Carver felt re-invigorated.

That destination turned out to be a fifty-two foot Princess yacht with the name *ELVIRA* painted in bright gold lettering on the transom and *San Diego, CA* in smaller letters beneath the name. Carver laughed when he caught sight of it.

"Let me guess," he said, as Perricone throttled back for their approach and the engine noise died down, "you guys picked this thing up in a drug bust from a dealer whose favorite film was *Scarface.*"

"And who had a thing for Michelle Pfeiffer," Perricone added as he maneuvered close to the imposing boat. "We still see stuff like that all the time, at least among some of the older guys we nab."

As the Whaler's starboard hull lightly touched the yacht's swim platform, another man came out through the sliding glass doors from what Carver imagined was *ELVIRA's* salon and walked across the teak decking to take the line from Perricone. Carver grabbed the man's outstretched hand and, once he had his footing on the platform, reached back down into the Whaler for his suitcase.

"Jeez, when we heard there was a spook coming, we figured we'd have to carry *his* bags," the man, a thirty-something Latino with two days' growth of beard, dressed in blue jeans and an untucked white linen shirt, his feet bare and his smile showing very white teeth, told him. "Alex Granda, at your service."

"Rip Carver, and I'm not a spy."

Granda shrugged.

"I heard," he said, "you're in some kind of special services division. But that's like me saying that at the end of the day I'm not really a cop. You bring any boat clothes by the way, Mr. Bond? I don't think a tuxedo's gonna work around here."

"I'll figure something out," Carver, a tight smile on his face, replied.

By then Perricone had secured the Whaler and joined them on the aft deck.

"Can we interest you in a welcome cocktail?" Perricone asked as he walked past them and opened the sliding glass doors that led to the main cabin of the yacht.

Granda and Carver, pulling his rolling suitcase behind him, followed.

"It's been a long day," Carver told them, "and it's three hours later for me. How about a rain check?"

"I think we can work that out," Perricone said. "Anyway, there are two master suites and a third, smaller cabin on this tub. I think you can guess who has the two masters," he went on, leading the way through the galley and salon and down a narrow stairway.

At the bottom of the stairs he opened the polished wood door leading into the cabin that would be Carver's home for he was not sure how long. Two beds, close together, took up most of the cabin's floor space. He slipped between the two and hoisted his suitcase onto the slightly narrower of the two roughly twin-size beds.

"You and I will be sharing a head," Perricone told him, "which is just across from your doorway. Lucky bastard Granda drew the master with its own. Let's see," Perricone said, pausing to glance at his watch, "it's nearly ten-thirty. One of us'll come and wake you at eight if you're not up by then. Oh, and just so you know, there was some kind of big fundraiser shindig at Duff's place tonight although it's starting to wind down now. We'll tell you all about it in the morning."

As soon as Perricone left, Carver took off his pants and jacket, dropping them on the bed next to his suitcase, unpacked his toilet kit and walked out of the room and the half dozen steps to the head. It was apartment bathroom sized and ultra-luxurious, with gold-speckled black marble tile on the floor and the same highly polished wood on the walls as graced much of the rest of the boat. The toilet was black, as well, and the faucets and such looked to be gold plated. There was a good sized stall shower with a small window and the same marble flooring and multiple nozzles and knobs, also in gold plate, as at the sink.

Drug dealing had apparently been good to its former owner, Carver thought as he opened the door to the head and walked back across the teak floorboards to his cabin.

8

JIM MORRISON, ESPECIALLY when the Doors were first starting out, performed with absolute abandon, and on the night that Edan and Sim watched him go for it at the Whisky A Go Go, he displayed complete indifference to what his singing style might be doing to his vocal chords and no apparent thought to the sprains and broken bones that his physical moves might well have brought about. Edan was pretty sure he was high.

Sim kept repeating *Holy shit* throughout the two-hour-long show. Edan did nothing but smile, and scream occasionally. He had thought the walls would come down during the band's opening number when they played *Break On Through*, and he was sure of it halfway through their second set when they played *Light My Fire*. But the walls were still standing when the band ended the set, appropriately, with *The End,* although it was pretty clear to everyone there that they really had been trying to destroy the place.

The Doors were the opening act for Them, Van Morrison's band, but once the applause and shouting for the Doors' performance died down, Edan hooked a thumb toward the exit and he and Sim worked their way through the crowd and outside to the Sunset Strip.

"You knew that was going to be one of their best shows, didn't you?" Sim asked as they walked up Hilldale Avenue toward the house.

"I might have read something about that," Edan replied.

"Well, it was absolutely fucking amazing," she said. "And it didn't hurt things that they carded me on the way in."

"You don't look twenty-six," he said.

"I don't look nineteen, either," she said.

They walked on in silence but as they turned onto Shoreham Drive, Edan suddenly took her in his arms and kissed her, hard, passionately. She did not fight him, but she did not respond, either.

"Nice try, cowboy," she said in a hoarse whisper when they parted, and Edan could see that she was crying.

"I'm so sorry," he said softly, stroking her cheek. "I am such an idiot! Shit! I know better and I didn't mean to hurt you, believe me. Please, chalk it up to that show and a couple of beers. Please."

Sim coughed, wiped away her tears and managed the flicker of a smile.

"You gave me back my legs and you gave me back my life in more ways than one," she said softly, "but even you can't give me back...that, so stop trying."

"Sim, I--"

She put a finger to his lips, then took his hand and they continued on to the house in silence. After checking the area, they walked quickly up the driveway and into the garage.

Edan was first into the device but this time Sim followed immediately, as soon as he had disappeared inside. Once enveloped in the tomblike silence, watching as Edan brought up, then began making entries on the holographic keyboard, she resolved to be more observant than she had been earlier. Once again, as soon as he hit *Enter,* she had the sense of a slight ringing in her ears. A subtle vibration emanated from below their feet and steadily grew and the floor's already pinkish hue darkened. And once again the sides and roof of the device seemed to disappear entirely. She forced herself to try and see what lay beyond them, but, as before, all that was visible were ever-changing snatches of lines, forms and color, but nothing you could lock onto.

She felt the same dizziness, too, and as it and the other sensations continued to build, it became impossible to concentrate on anything more than remaining upright and, it seemed, staving off delirium. And as focused as she continued to try to be, she still could not discern the precise moment when the dizziness, the ringing in her ears and the vibration stopped. It was as abrupt and unfathomable as it had been before. Once again the walls of the device came back into view, giving off the same dusky cast as when they had first entered the device, and it was just as massively quiet as it had been then.

"Jesus," Sim said softly.

"That's what you said last time," Edan told her, continuing to make entries on the keyboard.

"And it's probably what I'll say next time," she said, "assuming there is a next time. We should talk about that, by the way, and about something else."

"What's that?" Edan asked, turning to face her.

"You're completely out of control in here, once it starts," she answered, "completely helpless, almost on the verge of insanity as far as I could tell."

"That might be a little strong," he said, "but basically you're right."

"I was afraid you'd say that."

"Why?"

"Because," Sim said, "if there's ever a problem after you hit the enter key, there won't be any way to stop it. You'll be paralyzed, everyone inside the device will be paralyzed, presumably."

"Okay, but other than the discomfort, why's that a problem?" Edan asked. "Once I hit *Enter* it's an automatic sequence."

"I don't know," Sim said, "but I've been in enough dicey situations to know it's not good to be that far out of control. And as your head of security, I think you should try to find a way to prevent it, if possible, or deal with it some other way."

"Duly noted," he said. "Now let's get out of here."

The van was there and the rakes and brooms were no longer in the corner. It took them less than five minutes to get the device back into the van and secure it, after which Edan opened the side door and they jogged to the house and ran upstairs to the bedroom. They changed back into the outfits they had been wearing earlier. Sim brushed her hair and pulled it back into a ponytail and Edan spent a few minutes in the bathroom getting his back to its usual style. He stuffed the period clothing and accessories they had worn to the Whisky, along with their leftover cash, the watches and the rest, into the nylon duffle bag and slung it over his shoulder. Downstairs, he set the alarm and locked the house, and they walked to the garage. He opened the accordion doors while Sim got into the driver's seat of the van and he closed them after she had backed out it of the garage.

As she maneuvered the van out onto Ozeta Terrace, he said, "I think I'll call Papa John's when we get about a half hour from home. I'm starving."

9

WHEN THE ALARM on Rip Carver's iPhone sounded at six-thirty on Sunday morning, he had been immersed in a dream that when he awoke he could neither adequately remember nor understand, so jumbled and absurd were the details.

"Par for the course," he said softly, as he threw the covers back and sat up.

His shared bathroom, he could not think of it as a head considering its lux design, was clean, but clearly had been recently used. When he went up to the main deck thirty minutes later, dressed in jeans and a logo-less navy blue golf shirt, he was confronted by a similar scene. The galley had been used, in fact a half pot of coffee was sitting in its heating tray, but the area had been thoroughly tidied up. There were several clean mugs with the logo of the Bellagio Hotel on the granite counter, presumably memorabilia of the former owner's gambling jaunts to Vegas. He poured himself some coffee and took it out through the sliding glass doors and upstairs to the flybridge.

Like the rest of the boat, the upper deck was larger and more luxuriously outfitted than was typical, even for a craft of that overall size. Perricone and Granda were seated on a white leather banquet at a table, their backs to the open ocean, gazing out at Edan Duff's compound. Two Bellagio coffee mugs sat on the table between them, along with a laptop computer and a pair of high-powered binoculars.

"Anything exciting?" Carver asked, slipping onto the banquet a few feet away from them.

"It appears there's a possibility that Mr. Duff and his gal pal might have slipped out last night," Granda replied without taking his eyes off the house.

"You don't know for sure?" Carver asked, taking a sip of coffee. "And for that matter, why should he have to *slip out* of his own house? And while we're at it, who's his gal pal, and why do you call her that?"

"That's a whole lot of questions," Granda said, picking up his mug and turning toward Perricone, "and I haven't even had my second cup of coffee yet. Tell you what, Joey. Why don't you brief our spook and I'll go down for more?"

Without waiting for an answer, Granda also picked up Perricone's mug and headed down to the main deck.

Carver took another sip of coffee. It was then that he noticed the other yacht, moored about a hundred yards to the northwest.

"Don't tell me we have competition," Carver said, holding his mug out in the direction of the other boat.

"I suppose you could call it that," Perricone, shifting in his seat to look over at it, replied. When he turned back to Carver, he added, "It's a Sunseeker Predator 53, nice boat, brought to you by the nice folks at Teknodyne."

"So his competition's keeping an eye on Mr. Duff, too," Carver said, drinking more coffee. "Interesting."

"Sons of bitches almost got to our downed drone before we did," Granda, appearing at the top of the stairway said.

He put the mugs he was carrying down on the table and again took his place next to Perricone, who took a sip of his hot coffee.

"And if they'd recovered it and figured out that a laser brought it down," Perricone said, "I suspect they would've been just as surprised as us that Duff seems to be getting into the weapons biz."

"Some of us weren't all that surprised," Granda said, picking up his own mug, "considering that Ms. Garrison's always at his side. She's the gal pal we were referring to."

"Ah, of course," Carver said, "the one they call Sim."

Granda nodded.

"So you know about her," he said.

"Your colleagues spent quite a bit of time talking about her when they briefed me yesterday," Carver said. "Nearly died from injuries sustained in a mortar attack in Afghanistan. They were barely able to put her back together--"

"With help from Edan Duff," Granda interjected.

"With help from Edan Duff," Carver repeated before going on. "Then, when she got home, she put a bullet in her head and managed to survive that, too. Quite a girl. Duff came to the rescue again, with a job this time rather than cutting edge stuff from his medical devices company. Anyway, apparently Duff has a thing for her."

"Which he can't do much about," Granda said. "That headshot might not have killed her but it apparently obliterated the part of her brain that's responsible for sexual function, among other things."

"Yeah, I heard about that, too," Carver said. "Almost makes you wonder why she didn't take another crack at it."

Perricone cleared his throat.

"Anyway, she has a thing for weapons," he said, "of any size, shape or color, as long as they're lethal. It was one of her specialties in the service, worked with government suppliers to develop enhancements and such. She likes getting dirty with the boys, too. The group she was serving with was beta testing some new toys when that mortar attack interrupted things."

"You'd think she would've wound up working for one of them, the weapons suppliers," Carver said, "rather than Duff. Maybe she's got a thing for him, too, even if sex isn't part of it."

Carver's coffee was gone and he went down to the main deck to refill his cup. When he got back to the flybridge, he stood next to the table, gazing out at Teknodyne's Predator yacht, and asked whether the FBI thought that Duff had developed the laser weapon because of the woman, Sim.

Perricone shrugged.

"Makes as much sense as anything," he said. "Her expertise includes weapons development and she seems to like to use them, and he seems to have an interest in her survival."

"On the other hand," Granda added, "it's not his first foray into something other than high-end consumer electronics and software. He's become huge in applications and operating systems, too, and another division of his company works with DARPA on computer and communications gear. And a lot of that stuff is intended for use by certain government agencies, yours among them if the rumors are true, although that doesn't get a whole lot of publicity. You could say it's only a hop, ship and a jump from there to something more lethal."

Carver sat down on the banquet, which extended past the end of the table, and crossed his legs.

"Have you guys ever considered the possibility that he might not be developing that laser weapon to sell, either to our government or another one?" he asked.

Neither FBI agent answered immediately but when a reply did come, it was Granda who made it.

"What, you think maybe it's a pet project he's doing just to keep Sim happy?" he asked.

"Seems possible," Carver said, pausing to sip some coffee. "On the other hand, maybe he does have something else in mind."

"Like what?" Perricone asked.

Carver uncrossed his legs and leaned forward, putting his mug down on the teak decking.

"Duff's not even thirty years old, he's a multi-billionaire," he replied, leaning back against the leather cushions, "he's got a world-class weapons expert working for him and spending all kinds of time with him, he seems to have developed a miniaturized laser gun that's eluded everyone else and he's got a hoard of materiel that you can't figure out the use for. All you need to do is add in some number of well-trained, well-paid mercenaries and you'd have the makings of some kind of coup or insurrection or whatever."

Granda and Perricone stared at him for a moment, slack-jawed.

"What, you're suggesting he might be planning to overthrow the government?" Perricone asked.

"From what I know about him, Duff's a patriot," Carver answered, "as is Ms. Garrison, despite her, ah, unfortunate experience, in the military. He's low key about it but if you read some of the editorials he's written and analyze his speeches, you'll also see that he's critical of the current Administration's foreign policies and how they've handled, or not handled, some of our enemies. He's more or less said he wishes he hadn't supported the President's campaign."

"So you think maybe he's planning to take matters into his own hands?" Granda asked.

Carver shrugged and reached down for his coffee mug.

"I get paid to put pieces of information together," he said. "From what I know so far, what I just suggested appears to be at least a possibility. On the other hand, I haven't looked at all the data yet, so maybe I'm way off base."

"In a way, I kind of hope you're right," Granda said.

Perricone said nothing, but continued staring at Carver.

"Maybe you could get me that list of materiel and show me where I can work," Carver said, "and I'll see what else might be in play. Oh, and you never did tell me about Duff *slipping away* last night."

10

THE SECOND OF the catering vans had been waiting on the side of the road when Sim made the left turn from Laguna Canyon Road onto Pacific Coast Highway at eleven on Saturday night. They had said little on the drive home from Los Angeles, each seemingly lost in thought about the astounding evening at the Whisky. But after they got off the freeway, Edan began explaining that the amount of time you were gone from the present did not have to be the same as the amount of time you spent in the past, although you could not spend more than the elapsed *gone time* in the past. It related somehow to his earlier explanation about not being able to go into the future, the *actual* future, but Sim tuned him out about halfway through the explanation.

The same black Chevy Suburban, she knew by the dent in its front bumper, was parked near the intersection of the Coast Highway when the van Sim was driving, followed by the other van, turned right into the long drive that led to Edan's house. She drove slowly down the drive to the carport outside the catering kitchen. That was as far as you could go without triggering additional monitoring and security measures and countermeasures, which included a gantlet of pop-up steel blades and tire slashing barricades. She and Edan waited until the crew in the other van went inside before getting out and hastily transferring the device from the back of the van into the house through the same mostly hidden and well-secured side door they had used when they left. From there, they pushed it along, retracing their steps down a short corridor and then into the long, windowless white hallway to the gray steel door to Edan's lab at the end, the fluorescent lighting blinking on in segments as they moved through it.

When they got to the lab door, Edan entered a five-digit code into the keypad, pressed his left index finger against a biometric fingerprint reader and leaned in to bring his left eye close to an iris scanner. After a moment he backed slightly away and entered yet another five-digit code into the keypad. The sound of bolts unlocking echoed down the hallway. Edan pushed the heavy door open and he and Sim rolled the device through and put it back in its original position, to the right, not far in from the door and close enough to the wall so that a special charging pad attached to the wall could top off the batteries.

They closed and locked the lab door, and as they walked back up the long hallway Sim reminded him that they had agreed to discuss the uses to which the device might be put. She also reminded him that he owed her an explanation as to how he knew that the house in LA would be empty in June of 1966.

"I don't know about you, but I'm exhausted," he said.

"I was wondering why you didn't call for pizza from the van," she said as she entered numbers into the keypad at the door to the residential section of the house.

"Can we talk about it in the morning?" he asked.

She agreed and each headed off to their own bedrooms.

Sim slept better and awakened later than she usually did and Edan was already at the table on the terrace behind the house, eating breakfast, when she walked outside at nine on Sunday morning.

"If you must know," he said as Sim stepped out onto the terrace, "there was a nasty murder in the house on Ozeta Terrace in November of 1965. A fifteen-year-old boy killed his parents with a machete. The house was vacant for nearly two years after that."

She was dressed in black yoga pants and a Lakers tee shirt, her feet bare, and she nodded and walked to the credenza that ran along the side of the house. There was a coffee urn with a low flame going underneath it and a dozen or so mugs nearby, all with the logo of one of Edan's companies. She took one, filled it nearly to the brim and sat down next to Edan, who was seated at the head of the table, with her back to the ocean.

"Interesting," she said, taking the mug in both hands and bringing it to her lips. "By the way, we have a new watcher out on the boat."

"New as in a replacement or new as in there are now three?" he asked, taking a bite out of the toasted English muffin that sat on a small plate next to a folded paper copy of the weekend *Wall Street Journal*.

She held up three fingers in reply.

"Now why do you suppose that is?" he asked.

She took a bite of his muffin and another sip of coffee before answering.

"They're getting nervous I imagine, which is understandable," she told him. "I know I would be if I was the government and I found out that some twenty-eight-year-old billionaire beloved by one and all who makes consumer gadgets and applications, whatever the hell that means, for a living now has a miniaturized laser weapon."

Edan laughed.

"But it's one guy," he said. "It's not like they've called in the cavalry. They haven't called in the cavalry, right?"

He looked concerned and Sim shook her head.

"No, there's no Marine division or SWAT team staged in the driveway," she said. "I can tell you that because I spent some time in the command center staring at the monitors before I came out here. There are now two black Suburbans up on the Coast Highway, though."

"Great," Edan said, "although I suppose that's not surprising in light of the arrival of the third man. I guess we'll just have to be even more careful than usual, if that's possible. The audio jammers are working okay, right?"

Sim nodded.

"I double-checked," she said. "Feel free to speak freely."

"About our new arrival," Edan said, "this third guy, he's not wearing a spandex suit with a big, red **S** on the front, is he?"

Sim shook her head.

"Jeans and a golf shirt," she replied.

"That's a relief."

"It doesn't mean he's not Superman, though," Sim said. "I mean, since they didn't exactly need a third set of eyes just to stare at us through binoculars and take notes, I'm guessing it's someone with a totally different and probably very specialized skill set."

"Okay," Edan said, "Heckle and Jeckle out there are your run-of-the-mill, knuckle-dragging field agents, so would you care to venture any guesses about what the new guy's very specialized skill set might be?"

"He's probably some kind of analyst," Sim replied, "tasked with figuring out either what it is you're planning to do with that laser or, since you seem to have built something that they haven't been able to build, what other surprises you might have up your sleeve, or maybe both."

Edan stared at her for a moment. Her hair was pulled back into a long ponytail and her gauged ears were held open by round, gold tunnels. You could look right through the inch-across openings in her earlobes at the tiny tattoos on the sides of her neck which, if you peered at the correct angle, made it look pretty much like the view through a telescopic gun sight.

"Maybe I should offer to sell them the technology," he finally said, taking his eyes off Sim and looking off toward the FBI yacht. "That might get them off my back."

"Maybe, maybe not," she said. "It wouldn't answer the question of what you might still have up your sleeve."

"So one way or another, I'm stuck figuring out how to get out of my own house unnoticed with the device if I ever want to use it again," he said. "After all, the old catering truck ruse will only work so often."

"True," she said, "but you're a clever fellow, I'm sure you'll think of something."

She finished the half English muffin that she had taken a bite out of and reached for the partially eaten other half, but Edan caught her hand and stopped her.

"Muffins and toaster are over there," he said, gesturing toward the credenza.

She gave him a dirty look but got up and walked back over to it, taking an English muffin from a basket of various breads that sat next to the coffee urn, splitting it and dropping it into the toaster. When it was done, she buttered it, set it on a small plate and returned to the table. She sat down, put half of the muffin on Edan's plate and bit into the other half.

"You can get the coffee," she said as she chewed.

Edan sighed and looked at her askance, but took their mugs to the credenza, where he poured a fresh cup for each of them.

"So," Sim said when he put the mugs on the table and sat down, "unlike the feebs out there, I do know what it is you still have up your sleeve. What I don't know is what you're planning to do with it, other than impress girls with funky shoes, bohemian Mexican peasant bags and concert tickets. You did say we were going to discuss that, you know, what you're planning to do with the, ah, dingus."

"I remember," he said, taking a bite of muffin and washing it down with coffee. "But I wasn't just trying to impress a girl, even though I'm extremely glad you had a good time. It was a serious test. I'd been planning a series of them to study what really happens when you change things."

"*Had been* planning?" she asked.

"I think we can skip a few steps," he replied, "given the apparent success of last night's trip."

Sim looked at him askance.

"So, first it was you going and pounding in that nail," she said, "then it was us going further back to go somewhere we hadn't been when it first happened. You never said what was supposed to come after that but now that you've decided to *skip a few steps*, what is it now, killing Hitler?"

Edan smiled.

"Not quite," he said, "at least not yet. You're sure the watchers can't hear us?"

Sim nodded.

"Or the assholes?" he asked, and she knew he was referring to the Teknodyne people on the other yacht.

"I'm sure," she replied.

Edan cleared his throat.

"What do you know about the Suez crisis of 1956?" he asked.

Sim looked at him quizzically for a moment before responding.

"Just what I learned in Command and General Staff School," she finally said.

"Which is?"

Sim stared at him for a moment.

"You really want to know?" she asked.

"I really want to know," Edan assured her.

Sim shook her head.

"Of all the memories I lost, I can't quite believe I still have this one. Anyway," she went on, clearing her throat, "as I recall, the UK controlled the Suez Canal back then and had a major presence and interests in the region other than that, too. So in kind of a fit of anti-Brit and pro-Arab rage, Nasser, who was president of Egypt at the time, decided to seize it. I'm pretty sure that was in 1956, so that must be what you're talking about."

Edan nodded and she continued.

"I'm also pretty sure that at one point he scuttled some ships in the canal to block traffic," she said. "It was a big problem for the Brits since most of the oil from around there going to Western Europe was transported through the canal."

She stopped, but Edan was staring at her intently and asked her to go on.

"Anyway, I think the Israelis then went and invaded Egypt, and the UK and France kind of piled on. They wanted control of the canal back and Nasser out of there. I think they all figured the US would join in, but we didn't. In fact we made them back off, and the whole thing turned into kind of a disaster."

"From what I know about it," Edan said, "that's kind of an understatement. It was essentially the end of the road for the UK as a global power."

"Right, now I remember," Sim said. "Their prime minister had to resign and UN troops wound up on the Israeli-Egyptian border, among other things. Oh, and while everybody else was kind of distracted, the Soviets took the opportunity to invade Hungary. So, why do you ask?"

Edan smiled.

"There are those who think that most of our current problems in the Middle East can essentially be traced back to the Suez Crisis," he replied, "and in my short life, at least, most of the problems in the world can be traced back to the Middle East."

"Jesus Christ, Edan!" Sim said, suddenly on her feet. "I'm only working with about eighty percent of a brain here but--"

"I hate it when you say that."

"I know," she said, "but, damn it, Edan, it sounds to me like you're thinking about going back there and somehow trying to change things."

"Can you think of a better use for the device?" he asked, picking up his mug and finishing his coffee. "I know I can't."

"This isn't the discussion I envisioned when you agreed to talk about how the device was going to be used," Sim said.

Edan got up, took both their mugs to the credenza and poured more coffee for both of them.

"Fair enough," he said, coming back and handing one to her, "but can you think of a better use for the device?"

"I don't know," she replied, sitting down, "maybe going back and advancing medical breakthroughs."

Edan smiled.

"I've thought about that, believe me," he said.

"And?"

"Well, starting with vaccines and such," he replied, "the problem would be one of integration into the existing systems. I mean, if a few pallets of antibiotics showed up a long time ago, how could that be explained? And if you could figure out how to explain it and you could convince people it was all right to use them, what would happen when they ran out? I mean, there would be no infrastructure that could take over, either to manufacture or deliver them. And whatever caused whatever outbreak it was would still be there. It would be the same thing for certain surgeries and other procedures. Maybe you could teach the technique but the facilities almost certainly wouldn't be up to the task, not to mention the surgeons' foundational training. I could go on."

"I'm sure you could, but--"

"Besides, what encourages positive developments of all kinds," he went on, "whether medical or something else, more than a relatively peaceful, stable environment in large parts of the world where minds are free to flourish and all that?"

"And you're saying that disabling the Middle East hate machine might help provide that?" Sim asked.

"I'm not saying it's been the only source of trouble in the world in the last century," Edan said, "and I'm not talking about disabling it, I'm not sure anything could do that. But I am talking about mitigating it, which would likely have an outsized effect. And doing it in the way I've been thinking about would avoid the kind of shock that might be caused by a sudden, momentous event."

"Good to know that you're not planning a sudden, momentous event that might cause a shock," Sim said, her tone oozing with sarcasm. "You know, you could just go back and stop the assassination of Archduke Ferdinand and maybe prevent World War One. Mountains of bad shit came out of that. Or maybe keep the Japanese from attacking Pearl Harbor."

"I hear you," Edan said, his tone conciliatory, "but I wouldn't have the wherewithal to do those things."

"And you have the wherewithal to prevent the Suez crisis?" she shot back.

"Yes, I think I do," he replied, "and in a way that would very likely avoid a sudden shock, at least a major one."

Edan drank some coffee but said nothing further. Sim broke the silence a few minutes later.

"What about preventing the assassination of Doctor King?" she said. "That would be accomplishing something really important closer to home."

"It's on my list," Edan said, "but other than undoing the short-term fall-out, I'm not convinced it would make things all that much better than they've turned out."

"But I could lobby for it?" she asked, arching an eyebrow.

"Why not," he replied. "But first I need you to buy into my Suez plan."

"And how do you expect to get me to do that?" she asked.

"There's someone I'd like you to meet," he replied. "He's a professor at Berkeley and he's got a lot more credibility than me on the topic."

"And if I'm not convinced?" Sim asked, her eyes locked on Edan's face.

"We won't do it," he replied.

11

RIP CARVER WAS working at the dining table in the salon of the *ELVIRA* at nine on Sunday morning, the sliding doors open to let in a pleasant breeze, when he heard Granda call out from the flybridge.

"Speak of the devils," the FBI man said.

Carver was facing the shore and there was a wide window on each side of the salon, but Edan Duff's compound was up the hillside and Carver could not see it from where he sat. He eased himself off the banquet that encircled three sides the table and leaned over the white leather sofa on the other side of the salon to get a better view. He could only see the house well enough from there to tell that there were people seated at a table on the broad terrace that ran along the back of the house. But it was difficult to make out any detail from that distance. There was a pair of binoculars

sitting nearby, though, on the edge of the granite coun-
tertop in the galley, and he reached up for them.

Jane Garrison, the woman known as Sim, was
seated with her back to the ocean so Carver got a good
look at some of the tattoos on her back and her hair,
but not much else. Duff was at the head of the table
and Carver got a somewhat better view of his face, in
profile for the most part but more than that when he
turned toward the woman.

"I don't suppose there's any audio," Carver called
out.

"You don't suppose right, or however the fuck you
answer a double negative or whatever the fuck that
was," came Granda's answer.

Carver continued to watch the pair eat and talk for
a few more minutes, but then put aside the binoculars,
poured himself more coffee and sat down again in front
of his laptop.

Achieving his goal of figuring out what Duff was up
to was not dependent on his familiarity with the billionaire's face or even his proximity to the man, although
Carver hoped that something might happen in Duff's
vicinity that could help shed some light on his activities. The FBI team was putting a good deal of weight
on his having slipped away the previous evening, but
as far as Carver was concerned, it proved nothing.
Duff was aware that he was being watched and might

simply have wanted to go out and see a movie or have dinner at a restaurant without uninvited company. And Granda and Perricone's explanation of Duff's alleged absence had not convinced Carver that, for certain, he had actually had left the property. The fact that he had not attended the fundraiser, a piece of information for which the Bureau had overpaid someone who had been there, did not necessarily mean he was not in the house.

Maybe he and the woman had left in one of the catering vans, as the FBI suspected, and maybe they had not.

The possibility that they had left, and that the purpose of their covert outing had been to attend some sort of clandestine meeting with who knows who, was a matter for his FBI colleagues. But unless they could learn exactly where Duff had been and why, the whole thing was pretty much irrelevant to Carver's task.

So he took a sip of coffee and took up where he had left off, which was analyzing a list of all the items that the government believed Duff had acquired and that had been delivered to the lab in his house, and another list of the items that would likely be needed to produce a miniaturized laser weapon from among the items on the first list. Each list was extensively footnoted, either to explain the nature and general or alternative uses of particular items, or to comment on the likelihood of an item's need in building the weapon, with each item ranked on a one to five scale. Many of the footnotes had footnotes of their own.

Most people would have either laughed or thrown their hands up in despair in the face of what now confronted Carver, but he had been there before and was undaunted. As long as the coffee held out and he could eat and sleep decently, he was reasonably confident of success. And if the past was indeed prologue, the odds of success were quite good.

Carver worked through the lunch hour, stopping only to make himself a ham and cheese sandwich, which he washed down with a Diet Coke. He was planning to have dinner with the two agents and was hoping that Granda and Perricone could fill the role of useful sounding boards, something of which Carver was thus far uncertain. But he hoped a few stiff drinks might help, him if not them.

He sat at the table and worked through the afternoon, getting up only for bathroom breaks and to pour more coffee. He did not look out at Duff's house again and his two companions left him more or less in peace. It was Southern California, with its early dinner hours, earlier even than the conservative city of Washington, so he was not overly surprised when Granda announced at five-thirty that the yardarm was down and the bar was open. Carver yelled up to them that he would be there in a few minutes, made a few final notes, closed out of the files he had been working on and went up to the flybridge.

"We'd love to have shaken, not stirred, a martini for you, 007," Granda told him as Carver appeared at the top of the ladder, "but technically we're not supposed to have alcohol on board at all."

"Any port in a storm," Carver said, taking a glass of what proved to be rum and Coke from Perricone and sampling it.

"This'll do nicely," he told his hosts.

They gathered around the table where the two agents seemed to spend most of their time, rum and Cokes in crystal lowball glasses all around and an open bag of Doritos in the center of the table, and made themselves comfortable.

"So, whatcha got?" Granda asked after taking a sip of his drink. "Or have you been playing computer solitaire and visiting porn sites all day?"

Carver ignored the comment but answered the question.

"What I've got," he replied, "is more than I had this morning but not nearly as much as I'm going to need."

"Do tell," Granda said, stretching his arms out along the top of the banquet where he and Perricone sat.

Carver sat across from them in a chair that swiveled and he leaned forward and put his elbows on the table.

"Whatever he might be building with what I might as well call the leftovers," Carver said, "it's probably fairly big or heavy or both."

"And you deduced that from…," Granda said.

"You know the roller arrays they have on the equipment they use to load those big aluminum shipping containers onto airplanes?" Carver asked.

"I've seen them being loaded, yeah," Perricone replied.

"Well, Duff's got enough of those to cover the bottom of at least one standard size container," Carver told them. "Since you don't usually see those things being wheeled down the street, there's a good possibility that he expects to have to move whatever it is he's building around and probably load it onto an aircraft, and that there won't be commercial cargo loading equipment around."

"So, maybe he expects to be loading it onto a private plane," Perricone said.

Carver nodded.

"I'm told he's got one of those," he said, "a big one. And if that's the case, it would mean he's probably planning to use whatever it is he's building somewhere other than here, maybe someplace very far from here."

Carver paused to eat a few Doritos and take a sip of his drink and Perricone and Granda waited for him to go on. When he did not, Perricone stepped in.

"Okay, so it's probably fairly big and fairly heavy," Perricone said, "and probably doesn't need any form of packaging to travel."

Carver nodded and sipped his drink.

"Okay, so maybe we know how he plans to move it," Perricone continued, "but that doesn't exactly tell us what it is."

"One step at a time," Carver said. "Next, we have the batteries."

"There were batteries on that list?" Granda asked.

Carver smiled.

"Not exactly," he said. "There were chemicals and other, ah, substances, and certain materials, that could be used to build batteries, a whole lot of them, and batteries of a type that are on a lot of companies' and governments' wish lists at the moment."

"Why am I not surprised?" Granda said, shrugging and leaning in to pick up his glass. "I mean, he built that laser that no one else has been able to build, right, all by his lonesome."

"How did you know all this shit about batteries?" Perricone asked Carver. "I mean, obviously you know a lot, but you can't know everything about everything. Maybe those chemicals and all can be used to make something other than batteries."

Carver took a handful of Doritos and started eating them one by one.

"I spent a lot of time online with Mary McKinney--"

"Ah, the one with the tits that won't quit," Granda chimed in.

Carver smiled.

"That would be her," he said. "And I think her brain is even bigger, by the way. Anyway, I spent a lot of time online with her and she looped in a few of her DARPA people and a couple of folks from Harvard. Batteries was the consensus."

"Got it," Perricone said. "Okay, I assume that batteries, even really advanced ones, are heavy. Maybe that's why he needs the rollers and all."

"I agree," Carver said, finishing his drink and rubbing his hands together to get rid of the excess salt from the chips, "but it's probably only part of the reason."

Then he stood up, glass in hand, and asked if anyone else wanted a refill. Both Perricone and Granda finished what was left in their glasses and handed them over to Carver, who turned and walked to the small wet bar adjacent to the pilot's seat. There was a half-full ice bucket on top of it and some cut-up lime wedges, but no bottles.

"There's a bottle of Myers's rum in the cabinet under the sink," Granda told him.

Carver found the bottle and made the drinks, then came back to join them.

"Where were we?" he asked when he sat down.

"Consensus on advanced batteries," Perricone said, grabbing one of the glasses Carver had set down in the center of the table.

"Right," Carver said, reaching into the Doritos bag again. "The next one's a little strange. According to the DARPA people, some of the other compounds he procured could be used to make certain types of minerals, if he has the right equipment in that lab of his."

"Minerals?" Granda asked. "Like what, exactly?"

"Probably some kind of gem-type mineral," Carver replied. "You know the sapphire they use on parts of the iPhones?"

Both men nodded.

"That's man-made in special furnaces--"

"And you think Duff's making it in his lab?" Granda asked.

"Not sapphire exactly," Carver replied, "but something along the same lines, and he's probably not making small pieces of it, either."

"Let me guess," Granda said, taking a long swallow of his drink, "and it's some kind of stuff that's never been made before."

Carver laughed.

"Pretty much," he replied. "Let's just say that its chemical constituency doesn't seem to exactly match anything else that's out there."

They sat in silence, drinking and eating chips for several minutes, until Perricone's eyes went wide open.

"Holy shit," he said softly. "If Duff's got all these things that no one else has been able to make and if he's using them to build another kind of advanced weapon--"

"Then it might put anyone who doesn't have it at a real disadvantage, like fighting off guys with rifles using bows and arrows," Granda said, finishing the thought, "or taking a knife to a gun fight."

"If it's a weapon," Carver said.

"Hey, he's already demonstrated his willingness to build a weapon that no one else has by building that laser," Perricone said, "so there's no reason to think he wouldn't try it again."

"I didn't say I was ruling out the possibility," Carver said.

"Jesus," Perricone said softly.

"What else?" Granda asked.

Carver sighed.

"There's still quite a bit more to evaluate," he replied, "but I need some time with a particular guy at DARPA before I can be sure and he wasn't available today."

"Give us a hint," Granda said.

Carver took a sip of his drink.

"It would be an unusual configuration," he said, "a *very* unusual one, but one possible grouping of the components suggests some kind of computer, or maybe a very sophisticated control unit of some kind."

"What the hell kind of weapon is big and heavy, is powered by batteries and controlled by a computer and is made with sapphire, or something like it?" Granda asked, shaking his head.

"How about metal?" Perricone asked without waiting for Carver to reply to Granda's question. "Has Duff got a lot of stuff that could be made into some kind of metal on that list of his?"

"Four titanium rods," Carver replied, "that's it."

"Rods," Perricone said, sitting up straighter, "maybe for some kind of reactor?"

"I asked," Carver replied. "The rods inside a nuclear reactor are made out of things like boron, indium or cadmium, something that absorbs the nuclear material itself to control the reaction. Titanium wouldn't work. Plus, these are probably too short."

"Yeah, but with Duff, who knows," Perricone said. "He doesn't have nuclear material though, right?"

"There's nothing fissionable on the list and nothing fissionable that could be created with the things on the list, or so I'm told," Carver replied.

"Okay, so assuming he didn't already have nuclear material, and we're pretty sure he didn't, what the hell kind of weapon is big and heavy, is powered by batteries and controlled by a computer and is made of sapphire, or something like it, and has almost no metal parts?"

"Again, assuming it's a weapon," Carver said.

"You said you hadn't ruled out the possibility," Granda said.

"And I haven't," Carver said, "but I also need to consider every alternative."

"Fine," Granda said, "so, what the hell kind of... *thing*...is big and heavy, powered by batteries, controlled by a computer and made of sapphire, or something like it, and has almost no metal parts? And what the hell is it for?"

"That, gentlemen, is exactly what I'm trying to figure out," Carver said.

12

THE UNIVERSITY OF California at Berkeley is home to one of the top rated graduate history programs among all universities in the United States, surpassed, in the opinion of some, only by Princeton. But Berkeley had the distinction of having on its staff Harry Taylor Lee.

Lee traced his ancestry directly back to Richard Lee, who had emigrated from England in 1639 and made a fortune in tobacco in Virginia. Harry's branch of the family tree skirted the iconic Civil War General Robert E. Lee, also a descendant of Richard Lee, but his parents had named him in honor of the General's father, Henry "Light-Horse Harry" Lee, who fought in the Revolutionary War.

Harry Taylor Lee had been a CIA Middle East analyst and former field agent who had fallen into a comfortable role at the University of Virginia in Charlottesville when he retired from the Agency at fifty-five. The nascent Duff Foundation's offer several years later of a generously endowed chair in Middle East studies at Berkeley, Edan Duff's alma mater, found Lee surprisingly receptive, perhaps due to the then-recent death of his wife. Edan believed that Lee's experience and global outlook would translate well into the areas of research and marketing, and experience had proved him right. Several of Edan's colleagues met with Lee regularly, generally at his office in Berkeley but occasionally at the Duff Group's corporate campus in Carlsbad. Edan had met him only once before, though, when the university had arranged a reception in his honor shortly before he joined the faculty.

As Edan walked across the terrace behind his house after breakfast on Monday morning, he was thinking about how their second meeting, set to take place in a mere half hour, would be of a rather different sort. And to him, at least, it would be more important. Its purpose was to get Sim to buy into the Suez plan.

He was heading toward a stairway that led down to the helipad, and as he descended the stairs he could see that Sim had already undone the tie-down lines and was performing her pre-flight inspection on Edan's Robinson R-66 helicopter. She had come outside while he was eating breakfast and had stopped to fill a cardboard cup with coffee. They had both smiled then, so there were no further morning greetings to be made when Edan reached the pad. Wordlessly he climbed aboard through the left side door as Sim entered through the right. They belted themselves in and each donned a headset with built-in mics.

"The usual twenty minutes," she said through the craft's intercom system as she threw the switches that brought the small helicopter's electronic brains to life. "Not much of a breeze so it should be pretty smooth, clear skies all the way."

She spoke briefly with air traffic control and began flipping more switches. Within moments the whine from the craft's single turbine engine began to rise in pitch and the rotor began to rotate above their heads. Edan absently tugged his seat belt tighter, Sim brought up the engine speed, pulled back on the collective lever and pushed down on the left foot pedal and they slowly rose into the air and headed out over the Pacific, turning southeast almost directly above the FBI's observation yacht.

The flight was indeed smooth and the sky was unusually clear, and Edan was savoring the ride when, barely fifteen minutes later, Sim began a descent and aimed them directly toward the Duff Group's helipad. It was located next to a volleyball court behind one of five nearly identical low-rise glass office buildings. The craft touched down gently at the center of the big white **H** that was painted on the concrete pad and Edan stepped out, jogged away from the arc of the rotor blades and stretched. Sim went through her post-flight checklist before joining him for the short walk to the building that housed Edan's official workplace.

Despite being much further south, like many of its Silicon Valley corporate counterparts the Duff Group's buildings had no offices, as such, and the support pillars in the open space were as narrow as possible, a design that maximized the amount of natural light that reached into all areas and further enhanced the sense of openness. There were a handful of bright, white partitions with surfaces you could write on with special markers, which were angled to preserved as much of the open feeling as possible. Workspaces consisted of scattered modular desks, communal tables, some sofas and club chairs and the occasional low-walled cubicle.

Despite its five stories, the building had no elevators save for a single one reserved for freight and emergencies. Instead, there were what Edan and the architect had dubbed tubelifts. These consisted of small platforms, about two feet square, that were attached to a moving conveyor belt that ran vertically through carbon fiber tubes. The tubes spanned the height of the building, passing through large, circular openings in each concrete floor. The tubelifts, which were scattered throughout the building, operated continuously, essentially like a vertical airport luggage carousel. From the building's lobby you simply stepped on the next upward bound platform that came along, took hold of a small handle, and stepped off at whichever of the floors above was your destination. Descending platforms extended from the opposite side of the carbon fiber tubes. They were efficient and they were a great deal more enjoyable to use than an elevator, but they were not very practical if you were carrying much. For that, there were stairs, made of glass and of a very open design.

"I still say these things are a safety hazard," Sim said as they walked, largely unnoticed, toward the nearest tubelift.

"Says the former black ops helicopter pilot," Edan said as he lightly stepped onto a rising platform.

They rode the tubelift to the top floor, which, unlike the other four, was taken up entirely by conference rooms and a café. The conference rooms were of varying sizes but all of their walls and doors were made of glass. Sim checked an electronic board in a central foyer to see which conference room had been assigned to them and Edan followed her to a sparsely furnished square room in one of the corners of the building.

Harry Lee was already there, seated at a round table that could seat six, his legs crossed and a mug of coffee in hand, gazing out the windows, his back to them.

"Good morning, professor," Edan said

Lee turned abruptly, stood up and smiled. The old man was trim and fit for his age, had a full head of snow white hair and seemed equally at ease in his wool trousers, pale blue Oxford shirt, bow tie and tweed jacket as Edan was in his jeans and hoodie. They all shook hands and Edan made clear that he preferred to be addressed by his first name. He then introduced Sim, as Jane Garrison, Lee's eyes lingering on her for longer than Edan, and apparently Sim, would have preferred. She did not invite the professor to call her Jane.

"Thank you for making the trip down here on such short notice, professor," Edan said, as he and Lee sat down.

Sim walked to a table in the corner that held a carafe and several mugs, as well as thimbles of cream and sugar packets, and poured coffee for herself and Edan before coming to join the two men at the conference table.

"To be honest, it's a welcome change of pace, Edan," Lee said, re-crossing his legs and picking up his coffee mug. "Being whisked away from campus in a limo and escorted onto a private jet makes it rather painless, as well. And I must say I'm rather impressed with your facilities. I'd say you've one-upped most of your Silicon Valley contemporaries. Ms. Garrison's presence perks things up, as well. Should you ever find yourself up north with time on your hands, my dear," he added, turning to face Sim, "you're always welcome to sit in on one of my classes."

"To perk things up?" Sim asked dryly.

Lee smiled.

"Indeed," he said.

"That's only because you don't really know me, professor," Sim deadpanned.

"I'll take my chances," Lee told her.

"Well," Edan said, "you've come down here for a reason, professor, so why don't we get started. As you know, the subject is the Suez crisis and we'd like to get your insights, anything and everything you're willing to share."

"Given what you're paying me for the day, believe me, I don't plan to hold back," Lee said, flashing a brief smile. "In any case, at one time or another I've studied everything that's ever been written about Suez and know the history quite well."

Lee then launched into a full-fledged lecture, standing up at one point to pace back and forth as he spoke. Much of what he told them confirmed what Sim had already known or what Edan had told her the previous day, but Lee was able to add quite a bit of nuance and detail. For example, he told them that the tankers using the canal were foreign and had mainly British and French crews. All that Egypt, Nasser, got out of their passage was the tolls they paid.

"Made it look like Egypt was still a colony," Lee told them.

He went on to give them an idea of the size of the British military presence in the region and he went into some detail describing the raids, kidnappings, and other tactics that Nasser adopted when he decided it was time to get the foreigners out, telling them that the Brits were pretty much powerless to stop it.

"So Anthony Eden, who was Foreign Secretary at the time," Lee said, "Churchill was still Prime Minister, went to Cairo personally to have a word with Nasser, in Arabic if you can believe it. It was an attempt at appeasement, pure and simple, and he put together an agreement for British troops to pull back from the Canal Zone. I'd love to have seen his face when he found out not long after that Nasser had rewarded him by turning around and starting to buy weapons from the Soviets."

Lee went on to explain that Nasser kept the pressure up, demanding larger canal tolls. To try to placate him once again, the Brits, with help from the US, offered to get the World Bank to back a loan so the Egyptians could build the Aswan Dam, which according to Lee, Nasser really wanted very badly. He told them that John Foster Dulles, who was Secretary of State, pulled the rug out from under the loan deal, making Nasser angry enough that he ordered the Egyptian army to seize the canal. Lee then explained that everyone was worried that Nasser would eventually stop traffic through the canal entirely, cutting off the flow of oil. And since the Brits and French were dependent on that oil, President Eisenhower worried that the British and French might try to get the canal back by force and replace Nasser with someone who would be more accommodating to them. And while Eisenhower had no particular love for Nasser or the Arabs, he seemed to realize that military action was probably going to be counterproductive. It would alienate the Arabs and might even draw in the Soviets. And he knew that if Nasser cut the flow of oil, the U.S. would have to make up for it, like it or not.

"We had a lot of oil back in those days, remember," Lee told them. "We're moving in that direction again today, which is a very good thing in my opinion, by the way."

Lee moved on, telling them that Anthony Eden had become PM by then, decided to be clever and came up with a plan was to get the Israelis involved and make *them* out to be the bad guys by getting them to agree to undertake a military operation in the Sinai. The idea was to make it look to Nasser as though the canal might be the Israelis' real target. That gave the Brits and the French an excuse to go in and say they were protecting the canal from the Israelis.

Lee paused to pour himself more coffee. After he had sipped some, he sat back down, crossed his legs and continued.

He told them that the Brits and French announced their plans to protect the canal from the Israelis but for some reason delayed the start of militarily action for about a week, which gave Nasser the opportunity to scuttle a number of ships in the canal, which essentially closed it down. When the Brits and the French finally did attack, the whole thing failed miserably. As a result, their oil was cut off, Arab hatred of the West intensifies, Nasser became a hero, Anthony Eden had to resign and Eisenhower wound up having to supply Europe with oil.

"Okay," Sim said, "the Brits and the French lost their remaining credibility, both as military powers and as countries that can be trusted by the Arabs, but what about us?"

"We weren't viewed as badly as the British, French and Israelis were," Lee replied, "but we got stained, too. After all, looking at it from the Arab perspective, they must have thought we had been supporting the Brits and French all along. After that, things kind of went from bad to worse. And, of course, Nasser's star rose like crazy."

"Question," Edan, speaking for the first time, said. "I know that Anthony Eden wasn't exactly fond of John Foster Dulles and that he blamed Dulles for America's opposition to his plans. I also know that Dulles was diagnosed with stomach cancer a few days after the invasion started. What do you think would have happened if Dulles had been too ill to function, or had succumbed to the cancer earlier, while all this stuff was developing?"

"You do know that Dulles lived another three years, right?" Lee asked.

"I know," Edan said, "but still, you've got to wonder."

"It would be pure speculation, of course," Lee said.

"Of course," Edan assured him.

Lee paused for a moment and seemed to be organizing his thoughts. Sim had her eyes locked on Edan.

"Well," Lee finally began, "as I alluded to, Eisenhower was dead set against military action. He thought it would play into Nasser's hands, build him up in the region, which was exactly what happened, of course. Having said that, though, it was Dulles who did almost all of the talking for the U.S., publicly and privately, and Anthony Eden thought Dulles was giving the Brits mixed messages about the American position. It's possible that if Dulles had been removed from the mix at the right time, those messages might have been conveyed more clearly and Eden and the French and Israelis might have held off."

"And?" Sim asked, her eyes back on Harry Lee.

The professor looked at her and shrugged his shoulders.

"If you were a pessimist, my dear, you'd probably think negotiations over the canal would have dragged on for a while and then there would have been an invasion anyway, maybe better planned and maybe even with US help."

"Which might have solved the short-term problem but hurt our reputation in the region in the long run," Sim suggested.

"No doubt," Lee agreed.

"And if you were an optimist?" she asked.

"You'd think Eisenhower and all those big brains he had around him could have come up with a way to diffuse the crisis, tarnish Nasser's reputation and keep the rest of the Arab world happy, or at least reasonably satisfied."

"Do you think we would be better off today if that invasion hadn't happened?" Edan asked.

Harry Lee paused and took a sip of coffee. Sim stared at Edan.

"You're asking whether our problems in the Middle East can essentially be traced back to the Suez Crisis, aren't you?" he asked.

"Yes, I am."

"That's a hell of a question, Edan," Lee said. "I mean a great many other things have happened in the region in the last fifty-some years, and US policy hasn't always been very effective."

"All I'm asking, professor," Edan said, "is whether, in your considered opinion, you think we'd be better off today if the invasion hadn't happened?"

Lee cleared his throat before answering.

"Assuming Eisenhower had come up with a way to diffuse the crisis," he said, "in the immediate aftermath we would have been one hell of a lot better off. Nasser's position would have at least been weakened, the Soviets', too, most likely. Britain and France would have averted a disaster. The Israelis would have been better off, as well, although I'm not sure how much that really would have mattered in the longer term. And we wouldn't have had to sell oil to the Europeans. That alone could have had significant, positive consequences since the Arabs probably saw it as evidence that we'd been colluding with the Brits all along."

"And longer term, professor?" Edan asked.

"We've assumed Dulles had been removed from the mix, right?" Lee asked.

Edan nodded.

"Well, in that case Eisenhower might well have figured out how to take an already improved situation and manage things better with the Arabs going forward. And that might well have provided a more solid foundation for Kennedy, Johnson and their successors to build on. So the simple answer is yes, under those circumstances, I do think we'd be better off today. Of course it also assumes that there wasn't another Suez, or something like it, later on. So even if you believe that Suez was the seed of the mess we're in today, we could be in the same mess, or a worse one, if something even more destructive than Suez had happened later on."

"But you implied that the likelihood of that probably would have diminished if Suez had been averted, professor," Edan pointed out.

"Yes, I suppose I did," Lee said, frowning. "Of course, it's all pure speculation."

"Yea, of course," Edan agreed.

13

"I WASN'T EXPECTING *that*," Carver said as the Robinson helicopter lifted into the air from the hillside just below Edan Duff's house on Monday morning.

"Yet another in the long line of endless perks of being a billionaire," Granda said. "After all, you wouldn't want the poor kid to have to drive everywhere he goes, now would you?"

"It's not that I'm surprised he has a helicopter," Carver said. "It's just that I never noticed where there might've been a helipad."

"Well, as you probably figured out, it's down the hill from the house and off to the side," Perricone said. "We got a look at it before the drones were shot down. There's some sort of hard shell awning that retracts into a structure set into the hillside. Plastic sheeting drops down from the edges of the awning when it's extended, which makes it into kind of a hangar. We assume the structure that it's attached to is for storage or whatever. Anyway, from here you really can't see that there's anything there until they retract the awning, and even then all you can get is a glimpse of the rotor blades above the hedges. Like I said, we only know the details from some video one of the drones sent back."

"We actually did manage to get some decent intel before the shoot-downs," Granda added. "Now, not so much."

"So, where do you suppose he's off to, his office?" Carver asked. "That's in Carlsbad right?"

They watched the craft arc out over the ocean and cross almost directly above them, settling on a southeasterly course, before either of the FBI men replied.

"The direction they're headed suggests that's where he's going, yes," Perricone said, "but we won't know for sure until he gets there."

"You've got eyes at his office?" Carver asked.

Granda smiled.

"That's the thing about these high-tech marvel companies," he said. "Everyone gets rich, or at least that's what the young ones are conditioned to believe. But the junior people don't start getting any benefit from their stock options for at least a couple of years. Some of them get tired of waiting so they take our cash to fill in the gap, so to speak, at least if we don't ask them to do anything that seems too underhanded. So far we've found most millennials' morals to be pretty flexible, up to a point, anyway."

They were seated around the table on the aft deck of the *ELVIRA*, finishing breakfast. As the helicopter disappeared from sight, Perricone picked up his iPhone and sent two text messages.

"Contacting your guy at his office?" Carver asked, getting up from the table.

Perricone nodded.

"And our boss," he said.

Twenty minutes later, when Carver was settled in at the table in the salon, immersed in his research, his laptop open in front of him, the sliding glass doors opened and Perricone stuck his head around the edge. Carver looked up from what he was doing.

"Duff just got to his office," Perricone said. "I'll let you know if anything interesting happens."

Carver nodded and went back to what he had been doing, which was arranging certain of the compounds and materials on his list into yet another subset. He was still struggling to make sense of this new list an hour later when Perricone reappeared to tell him that Duff was attending a meeting with an older man who had been brought there for the occasion.

"Everything in that building is either open plan or has glass walls and doors," Perricone told him, "so our guy was able to get a cell phone photo. We're running facial recognition now."

"Might be easier to just get a look at the building sign-in sheet," Carver said. "Place like that probably doesn't let anyone in without going through some kind of security procedure."

Perricone, who was usually about as even-keeled as they come, flashed an angry look.

"Gee, I sure as hell wish I'd thought of that," he said, with just the right amount of sarcasm to make Carver immediately regret he had said it.

"Sorry," he said.

"Whatever," Perricone said. "Anyway, it seems Duff's guest was taken to a conference room without going through security or signing in. Happens there from time to time."

"Interesting," Carver said as Perricone slid the door shut and walked away.

Granda was prone to the occasional outburst, but when Carver heard a particularly loud *What the fuck!* emanate from the agent a half hour later, he got up, slid back the door and joined Granda and Perricone up on the flybridge. Both men turned when they noticed him at the top of the ladder but neither said anything until Carver walked to the table and craned his neck enough to catch a glimpse of the screen of the laptop that was open in front of them.

"Meet Harry Taylor Lee," Perricone said, glancing at the photo of Lee that filled the computer's screen.

"Doesn't exactly look like a Chinese or Iranian spy," Carver said.

"History professor up at Berkeley, so maybe not so far off," Perricone said without a trace of irony, "holds the Duff Foundation chair in Middle East studies. Also consults for the company on a fairly regular basis."

"And he's one of you spooks," Granda added, looking away from the screen and standing up and stretching. "That picture came with some interesting info from DC."

Carver shot a questioning look at him, but it was Perricone who answered.

"Lee was a senior Middle East analyst for your esteemed employer," Perricone said, reading as he spoke, "until he retired about fifteen years ago to go teach at the University of Virginia in Charlottesville. Let's see...it seems Duff apparently made him an offer he couldn't refuse a couple years ago to get him to come out here. This says it surprised a lot of people since Lee's about as Virginia as they come. Robert E.'s somewhere up there in the family tree."

"Does Duff *consult* with him often?" Carver asked.

Perricone turned away from the screen and looked up at Carver.

"For what it's worth," he replied, "our guy there says he's never seen Lee in the building before. We asked DC if they have any more, though. You know, he may not be connected with the Chinese, but I'm not especially thrilled to hear about his Middle East background, either."

"You're thinking Duff's customer might be a Middle Eastern country, like maybe Iran, and not China?" Carver interrupted to ask.

Perricone nodded.

"The thought of Iran or someplace else over there had occurred to us," he said. "But there's nothing in the stuff DC sent, so far at least, to suggest that Lee's any more than just a professor and a consultant to Duff. On the other hand, anyone who was with the CIA for as long as Lee was must have some other, *ah,* skills or connections or whatever."

Perricone looked expectantly at Carver, but all the color had suddenly gone out of Carver's face and he was staring off into the distance, vaguely in the direction of Edan Duff's house. Perricone thought he saw small beads of sweat forming on Carver's upper lip.

"You with us, Carver?" Perricone asked.

But instead of answering, Carver turned away and hurried back down the steps, taking his iPhone out of his pocket as he did.

14

"I DON'T REALLY care who he is, it's still just one man's opinion," Sim said as they walked outside toward the helicopter after their meeting on Monday morning with Harry Lee.

It was the last time either spoke until they were back on the broad terrace behind Edan's house a half hour later. A tray of cold cuts and breads, a bowl of salad, and various condiments, along with an assortment of soft drinks, had been left for them on the credenza and wordlessly each put together a lunch. It was warmer now and Sim had discarded the fleece vest she had donned earlier, revealing the yellow racer-back tee shirt she had worn beneath it. That, in turn, revealed parts of the tattoo that covered her entire back and much of her arms. And as they stood at the credenza and fixed their lunches, Edan had a difficult time keeping his eyes off it.

"I take it you'd like me to get a second opinion," Edan said, as he walked to the table carrying the turkey and Swiss cheese sandwich on rye he had put together.

Sim followed him and when she sat down, pushed the salad around on her plate and shrugged before answering.

"As the great man told us," she said, "it's all pure speculation."

Edan smiled and took a swig from a small bottle of Pellegrino water. When he said nothing further, Sim asked if he had considered speaking with a professor of ethics.

"You've got one of those on the payroll, too, right?" she said, finally taking a bite of her food.

"We do," he replied, "and we use him a lot more than we use Lee. I've thought about it in the context of this...project...but there's really no point."

"Really? No point?" she said. "Why's that?"

Edan put down his sandwich, pushed his plate away and folded his arms on the table.

"Because there's no ethical justification for doing any of what we're doing, what *I'm* doing," he replied. "And when I say that, I don't just mean thinking about changing Suez, I really do mean *any* of it."

"Eighty percent of a brain here, remember," Sim said. "You're going to have to explain that to me."

Edan sighed.

"When I went back and hammered in that nail," he said, "I had no way of knowing whether it was going to do absolutely nothing or cause a calamity of epic proportion. Objectively, I had no right, there was no possible justification, for me to take that kind of risk with the lives of countless people who had no idea that someone was gambling with their whole existence."

"But nothing bad happened," she said, "and then when we went back further and went to the Whisky and still--"

"I felt a lot better about it, sure," he said, completing her sentence, if not her thought, "but I still didn't really know for certain whether the universe has a mechanism for dealing with two people going back much further, for longer, and interacting with other people. The fact is that in its own way it was probably nearly as indefensible as the first trip. And I can say the same thing for the next trip back, whether it involves Suez or not, because it's going to be even further back, for longer, with more people, and therefore it going to be more potentially disruptive of the fabric of things."

"As far as I'm concerned," Sim said, "you've already proved that the universe really does have some sort of mechanism to, I don't know, *absorb,* what you're doing. I mean, if that mechanism or whatever you want to call it works at all, I find it hard to believe that there's some sort of cosmic tipping point beyond which there will be hell to pay, regardless of what you might have told me before. It either works or it doesn't and I don't think it's a matter of degree. Don't misunderstand me, I'm in violent agreement that doing it the first time was one big fucking unjustifiable roll of the dice, but that's done and gone, as they say, and it worked out okay."

"But for all I know," he said, "it did change things and maybe not for the better, at least for some people."

Sim shrugged.

"What's meant to be will always find a way," she said.

Edan stared at her for a moment before saying anything further.

"Who said that?" he finally asked. "It sounds like some famous philosopher."

Sim laughed.

"I suppose you could say that," she told him. "It's a line from a Trisha Yearwood song, *She's In Love With the Boy.* I don't think she wrote it, though."

Edan shook his head slowly and smiled.

"Okay," he finally said, "if you don't think there's a problem, why the snide remark about talking with an ethics guru?"

"Well, for one thing," Sim replied, shifting in her chair to face him more directly, "you're planning to kill someone."

"How do you know I was planning to kill John Foster Dulles?" he asked. "Maybe I was thinking about another way to get him out of the picture."

""For months, maybe longer?" came her reply. "Give me a break. The only way to ensure that Dulles is really *out of the picture* is to kill him. You know it and I know it. Anything else would be stupid, and you're not stupid."

Edan hesitated before going on.

"He was already very sick and--"

Sim held a palm out to him and he stopped talking.

"You're planning to kill someone, Edan," she went on, "and the someone you're planning to kill is a historical figure, and killing him may change the outcome of a very large, complex event that--"

"Whoa!" he said. "You just said there's probably no *cosmic tipping point* and--"

Her hand shot up again and again he stopped talking.

"If you kill John Foster Dulles and the Suez crisis is diffused," she went on, "people who would have died aren't going to die, which means that people who wouldn't have been born are probably going to be born, events are going to unfold that have already unfolded in a different way. Jesus, Edan, it's not just a matter of degree, or when you get to some tipping point. It's a matter of intrinsic change. Come to think of it, maybe *that's* the trigger for the calamity you were so afraid of."

"Or maybe it's not possible to trigger a calamity no matter what," he said. "After all, there's so much we don't understand about the quantum world, about time."

"But maybe going back to hammer in that nail and then going to see the Doors have already caused some of the same...ripples," she said, "and like you said, we just don't know about it, and we never will."

"Look," he went on, reaching across the table and taking her hand, "there's probably no ethical justification for building the device in the first place considering all the issues it raises. Of course, even I didn't think it was really possible to build it. Anyway, the device now exists and it's awfully hard to ignore it, and maybe harder still to avoid trying to using it beneficially."

"And it's hard to believe the whole thing's just some big video game that doesn't really matter and just happens to come out differently every time you play it," she said defiantly, pulling her hand away and folding her arms across her chest. "Just because some physics professor or scientist or whoever says that there are all these quantum universes doesn't mean it's true! And even if it is true, it still doesn't mean you should fuck with them!"

Edan let her calm down for a moment before saying anything.

"Getting back to your original point," he finally said, his tone conciliatory, "I can't speak with the professor of ethics."

"Why?" she asked, barely looking at him.

"Because if I did I've have to kill him, too," Edan said with no trace of humor.

"Let me guess," Sim said, "because you couldn't have a serious conversation about all this without him realizing, or at least suspecting, what you're up to."

Edan nodded.

And with that she began laughing, half-heartedly at first, but then she let go and the laughter flowed until it eventually turned to tears. Edan was so surprised that he just sat still, saying nothing, watching her. When she finally got herself back under control, she turned to him and asked, "So, what's the plan for going back and killing John Foster Dulles?"

15

CARVER HAD SPEED-DIALED Mary McKinney's number as he hustled down the ladder of the *ELVIRA* after his meeting with Perricone and Granda, telling her that it was urgent that they meet as soon as possible and that it was matter of national security. McKinney insisted that they meet in the same conference room at the FBI field office in Los Angeles where they had met when Carver had first arrived from Washington.

"It's the only place where I can be absolutely sure we won't be overheard," she said. "I put together the jamming system and supervised the installation of the equipment, and I wrote the protocols myself. If it really is a national security matter, that's got to be where we talk."

Carver was relieved that she had not insisted on hearing any specifics prior to agreeing to meet and did not even attempt to change the venue.

When Perricone tied the Boston Whaler up at the marina in Dana Point on Monday afternoon, he handed Carver off to March, the same young agent who had picked him up at LAX. Much as before, their conversation during the ninety-minute drive to L.A. was strictly limited to the occasional comment about the weather or the traffic. Carver held his laptop firmly against his thighs for the entire ride, treating it more like a bomb that might go off at any moment if it was jostled than a computer. And when he got out of the car in the building's parking garage, he cradled the laptop under his arm rather than carrying it by the handle of its waterproof and shock-resistant case.

McKinney was already there, drinking tea, when Carver was led into the conference room by Roscoe Kemp's assistant, a mug of coffee in one hand, the laptop still cradled under his other arm. For her part, McKinney appeared rather more relaxed, her chair pushed back from the table and her legs crossed at the ankles. She was wearing a loose-fitting shift, not unlike the one she had worn at their initial meeting but for its color, and, like the other, it failed to hide her enormous breasts with what he suspected was the desired degree of effectiveness. The sight of her remarkable body, swaddled though it was, brought him out of the milky haze in which he had been immersed since having the epiphany about Edan

Duff's plans. He put the laptop case and coffee gently down on the table, greeted McKinney and took a seat across the table from her.

"Thanks for arranging this on such short notice," Carver said.

McKinney shrugged.

"Hey, I work right upstairs these days," she said. "You're the one who had the pain-in-the-ass trip to get here."

"I wasn't sure how safe the yacht was for having this discussion," Carver said, opening his laptop case and turning on the computer, "and I didn't want to take a chance on Granda and Perricone maybe listening in."

"Well, we're here, we're alone, the room is as secure as they get and you've got my complete attention," McKinney said, taking a sip of tea.

Carver opened his laptop case, booted up the computer and opened a file on it before looking back up at her.

"Before I say anything," he said, "I'd like to talk about the woman, Jane Garrison, the one he calls Sim, first. Bear with me please. I know you know a little bit about her, but there's more that you might not know. I promise you'll see later why I need to lay it all out for you before I get into the, ah, the other thing."

"Now you've got me even more intrigued," McKinney said, taking a sip of tea, "and a little worried."

Carver did not respond to her comment but cleared his throat and began.

"She was born Courtney Jane Garrison in 1988 in Briarcliff Manor, New York, which is an upscale bedroom community in Westchester, maybe thirty miles north of Manhattan. Father was an orthopedic surgeon, mother was a partner at one of the big Wall Street law firms, only child of older parents. High school valedictorian, Fulbright scholar, top five percent of her class at Yale. My people tried to recruit her in the spring of her junior year."

"What was her major?" McKinney asked.

"Pre-law and international relations," Carver replied. With a meagre smile he added, "Why, are you planning to apply for a job at the Agency?"

"It's a little late for that," McKinney said. "So, you were saying...."

Carver cleared his throat again and continued.

"She turned us down cold," he said. "Then, that summer, her parents were killed in a car accident. Over Christmas break she got back in touch with the person who'd tried to recruit her and said she'd changed her mind."

"Not shocking, under the circumstances, I suppose," McKinney said. "I assume your people brought her on?"

"They did," he replied. "They put her in a kind of extracurricular program during the Spring semester of her junior year and over that summer and she caught the eye of a few people. Let's just say she demonstrated certain aptitudes that we hadn't expected and that the powers that be decided to try to steer her in a different direction. To some peoples' surprise, she agreed."

"I take it that it was something a little less, ah *academic*?" McKinney said.

Carver nodded.

"Is that how did wound up in Afghanistan?" she asked.

"Pretty much," he replied. "They put her into a different part-time program during her senior year. As it turned out, she excelled. One thing led to another and after graduation she came in full-time and wound up in a secret unit that before too long was doing black ops missions over there. They were extremely successful until the day they weren't."

"That's how she met Duff, right?" McKinney, getting up and standing with her back against the wall, nearby, asked.

"He and a group of doctors and technicians from his medical devices subsidiary were in Landstuhl, which is a big D-O-D hospital in Germany, demonstrating their latest and greatest to a joint services group of physicians from all over Europe when they brought her in, all but dead," Carver replied. "I'm told it was the combination of having just about every specialist on the Continent in the same place at the same time as Duff's equipment and scientists were there that saved her, kind of rebuilt her, actually. On the other hand, since she tried to take her own life not long after she was released from the hospital, it seems she hadn't really wanted to be saved. Not that I can blame her, considering what she went through."

"That didn't work out so well, the suicide attempt," McKinney said, going back to her chair, "and from what I heard the side effects were nothing to write home about, either."

Carver could not help but smile and shake his head slowly.

"Ironically," he said, finishing his coffee as McKinney sat down, "suicide might be the only thing she failed at her whole life, which brings us back to Edan Duff. As you probably know, he brought her into his organization after she recovered, she moved out to California and she's been his head of security ever since."

"I've always wondered what the head of security for a twenty-something, high-tech billionaire really does," McKinney said.

"Other than playing bodyguard and being responsible for security systems design and implementation," Carver said, "all we have is suspicions."

McKinney leaned forward in her chair.

"Do tell," she said.

"In addition to her fighting skills," Carver said, "which I understand are pretty amazing for--"

"For a woman?" McKinney interjected.

"For anyone without a true military background," he said, "Garrison's apparently something of a whiz at strategy and project management. The rumor is that a few of those projects have involved putting together and leading small but elite private forces to undertake their own covert operations in Afghanistan, as well as Iraq and Syria, oh, and Ukraine, too."

"You're serious?"

"It's not something I would joke about," Carver replied.

"Helping *us*, right?" McKinney asked.

Carver nodded.

"Not that they were asked to help," he said.

"But you said these are only suspicions, right?" she asked.

"I'm afraid that's all I can tell you," Carver said, "but I think it'll be enough for now."

"I think I might need to switch to coffee," McKinney said, picking up her mug and standing. "Want some more?"

"Black," Carver said, handing over his mug.

While McKinney was gone, Carver closed the file on his computer that he had been referring to and opened another one, the one he had used to analyze the list of materiel acquired by Edan Duff that had not been consumed in creating the laser weapon. When McKinney returned, she put the mugs of fresh coffee down on the table, closed and locked the heavy door to the room and sat down.

"My head is still spinning from your last revelation," she said, taking a sip of coffee, "I'm not sure I'm really ready for more."

"And I'm not sure I'm ready to actually say what I'm about to say out loud," Carver said, picking up his mug, "but I'm not sure I have a choice. I need to run it by someone I can trust. Anyway, put your seatbelt on."

McKinney smiled a nervous little smile and drank some more coffee. Carver glanced at his computer screen and took a deep breath.

"Okay," he said, "I've spent most of my time out here parsing through the list of things that Duff had delivered to his lab at the house, trying to isolate discreet inventories of items that might be used to produce a certain finished product. And as you know, I've been consulting with a large number of noted scientists and other experts on a regular basis. Thank you for the introductions, by the way."

McKinney nodded and he then proceeded to review for her his initial thoughts as he had explained them to

Perricone and Granda, concerning what he had called the leftovers, the items that Duff had not used to create the laser gun.

"At that point," Carver said, "I'd figured out that whatever it was Duff was building was probably fairly big and heavy and that it incorporated a system by which it could be easily moved onto a private aircraft or other vehicle without the need for any sort of container. Also, that it incorporated enormously powerful and long-lasting batteries and that it was controlled by some kind of computer."

"Some kind of computer?" McKinney asked.

Carver smiled but it disappeared quickly.

"It's probably stretching the term," he replied, "at least if you use the basic definition, which, by the way, is a general purpose device that can be programmed to carry out a set of arithmetic or logical operations automatically."

"It doesn't do that?" McKinney asked.

"Oh, it does that, I think," Carver told her, "but it's apparently capable of doing so much more that it really should have a different name, at least according to the people I spoke with. It's apparently like nothing that's been seen before. I mean, it took a small group of your brainiacs to even conclude that it was probably some kind of computer."

"Okay, so there are amazing batteries and an even more amazing computer," McKinney said, sipping her coffee. "So maybe he's developed some sort of super computer that's big and heavy but capable of being moved around independently, not a weapon at all."

Carver shook his head.

"There's not enough of the stuff he used to make the batteries and the computer to fill up something the size I think this thing is," he said.

"Which is?" McKinney asked, a skeptical look on her face.

"My best guess is somewhere between a hundred and a hundred-and-thirty cubic feet," Carver replied.

"Okay," McKinney said, "so what takes up the rest of the space?"

"Air," Carver replied.

"Air?"

Carver nodded.

"Whatever the thing is," he said, "I also knew that it was made of some sort of manufactured mineral, something more or less like industrial sapphire. Unless it's needlessly thick, which doesn't seem likely since stuff like that would be extremely strong, it's a whole lot bigger than the space needed for the batteries and the computer. That suggests the rest is empty space where maybe the person or people who operate it could sit."

"And since it's not logical to think the operator would need to sit inside a supercomputer," McKinney said, "you went back to thinking it might be some kind of weapon."

Carver nodded.

"My assumption at that point in the analysis was that it *was* probably a weapon of some kind," he said, "especially since we already knew that Duff had developed the laser weapon."

"But batteries and a computer alone don't make a weapon," McKinney said.

"Exactly," Carver agreed, "but at that point there were still a lot of items on his list of supplies that hadn't been accounted for."

"And when you accounted for them?" McKinney asked.

"I got nowhere," Carver replied. "There was always a piece missing. In fact, I kept typing out, *What's the fucking think for?* on my laptop."

McKinney laughed.

"But now you think you know what it's for," she said. "What changed?"

Carver smiled, and this time it was a real smile.

"Two things," he replied, "and they happened almost simultaneously."

"Out with it," McKinney said.

"The first was realizing that Duff might not have used up his entire supply of each of the items that were used in building the laser," Carver replied, "along with the possibility that he might have had some other interesting things already floating around in that lab of his before the FBI took notice."

"And the second thing?"

"The second thing was learning the identity of a man he met with down in Carlsbad this morning," Carver replied, "someone her flew in from Berkeley for the occasion.".

"Who was?"

"A fellow called Harry Taylor Lee," Carver replied, going on to explain who Lee was.

"But if Harry Lee's a historian, what--"

Carver held up his palm.

"Bear with me for a moment," he said. "When I started expanding the list of unused items to include a few of the things that Duff had used to build the laser, the brainiacs started thinking about high-energy magnetic fields. They had to make a few assumptions about what other items might be floating around Duff's lab that weren't on the inventory, but they were reasonable assumptions."

"And?"

"They suggested that whatever the thing is, it might be capable of producing prodigious amounts of energy," Carver replied.

"Okay, but to be used how, or for what, exactly," McKinney asked, "because what you just said could suggest some kind of new, efficient power source as much as some kind of weapon."

"Fair point," Carver said, "but not what the scientists are thinking. For one thing, there don't seem to be any materials that would lend themselves to directing the flow of forming some kind of transmissions system."

"You mean like power lines or something like them?" McKinney asked.

"Right, but it not just that," Carver said. "The people I spoke with weren't at all convinced that the output of the thing would be in the form of electricity, or even a type of gas or other element that could be burned to produce electricity. The fact that the thing seems to be made mostly of a glass-like substance and incorporates almost no metal in its structure, along with the fact that it's controlled by a very advanced computer led a couple of the scientists to wonder whether the energy it appears capable of producing could be aimed externally as maybe some sort of plasma beam."

"So it really is a weapon," McKinney said.

Carver smiled again.

"Maybe not," he said.

"Okay, if it's not a new kind of power source and it's not a weapon, then--"

"Then this is where your seat belt might come in handy," Carver said. "One of your geniuses started wondering if instead of being expelled from the thing, as he put it, all that energy might somehow be recirculated within the thing itself, resulting in some sort of high-energy magnetic field. Theoretically, if certain chemical compounds were being circulated through the glass-like shell of the thing and super-charged within that small of an area, he thinks it might be enough to create artificial gravity and actually curve space-time, at least locally."

McKinney stared at him wide-eyed.

"Hang on," she said softly, "you're suggesting it might be a time machine?"

"When I found out that he met with a noted historian like Harry Lee this morning," Carver said, "that's the conclusion that kind of clicked into place."

"Is that even possible, really?"

Carver shrugged.

"Hey, we're dealing with Edan Duff and some very strange formulations of materials and exotic compounds here," he replied. "For that reason alone, we can't rule out the possibility. By the way, the other geniuses were, shall we say, intrigued with the internal circulation theory."

"But it could still be a weapon?" McKinney asked.

"I suppose," Carver replied, "but then why did Duff need to speak with a historian?"

McKinney said nothing and her gaze was fixed somewhere off in the distance.

"Henry Lee's specialty is the Middle East," she said, refocusing on Carver.

"Yes, but from a historical perspective, not a current day, military perspective," Carver told her. "Besides, Duff has already used Jane Garrison to put together small armies for military-type operations in the Middle East. He didn't need a historian, or a high-tech cannon, for those. I think he has something completely different in mind."

Again, McKinney said nothing and her gaze was fixed somewhere off in the distance.

"Okay," she said a moment later, still staring off into the distance, "if you could go back in time and change something about history in that region, what would it be?"

16

EDAN SAT AT the table on the terrace behind his house on Monday evening, working at what appeared to be some sort of tablet computer, when the sound of the Boston Whaler's engine, carried to shore on an easterly breeze, caught his attention.

He looked up as the Whaler approached the Princess yacht that had been anchored offshore for months. The small boat throttled back and one of the two men aboard threw a line to a man who was standing on the yacht's swim platform. Edan got up and walked to the credenza, where there was a pair of binoculars, and took a closer look as the Whaler was tied up to the yacht and both of its occupants stepped gingerly onto the bigger boat. He then watched all three men disappear into the yacht's salon.

Edan entered a three-digit number on the tablet's keypad and seconds later Sim's face came up on the screen.

"Small boat just delivered a guy to the Princess," he said. "They must've gone in while we were down in Carlsbad this morning and now they're back. The passenger was the same guy who came aboard the other day and the guy running the boat was the same one who ferried him out before, one of the two who've been there all along."

"And there's now a second black Suburban parked on the shoulder up at the intersection," Sim told him. "Stay there, I'll be right out."

Moments later, she came out of the house and joined Edan on the terrace. She wore pink nylon gym shorts and a black sports bra and her hair was pulled back into a ponytail. She had obviously been working out and the setting sun caught the slight sheen of sweat on her face and body. Edan could not take his eyes off her.

"Maybe I should go shower and change first," she said.

Edan forced himself to look away, glancing out at the ocean.

"Sorry," he said. "Anyway, I'm guessing that they think something's up."

"Could be," she said, "and you've got to wonder if it has anything to do with our trip down to Carlsbad. If I were paranoid, I'd think they think something serious went down at your office. Or maybe they think we're planning to put laser guns on the helo and go do God knows what, God knows where. In any case, let me re-think our plan for tonight. I'll be back."

She went into the house and Edan's gaze followed her every step of the way. Once she was inside, he sat down, put his elbows on the table and rested his forehead on his open palms. Then he shook his head and resumed doing what he had been doing before he heard the Whaler.

Sim re-emerged twenty minutes later dressed in jeans and a cotton sweater, her still-wet hair slicked back and fashioned into a single braid.

"You think you can still remember how to drive?" she asked, taking a small bottle of water out of the small refrigerator that was built into the credenza and joining Edan at the table.

"Funny," he said.

"I'll take that as a yes. Good, now here's what we're going to do."

Not long after, a black Mercedes sedan with tinted side and back windows turned left from the Pacific Coast Highway into the long, winding drive that led to Edan's house. It ran the gauntlet of barricades, which Sim had disarmed for the occasion, and then waited, idling outside the main entrance to the house for several minutes. No one got in or out of the car. Then it retraced its course, turning right from the end of the driveway onto the Coast Highway. The driver watched in his rearview mirror as one of the Suburbans pulled off the shoulder and also headed south. As the Suburban kept pace a few car lengths back, the driver texted Sim to confirm that he was being followed.

She was standing next to Edan's immaculate dark green 1964 Pontiac GTO convertible when the text came in and he started the old car, let it idle for a moment, shifted into first gear and edged out of the crowded garage.

"Say hi to Dale for me," he said, pausing next to her.

"Sure," she said. "Have fun."

She had an idea of where Edan might be headed and the last thing she actually wanted was for him to have fun. She kept her face impassive as he revved the engine, let out the clutch and started slowly up the drive.

When he got to the intersection, he too headed south on the Coast Highway. Once he confirmed that he was also being followed, Sim walked back into the garage, got into her silver Porsche 911 and headed up the drive, but she turned left onto Pacific Coast Highway and headed north. The car's high-tech automated manual gearbox clicked off shifts quickly and firmly as she accelerated hard, well past the legal limit, all the while checking to see if another watcher appeared behind her.

While she drove north, becoming more certain that she was not being followed, the Mercedes continued south, stopping after a few minutes when it got to the Salt Creek Grille, just off the highway. The Suburban followed, driving slowly past the restaurant's parking valets and stopping just in time to watch a woman in jeans and a black hoodie who resembled Sim in height and build, and a somewhat more formally dressed and somewhat older Asian man, get out of the car and walk into the restaurant.

Edan's GTO continued further south to the Ritz-Carlton in Laguna Niguel. He tipped the valet to leave his car out front and watched as the black Suburban that had been trailing him pulled into the hotel's drive. Then he headed inside to the Bar Raya where he found an unoccupied white leather bar stool, ordered a vodka and soda and waited.

Sim savored the drive north in the powerful and stable sports car, finally turning off the highway when she got to Newport Beach, at the entrance to Mastro's Ocean Club. She, too, tipped the valet to leave the car out front and once she was sure there were no watchers, walked into the restaurant. She checked in with the *maitre d'* and was escorted to a generously sized two-top in the courtyard, under the soaring branches of a giant tree covered with twinkling white lights. Her dining companion, a large and muscular man of thirty-five with close-cropped sandy hair, dressed in jeans and a black cashmere jacket over a pale blue tee shirt, stood and smiled as she approached. They hugged briefly, and it was more of a hug between old friends or a brother and sister than one between lovers or former lovers.

"How you been, girl?" the man, whose name was Dale Bowdoin, asked when they parted, a hint of his native Mississippi and a trace of concern in his voice.

"My new parts seem to be holding up better than the old ones," Sim replied as she took her seat. "How about you? Been anywhere interesting lately?"

"Hell, my last serious outing was with you," he replied, smiling and lowering himself into his chair, "and that's going on eight months ago now. Since then it's all been baby shit. Bunch of Boy Scouts with a few merit badges could've gotten the same results we did."

Sim laughed.

"Well, if I was looking for a bunch of Boy Scouts," she said, "I wouldn't be having this meeting here with you."

"That's good news," Bowdoin told her, "real good news. And while we're about it, y'all'll be able to sample some of the very best steaks and martinis in southern California. Ever been here before?"

Sim told him she had not.

"Well, y'all don't know what you been missin'," he said. "And lordy, what's become of my manners? You must be thirsty as hell."

He gestured to a waiter who came over and asked how he could help.

"Two more of these, please," he told the man, holding up a nearly empty martini glass.

"Right away, sir."

"What are you getting me into?" Sim asked once the waiter had gone. "I've got kind of a long drive home."

"Nothin' fancy, just the basics, darlin'," he replied. "You just pour some Bombay Sapphire gin into a shaker, pass a bottle of dry vermouth over top of it—"

"Cap on or off?" Sim asked, smiling at him.

"If you want them to take it off, I can call the feller back," Bowdoin said, feinting a gesture toward another waiter.

Sim smiled again.

"That won't be necessary," she told him.

"Anyway," he went on, "shake with ice, pour into one of these here classic martini glasses, add two green olives with one of them little ole pimientos inside, no blue cheese or anythin' weird like that, and serve."

"Bring it on," Sim said.

They made small talk during the five minutes it took for the waiter to return with their drinks. He put them down and Bowdoin ordered two New York strips, rare, and a side of sea salt and vinegar fries.

"Hope that meets with your approval, captain," he said as the waiter walked away.

"If it hadn't, you'd have known about it, *captain,*" Sim said.

They held their glasses out and clinked gently, and each took a sip.

"Now then," he said, putting down his glass, "why don't y'all tell me what it is you're here to get *me* into."

17

"SO, YOU GONNA share what happened at your big powwow with princess tits-that-won't-quit up there in the big city, hoss?" Granda asked Carver as he slid the door to the salon closed on Monday evening.

Apparently there had been some sort of signal between Perricone and Granda to the effect that Carver had not shared the details of his L.A. meeting during the ride out in the Boston Whaler. But instead of answering, Carver stepped over to the galley, laid three crystal lowball glasses out next to each other on the counter, tossed several ice cube into each one, found a bottle of Myers's rum in a cabinet and began fixing three generous rum and Cokes. He cut up a lime and after he had squeezed some of its juice into the drinks, handed one to each of his companions, held his own glass out in a toast and polished off about half of it in one swallow.

"I'm sure you know the old joke about how I'd have to kill you if I told you," Carver said, taking another, much smaller sip of his drink.

"Oh for fuck's sake," Granda said, "you're gonna play the national security card on us?"

Carver nodded.

"Afraid so," he replied. "Anyway, drink up, boys, I hate getting drunk alone."

"It's that bad?" Perricone asked.

Carver's reply was to pour more rum and a splash of Coke into his glass. Perricone and Granda both took long sips from their glasses.

"By the way," Carver said once he had sampled his freshened drink, "I'll be leaving in the morning, for good this time. Looks like I'll need a ride back to that marina."

"Whatever," Perricone said.

They took the open and nearly empty bottle of Myers's, along with an unopened one, a few cans of Coke, a silver ice bucket filled to the brim with cubes and the already sectioned lime up to the flybridge and spread out around the table there, all three of them facing Edan Duff's house. They passed a pair of binoculars around and about an hour and two drinks later they saw Duff and Sim get up from the table on the terrace and go into the house. About ten minutes after that Perricone's iPhone rang. He set it down on the table and put it on speaker, as the caller, a watcher in one of the Suburbans, told them that a black Mercedes sedan had come to Duff's house and apparently picked someone up. They were following it south on Pacific Coast Highway. A few minutes later, another call came in letting them know that Duff had driven off, as well, and that he was also headed south, in a dark green Pontiac GTO, and that the team in the second Suburban was following him.

"Motherfucker!" was all Perricone said after the second call ended.

"Let me guess," Carver, who had gotten up to fix his third rum and Coke, said, "you think the woman wasn't really in the Mercedes, Duff hit the road to lure out the other Suburban and now Sim, Jane Garrison's, off somewhere with no one left to follow her. And she's probably where the action is."

"Something like that," Perricone said.

"Clever son-of-a-bitch," Granda added.

"Au contraire," Perricone said, slurring his words slightly, "clever *bitch*. She's the strategist in that duo."

"You gonna tell your comrades that it's probably not Garrison in that Mercedes?" Carver asked.

"Naw," Perricone replied. "Let 'em follow through and figure out for themselves what jerks they were. What the hell, right? I mean, by now that Sim woman's gotta be long gone. Even if they turn around now, they're not gonna catch up with her."

"Probably right," Carver agreed.

Perricone stared at his watch for a moment, then stood up and cautiously made his way down the ladder to the main deck. A few minutes later they heard the sound of pots and pans clattering, coming from the galley, below.

Carver and Granda drank in silence until Perricone called up to them a half hour later to say that dinner was ready and that they should come downstairs. It took two trips and a good deal of concentration on the steps for them to bring their glasses, the rum, ice bucket and Cokes down to the galley. Carver made fresh drinks while Perricone, using stainless steel tongs, scooped angel hair pasta out of a large pot of boiling water and into a serving bowl. Next, he unsteadily transferred a thick, red sauce from a smaller pot into a china gravy boat that matched the other dishes on the boat, all of which were logoed *ELVIRA,* the name of the yacht, in gold filigree.

Perricone had left three dinner plates, some silverware and a stack of paper napkins on the aft deck table and Granda set three places while Carver brought their fresh drinks out from the galley and set one down at each place setting. Perricone brought out the pasta and sauce and each man served himself dinner.

"Eat, drink and be merry, for tomorrow we will die?" Perricone asked, looking across the table at Carver with the eyes of a drunk.

"Pessimist," Carver said, twirling some angel hair around his fork.

Perricone shrugged.

"Hey, I'm just guessing we won't be able to stop Duff," he said, "whatever the fuck he's up to. What, you telling me you're optimistic?"

Carver hesitated before answering.

"I'm not sure I'd go *that* far," he finally replied. "It's just that I don't think it's necessarily *us* that are going to die."

18

EDAN DUFF WAS the kind of quasi-celebrity that, when he traveled, a great many people thought they recognized but that most could not quite place. In much of Southern California, though, his face was as well-known as any A-list movie star's, so he hid under base-ball caps a lot when he went out and tended to keep to low-key places where he might be casually acknowl-edged but where he was likely to be left in peace, and protected from prying paparazzi if necessary.

The Ritz-Carlton in Laguna Niguel was one such place, but he had been at its bar on Monday night, sans ball cap, for only ten minutes when a striking young woman strode into the room and sat down on the stool next to his. He seemed immersed in his thoughts and the bartender, who knew Edan from prior visits, was about to say some discouraging words to her. But then Edan noticed that she was there and when he did he turned, smiled and leaned in to kiss her lightly on the lips. As he did, the bartender moved away.

"It's good to see you, Pamela," he said. "You look fantastic, as usual."

She smiled, touched his cheek and told him he looked tired.

"Maybe a little," he said. "So, how was your day?"

As he said it, he signaled the bartender and ordered a cosmopolitan for her.

"Let's see," she answered playfully, tossing back her long, auburn hair, "I nailed my scene on the second take this morning, was picked up from work in a limo, driven down here, escorted to a beautiful suite, had a massage, followed that up with an hour at the pool and somehow managed to have my hair done and squeeze in a mani-pedi after that, so I suppose it wasn't too terrible. Thank you, by the way."

Edan smiled. From across the room, she was dead ringer for Sim. The likeness began to fade as you got closer to her, but it was still rather remarkable. She was an actress and had a small recurring role on a long-running cable TV drama. His personal assistant was a fan of the show and had mentioned the resemblance to Edan one morning about two years earlier. After Edan had checked it out, one of his attorneys contacted Pamela's agent and he had arranged for them to meet. They got along and had come to an understanding quickly after that. It immediately doubled her income, which did not even take into account the clothes, shoes and jewelry he supplied, or the massages, salon visits and occasional exotic vacation.

In exchange, as her TV production schedule allowed, she joined him when there was a business function or gala that demanded he arrive plus-one. And she would spend an evening or sometimes the night with him when he wanted something more intimate, which was becoming more frequent.

He liked her well enough but he did not love her. His capacity for love was expended entirely on Sim, the two women's physical likeness notwithstanding. But Pamela was a skilled lover and adventurous enough in bed and their couplings were satisfying for both of them. Still, he remained quite certain that making love to Sim would far transcend even that. But if he could not make love to Sim, a tragic impossibility, at least he could imagine he was, and there was comfort of a sort in that.

"Talk you into dinner?" he asked when her drink arrived.

"How about room service?" she replied. "I have to be on the set early tomorrow."

"Maybe just dinner tonight," he said. "I made a reservation here, at Raya. I think you'll like it. It's kind of pan-Latin and I booked a table looking out at the ocean."

She looked surprised but not disappointed.

"Whatever you'd like, sweetheart," she said.

They chatted for a few more minutes while she sipped her cosmo and he finished his vodka, then walked to the restaurant and were seated at a table near the windows. Outside, a half moon shined brightly enough to illuminate the choppy water. He ordered a bottle of Heitz Cellar cabernet and suggested they begin with the ceviche tasting, to which she readily agreed. She chose the achiote salmon and Edan the miso Alaskan black cod for main courses. Both the wine and their conversation flowed freely. They declined the offer of dessert and as Edan asked the waiter for their check, Pamela asked Edan if he was sure he did not want to go back to the room with her.

"The car is coming for me at five, but...."

"Not tonight," he said.

They walked to the elevators and he kissed her goodnight when the doors opened.

"Sleep well," he said.

"You, too," she said, stroking his face. "I'll see you soon."

Then he walked outside to his car.

19

THERE WAS ONLY one black government Suburban parked in what had become their usual watching positions when Sim turned into the long drive that led to Edan Duff's house at eleven on Monday night, and she smiled at how easy it had been to carry off the deception.

"Idiots," she said aloud.

But her smile was short-lived once she realized it meant that Edan must still be with the woman, Pamela, and Sim's mood darkened as she followed the twisting drive toward the garage. The narrow, serpentine road was well lit and it was easy, even for the casual observer, to pick out the cameras and other sensors that lined the route. That was by design, of course, since deterrents had their place. But so did countermeasures and Sim had taken care to much more carefully conceal the pop-up barricades and such. And the countermeasures now included lasers, added within the past few days.

The full arsenal could be controlled from a panel in the small command center in the house, not far from Sim's suite, or just as easily from her iPhone, or Edan's, if it came to that. For now, though, she used her phone only to make sure the barricades and other counter-measures were not triggered as she drove past, rather than to mount a full-scale attack on an intruder.

As she neared the garage, Sim used another app on her iPhone to open the wide door and, as the door closed automatically behind her, she parked her Porsche among the dozen automotive icons from which Edan had selected the GTO. To her surprise, the GTO was there. There was another surprise when she put her hand on the hood and discovered it was barely warm.

"Guess it was a quickie tonight, eh Duff?" she murmured as she walked to the door that led into the house. "Must be the happy couple in the Mercedes who aren't back yet."

There was a keypad next to the door and she entered a five-digit code, pressed her left index finger against a biometric fingerprint reader and the steel door unlatched. Lights came on as she walked down a short hallway that, unlike the longer one leading to Edan's lab, was carpeted, less harshly lit and furnished with a narrow parson's table on which there was a lamp and a wooden bowl into which she tossed her car keys. The doorway at the end of the hall required her to input a code into another keypad, although no fingerprint offering was required.

The exhaustion, or maybe it was ennui, that had settled over her meant that she should have walked directly to her suite and gone to bed but she instead walked through the kitchen and out to the terrace at the back of the house. She rarely saw any of the six people who shared the everyday responsibilities of keeping up such a house and its occupants, like house-keeping duties and meal preparation. But nothing was ever out of place or in need of cleaning and food and beverages, appropriate for the situation or time of day, were always left where Edan or Sim were most likely to want or need them. It surprised her at first, although it should not have. After all, everyone who worked for Edan was outstanding at his or her job, and well paid. But she had never come around to taking it for granted and it still sometimes surprised her.

There was an ice bucket on the credenza filled with perfect, square cubes. Lined up next to it were a dozen assorted Baccarat crystal glasses, a stainless steel cocktail shaker, a stack of elegant Caspari paper cocktail napkins and a tray of lemon and lime wedges and orange slices. Sim selected a lowball glass, opened a cabinet beneath the credenza and withdrew a bottle of Bombay Sapphire gin. She had stopped after a single martini at Mastro's, but Dale had talked her into a second glass of wine during dinner, so she was unsure whether another drink was a good idea and paused, bottle in hand.

"Fuck it," she said softly after a moment.

She put the Bombay bottle on the credenza, leaned over and found one of Campari and another of sweet vermouth and set those down next to the gin. She still had the crystal glass in her other hand and scooped a few ice cubes into it, then poured in equal parts of each of the three liquors. Using a folded orange slice she stirred the concoction, better known as a Negroni, and dropped the slice into the drink. Then she carried the glass and a napkin to the table and sat down facing the ocean and the two yachts that were perennially anchored offshore.

She took a sip of her drink and once more thought about the fact that it had not been Edan's assistant who had noted the uncanny resemblance between Sim and the actress Pamela Mitchell. TV shows and movies were Sim's only real escape, her head injury also having left her without the patience or the acuity for reading anything much more serious than a magazine. She had been a fan of the show on which Pamela appeared and it was Sim who had brought the woman's resemblance to the assistant's attention, making sure that he kept aspect that of it to himself.

Of course, once Edan and Pamela had begun seeing each other, Sim had stopped watching the show.

She took another sip of her drink, ran her tongue over her lips and then took a longer sip.

It was a cool, still night and once the clinking of ice cubes subsided it was as soundless as the outdoors could get. So soundless that Sim could even hear the very slight whistling sound that emanated from the artificial lung in her chest, something she rarely heard except when lying in bed. Now it brought back what she had become. And the thought of Pamela Mitchell brought back what she once had been. She was unaware of the tear trickling down her cheek until it splashed into her drink, a lack of feeling in parts of her face, neck and chest being yet another change bestowed by the mortar round and endless surgeries.

She stood up suddenly, swirled the ice in her glass and walked to the railing, where she took a long swallow of the Negroni and locked her eyes on the Princess yacht in the harbor.

She had told Dale Bowdoin nothing about the device, of course, and likely would not do so until he and his team were ready to get inside it. And she was still hoping that either she or Edan would somehow be able to come up with a plausible alternative explanation for its purpose to feed to Bowdoin's team before the mission to kill John Foster Dulles got underway. Bowdoin had not asked many questions when he was a member of their unit in Afghanistan and, more recently, had remained unquestioning of everything but operational necessities when he had followed her on the more private missions that Edan financed. For now, all he knew was that they would be going to a thus-far undisclosed location to undertake an assassination and that it would likely be carried out through the administration of poison.

And, of course, that he would still be on the side of right.

His reaction had been to smile and say, "Just tell me where and when and how many and what type of personnel to bring."

But after another sip of her drink, Dale Bowdoin was gone from Sim's mind and Pamela Mitchell had again taken over, and Sim had to wonder. Did Edan really think about her when he was with Pamela, when he was inside Pamela, and had he been inside her tonight?

She dropped her glass and her hands were shaking as she frantically worked to get the buttons and zipper of her jeans open. Once she had, she thrust her hand down, inside her panties, imagining Edan inside her and willing her fingers to somehow provoke the reaction that his body should, that even the thought of him should, the sweet wetness and parting that would have come to any normal girl.

But she was no longer a normal girl, had not been for quite a while now, and never would be again.

She zipped up her jeans and this time felt the tears as they began to stream down her face.

20

"YOU'D BETTER NOT be fucking with me, Rip," Roger Bates told Carver and McKinney as he paced back and forth across the front of the secure conference room at FBI headquarters in Los Angeles at noon on Tuesday.

Carver assured the CIA Deputy Director that he was not fucking with him. Mary McKinney felt no need to add anything to what Carver said and continued to stare at her hands, which were interlaced on the table in front of her. Bates was not about to let her off so easy, though.

"And what about DARPA?" he demanded, stopping his back and forth to look straight at her. "You agree with this, this preposterous conclusion of his?"

McKinney squeezed her hands together so tightly that they began turning red, but she forced herself to look up at Bates.

"Most of the analysis that Mr. Carver did was vetted through people at my agency or academics we use as consultants," she told him.

"Most of whom had no idea that they were looking at one piece of a much larger puzzle," Bates shot back, "so they had no fucking idea what that whole picture might look like!"

"That's true of most of them for most of the project," McKinney admitted, "but the most recent consultations included a peek at the whole picture and it was the scientists, not Mr. Carver, who came up with the internalization of energy theory and the potential effect on the localized gravity and warping of space-time. I've also gone over Mr. Carver's analysis and reasoning at every step of the process, several times in fact. So yes, preposterous as it may seem, I agree."

Bates stared at her for a full minute, during which she did not move a muscle, before finally shaking his head and walking to the credenza to pour coffee into a mug. He did not ask whether McKinney or Carver were interested in refills of the nearly empty mugs that sat on the table in front of them.

Bates was a tall, paunchy man of fifty or so with a well-trimmed fringe of gray hair around the sides of his large head. He wore a Glen plaid suit and a tie and had been visibly unhappy at Carver's choice of jeans and a sweater as his attire for the meeting.

"You two won't be offended if I spend some time challenging those conclusions, I trust," he said, finally sitting down and taking a swallow of coffee.

"Of course not," Carver and McKinney replied in unison, although Carver added *sir* after his. "But I've prepared a document," Carver went on, "that lays out all of the alternative conclusions at each step of the analysis, the reasons for choosing the conclusion that was selected and why that series of conclusions led inextricably to my bottom line deduction that Edan Duff had developed a device capable of warping time. It also addresses in more detail why certain of the alternative conclusions were rejected."

"It might have been helpful," Bates said, "if you had e-mailed that document to me before I left Washington this morning."

Carver looked away for a moment before focusing back on Bates.

"There were two reasons for that, sir," he said. "First of all, I didn't think it would be optimum for you to be made aware of my conclusion before we'd had a chance to meet and talk it through--"

"Because I'd've told you it was completely ridiculous and refused to come out here?" Bates demanded.

"Yes, sir."

"And second?"

"And second," Carver went on, "considering the nature of that conclusion, as well as certain other aspects of the process, I felt that, at this stage, the fewer people in possession of documentation making mention of and laying out the steps of the analysis the better. Of course, once you and the Director are on board with my conclusion, then it will be your decision to make."

Bates grunted his grudging agreement and suggested that Carver hand over the document. Carver, in turn, opened a file on his laptop and made a few keystrokes. A printer on the same credenza where the coffee was set up began to hum and a document began to print. When it was complete, Carver took it off the machine and handed it to Bates, who quickly skimmed the twenty-odd pages.

"This is obviously going to take some time for me to go through," Bates said. "One of you better order lunch."

"Already done, sir," Carver told him. "It should be here shortly."

Bates insisted that Carver and McKinney remain in the room while he reviewed the document in case he had any questions as he went along. They complied, but for bathroom breaks, and sat at the ready, although the tray on which a selection of sandwiches was delivered had been picked clean by the time Bates made his first query.

"Take me through the analysis of why he could have built that laser system without consuming a hundred percent of each of his stock of components that were on its initial build list," he finally said, standing up to get a can of Diet Coke. "I mean, according to this analysis, having leftovers, so to speak, is crucial to your conclusion. Unless he had access to a few of the same items that went into the laser system, he apparently couldn't have built the, ah, time warping system."

Carver had not pictured Duff's creation as a system, and Bates' use of the word caught him off guard. He had instead been picturing some kind of machine, a hyper-modern iteration of the rudimentary device described long ago by H. G. Wells. But he supposed Bates' characterization of the technology behind it was accurate enough and he dutifully took his boss through the issue, as well as several others during the course of the next two hours. Mary McKinney made the occasional comment, but Carver did the lion's share of the talking.

When Bates was satisfied that there were no apparent flaws in the analysis, his focus turned to the historian, Henry Lee.

"He's a Middle East expert, right?" Bates asked.

Carver confirmed that he was and laid out Lee's background, adding that in addition to his regional expertise, Lee was viewed as also having a great deal of knowledge about many other facets of world history. Again, Bates asked a few questions but mainly listened

At four o'clock Bates excused himself to go to the men's room and Carver and McKinney also took a break.

Bates had already returned to the room and was standing at the windows, looking out on the city, when they
returned. As soon as Carver shut and locked the door,
Bates turned around and asked whether they thought
that Duff had already used the device. Carver glanced
at McKinney before answering.

"We think we know what it's for," Carver said, "but
we have no way of knowing whether it actually works."

"I'm not in the mood, Rip," Bates said menacingly.
"Assume the fucking thing works as planned. Now I'll
ask again, do you think Duff has already used the thing?"

"Assuming he hasn't tested it right there in his lab,
he's only had one opportunity that we're aware of,"
he said. "There was a party, some big fundraiser, at
his house a couple of nights ago. Two catering trucks
arrived a few hours ahead of time, stayed there for
what seemed to the FBI watchers like enough time to
drop off the food and such, and then left."

"And you think he might have used one of those
trucks to get the, the thing, out of there?" Bates asked.

"Yes, sir."

"Were they followed when they left?" Bates asked.

Carver sighed.

"No, sir," he said.

"So we have no idea where they might have gone?"

"No, sir," Carver repeated. "Apparently the FBI folks
who've been sitting up at the end of his street didn't

think there was a reason to follow them. They knew that a hundred or so people were expected to attend the fundraiser, so the catering trucks--"

Bates made a sour face and held up his hand.

"So it was natural for the trucks to have come and gone before the party started," he said. "I get it. Go on."

"Anyway," Carver said, "the same trucks came back late in the evening, apparently to clean up after the party."

"What kind of trucks were they?" Bates asked.

"Ford Transit vans," Carver replied, "the somewhat smaller ones."

"You think they were big enough to hold Duff's creation?"

"Assuming he didn't already have more raw materials to make that mineral substance," Carver replied, "which is what we think forms its exterior, it's not all that large. Of course, we don't know its shape--"

"Land the plane, Carver," Bates said.

"Probably so, the truck was probably large enough, yes, sir," he said.

"Was Duff at the party?" Bates asked next.

"According to someone who was there, neither Mr. Duff nor Ms. Garrison, who also lives in Duff's house, attended," Carver replied.

"Garrison's his head of security, right?" Bates asked.

"Yes, sir."

"Anyone see them leave?"

"No, sir."

Bates stood up and resumed his earlier pacing.

"Logic would suggest that Duff and Garrison could well have left the house in one of those vans," he said, "and if they went to those lengths to make sure no one saw them leave, logic also suggests they probably had the thing in there with them. So, assuming it actually works, the son-of-a-bitch might already have used it, for God knows what."

"It could have been a test," McKinney said, "but the fact is, whether he's used it or not, it's still possible that Duff intends to bring this to us once he's satisfied with the technology. He's done that in the past with other new items and there's really no reason to think--"

"Has he come to you about the laser system?" Bates, who had stopped pacing, interrupted to ask.

"No, but that may mean he's not yet satisfied--"

Bates held up his hand and McKinney stopped talking.

"That laser worked well enough to shoot down two FBI drones," he said. "I'd call that pretty satisfactory. And we have reason to believe that he's at least tested the *thing,* and as Carver here alluded to, he may also have tested it in his lab, so he's just as likely as not to be satisfied with its performance, too."

"We don't know--" McKinney began but Bates cut her off again.

"The sad fact is we don't actually know shit!" he yelled, his face becoming flushed and his voice rising, "at least not about that machine or whatever the hell it is! We don't even know for certain exactly what it is, let alone what stage of readiness it's at! But the more important fact is that his little outing in that van could have been a beta test and the damn thing might work just fine! And if that's the case and he hasn't contacted you about it, that might well mean he's completely satisfied and he's planning on selling it to the Iranians or maybe the Chinese or the Russians or God knows who as soon as he can and that makes it my problem!"

McKinney and Carver said nothing as Bates strode to the credenza, opened a bottle of water, drank about half of it and then sat down heavily in his chair.

"Look folks," he said, in a more conciliatory tone, "we're talking about something that, assuming it is what you think it is and that it actually works, would make other things that we regard as *high-tech* or *cutting edge* seem about as modern as an abacus. More importantly, its existence would create a level of potential danger in the world beyond anything we've ever dealt with before. And in the hands of an enemy it's a danger that's frankly almost unimaginable, and unallowable. We can't wait for him to come to us."

21

"IF I DIDN'T know better, I'd say you were trying to make a statement of some kind," Edan said as Sim joined him on the terrace at noon on Wednesday.

"What makes you think I'm not?" she asked.

After she had stopped crying the previous night, Sim had prepared another Negroni and taken it to her suite. There she went on the internet and printed out a photo of Pamela Mitchell and another of herself from a file on her computer and taped them to a mirror, side by side. Then she had sat for hours, staring at the two images. Eventually she had torn them both into tiny pieces and gone to bed. She slept fitfully, waking alternatively from the same two dreams, one of Edan making love to Pamela and the other of Sim meeting Edan for the first time, at the military hospital in Landstuhl. At the time, she had been heavily sedated and filled with painkillers and that somehow made the dream even closer to her memory of the gauzy semi-reality of the actual event.

She had finally gotten out of bed at nine, quickly showered, dressed in cut-off jean shorts and a halter top and walked to the garage. She maneuvered her Porsche out of the garage and up the drive and made a left turn onto Pacific Coast Highway. One of the black Suburbans pulled off the shoulder and onto the road as she did, keeping pace with her a few car lengths back as she drove north.

Whatever the watchers might have been expecting her to do, Sim was reasonably sure it was not for her to park in the center of Laguna Beach and walk to a nearby barber shop. As she had stepped out onto the sidewalk twenty minutes after entering the shop, her long auburn hair having been buzzed off, she wondered whether the barber or the watchers had been more surprised.

"I needed a change, that's all," Sim said, as Edan's eyes remained locked on her.

"That certainly qualifies," he said. "Please don't tell me that you've got appointments to get your breast implants removed and get a Maori tattoo on your face."

She almost smiled.

"Not yet," she said.

What little was left of her hair was so short that you could see the curve of her pale scalp beneath it.

Edan could also make out the fading scar from where the bullet had entered her head, not far from her right ear, as well as where it had exited, although he doubted that a casual observer would have noticed it, or if Sim cared if they did. The haircut also left her ears exposed, of course, and somehow the sight of her stretched earlobes, held open with circular gold tunnels an inch in diameter, was somehow even more dramatic than it had been when she had pulled her long hair back. The gun sight tattoos seemed more noticeable, too. The halter top she wore left much of the tattoo on her back and arms exposed, as well, and as he gazed at her, Edan was becoming hard and he thought he felt his face begin to flush. He hoped she did not notice.

"It'll be easier to deal with on a mission, too," she said.

She turned away from him and went to the credenza. It was after ten but breakfast was still set out and she scooped scrambled eggs, crispy bacon and hash brown potatoes onto a plate. She set the plate down while she poured coffee into a mug, then carried the mug and plate to the table and sat down next to Edan.

"You look spectacular, by the way," he told her, "although I can't help wonder if that's the reaction you were going for." He reached out and ran his hand over her head and she could not help close her eyes as he did. "Feels good, too," he went on. "Softer than I would have thought."

"As I said, I needed a change," is all Sim said before shaking off his hand and digging into her breakfast.

Edan kept his eyes on her for another few seconds and then got up to pour himself more coffee, hoping once more that she would not notice the bulge in his jeans or the pink in his cheeks. When he sat down again, he forced himself to focus on the work he had been doing on his laptop before she arrived. For her part, Sim said nothing as she ate.

When she finished, she carried her plate and mug to the credenza, leaving the plate and pouring more coffee into the mug. When she returned to the table and sat down, Edan turned to face her.

"I had a call first thing this morning from Mary McKinney at DARPA," he said. "Remember her?"

"The one with the giant boobs," Sim said, pushing her chair back and folding her arms across her chest. "What did she want, some kind of help, no doubt."

"She said she'd like to get together to talk about a project they're working on," he replied. "She told me she was coming out here from DC and asked if we could meet today or tomorrow."

Sim stared at him for a moment.

"She said that, *coming out* here?" she finally asked. "She didn't say *flying out* here?"

Edan thought about it before answering.

"*Coming*, definitely," he finally said. "Why?"

"I think she may already be here," Sim said, standing. "Let me have your iPhone."

Edan handed her his iPhone and she went into the house. While she was gone, Edan went and stood at the railing, looking out at the Princess yacht, anchored at its usual spot offshore.

"She flew out here three weeks ago on a United flight from Washington National," Sim said when she joined Edan at the railing ten minutes later. "Right now, she's at 11000 Wilshire Boulevard in downtown L.A., or at least her phone is. 11000 Wilshire's the federal building. The FBI's local office is in there, along with several other agencies. For all I know, DARPA's got space there, too, although it's not listed as a tenant."

The flush disappeared entirely from Edan's cheeks and his mouth opened slightly, but he recovered quickly.

"Okay, given that, along with the trips on that Whaler our friends out there on the yacht have been making lately and the fact that the third guy left yesterday morning and hasn't come back yet," Edan said, "I'd guess that it's not a project *they're* working on that she wants to talk to me about as much as it's a project *I'm* working on."

Sim bit her lower lip.

"There's that second Suburban, too," she said. "You know, McKinney's always come to Carlsbad when you've met with her out here in the past. Did she happen to suggest where the two of you might get together this time?"

"Just that she'd be happy to come down to Carlsbad, as usual," he replied.

Sim turned around and leaned back against the railing and thought about it for a moment, absently running a hand over her shorn head.

"Tell her you can't make it this afternoon," she said, turning to face Edan. "Make it for tomorrow afternoon instead. I want to try and see what she might do between now and then. As far as the Dulles mission goes, Bowdoin is nearly finished with the playbook, although he doesn't know who the target is, but you and I should talk about the timing. I have a feeling we may want to accelerate things."

22

"THE BAD NEWS is that driving out of here without picking up an entire government entourage is going to be impossible," Sim told Edan on Wednesday evening. "I was followed when I went to get my hair cut this morning, of course, but now there are more of them out there, a lot more, so even the kind of subterfuge I arranged last night isn't going to work anymore."

They were in the command center, the small room near Sim's suite where the monitoring screens and controls for all the security and weapons systems for the house were arrayed. With a quick look at the screens and other equipment, the casual observer might not have noticed anything out of the ordinary beyond the additional black Suburbans parked along Pacific Coast Highway. But Sim was not a casual observer and she noted that there were also a few armed men hiding in the bushes in the outer portion of the driveway, right down to Edan's property line. And as she pointed to various monitors and other sensors, she told Edan that there were now five people in each Suburban, instead of the usual two or three, and that the FBI, or whoever they all were, also had infrared scanners trained on the house.

"Not that they can penetrate the Kevlar in the outer walls," she added, "but you get the idea. They seem to have gotten quite a bit more serious."

"What's the good news?" Edan asked when she was done.

But instead of answering, Sim asked another question, one that surprised Edan.

"So, how much do you suppose the dingus actually weighs?"

Edan laughed.

"What?" she said. "I'm not sure I see anything that's funny at the moment."

"Nothing, really," he replied. "Well, actually, two things."

"What"? she said again.

"Well, first of all, you said *dingus*."

"I watched *The Maltese Falcon* after we got back from the Whisky," she told him. "It was terrific, by the way. What's the second thing?"

Edan let out a breath.

"How much the device weighs is a question I hoped no one would ever ask me," he replied.

"I can understand why you don't have a commercial scale or something like that in your lab," Sim said, "but aren't there other ways to figure it out, at least to get close?"

Edan smiled.

"It's not quite that simple," he told her, "but then again, nothing about the, ah, *dingus,* really is. Let's see, where to start?"

"This is where I'm supposed to say *just start at the beginning,*" Sim said, an impatient expression on her face, "but I think I'll try *keep it simple and just cut to the fucking chase* instead."

"Fine," he said. "Remember I told you that the device is always *on*, at least in a manner of speaking?"

"I remember," she replied, "although I also recall having no fucking clue what you were really trying to get at."

Edan smiled again.

"But you did notice that when we moved it into the van, it was fairly easy to move?" he asked.

"I do," she said warily, "but I figured that was probably because you used the best rollers that money could buy along with those super cool lifting rod things."

"Not exactly," he said. "Let's just say that there's some space-time warping going on all the time, inside the device at least, and that not all of it is really there at any given time. Sorry, but if I go into it much more deeply, I'm going to have to start talking about quantum mechanics again and I'm betting you--"

"You're right, I don't want to hear that," Sim said. "But what I think you're getting at is that it probably doesn't weigh as much as you'd think."

Edan grinned.

"Excellent!" he said. "Why did you want to know, by the way?"

"Because I'm hoping we're going to be able to take it out of here with your helicopter," she replied.

Edan said nothing for a moment and appeared to be thinking about something. Sim kept quiet until he finally said, "Okay, what do you have in mind exactly?"

"The helo has a cargo hook, although we've never had reason to use it," she replied. "According to the specs, a Robinson R-66 like yours can carry a load of just under a thousand pounds, max, including fuel, and it doesn't really matter whether that weight is inside or outside the bird. I'd like to lift the dingus out of here tonight--"

"Tonight?"

"I'll get into the specifics of why tonight in a minute," she said, "but I can assure you that Bowdoin and his guys are ready."

"Okay, keep going," Edan told her.

"Anyway, I want to lift it out of here tonight for the simple reason that I'm reasonably sure that if we wait, we might not be able to get it out of here at all," she told him.

Again, Edan appeared to be immersed in thought and again Sim did not interrupt him. Eventually, he said, "Okay, I think you're telling me that despite adding more watchers and whatever else, they don't have anything in the air keeping an eye on us, is that right?"

Sim nodded.

"Not at the moment, anyway" she replied. "My guess is that since the drone business they're concerned that you might be tempted to shoot down whatever they might put up there. On the other hand, I wouldn't be surprised if they're trying to arrange for some satellite time, but assuming that request was made at more or less the same time they decided to step up their surveillance--"

"Which is only within the past day or maybe even less," Edan said.

"Exactly, because of whatever the hell it was that triggered this whole fire drill in the first place," Sim said. "Anyway, getting satellite time's not that easy, even for these people. It's not like there's free time whenever you might decide you want it. Those things are usually booked 24/7, way in advance. If you want to bump somebody, you've got to show that your need is more important than theirs. And that someone else is either another agency or a private entity that's paid a lot of money for the privilege and had to wait a while to get their slot, so even if these guys plead national security it's probably not going to happen right away. Bottom line, we would seem to have a window of opportunity, but it's probably a pretty short window."

"Okay, but move the device where?" Edan asked. "If they've got all these people watching us here, I have to believe they've got people watching my plane."

"I'm sure you're right, but it's not like your plane's the only plane in the world or that John Wayne Airport's the only airport in southern California, is it?" Sim asked, a larcenous glimmer in her eyes.

"Fair enough," Edan said, "but there aren't very many private jets out there with a large enough baggage compartment to handle the device, and even if a few of them do, they probably don't have a large enough cargo door to fit it through. You'd need something like my BBJ or the Airbus equivalent at least."

Sim smiled.

"It's kind of funny," she said, "after getting in the dingus, I'd've thought that thing would be able to fit itself through smaller openings."

"Unfortunately, it doesn't seem to work that way," Edan said.

"Too bad, but I figured that would be too good to be true. You know the Airbus ACJ319?" she asked.

He nodded.

"I almost bought one," he said, "but I like to buy American when I can, so I went for the Boeing."

"Then you probably know that it's about the same size as the Boeing 737 that your BBJ's based on," she told him, "seven thousand mile range, way more than enough cargo capacity. There's one based up at Long Beach. It's ours for the next twenty-four hours, and please don't ask what that's going to set you back. Anyway, a couple of Bowdoin's people are already up there standing guard."

Edan paused again and this time stared at the monitor that displayed the Princess yacht anchored offshore.

"You know, this wasn't supposed to be so difficult," he said.

"Best laid plans and all that crap," Sim told him.

"Sons of bitches on that boat must be smarter than we thought," he said.

"*Someone's* smarter than we thought," Sim said, "although if it's really FBI on that boat, I doubt it's them."

Edan smiled and turned back to her.

"Okay," he said, clearing his throat, "so let's say we get the device out of here tonight by air without being tracked and take it up to Long Beach. What then?"

Sim smiled and glanced at her watch.

"I'll tell you all about it over dinner," she said.

23

PERRICONE HAD JUST opened yet another bottle of Myers's rum, taken from the *ELVIRA's* seemingly bottomless semi-secret cache, and fixed two rum and Cokes when Perricone caught sight of Edan Duff's Robinson helicopter slowly ascending into the clear night sky. He put down the glasses and quickly sent an encrypted text to Mary McKinney, who sat in the back seat of one of the recently-arrived Suburbans with Roger Bates. Her reply, that they had just seen the craft appear over the hillside, came within a few beats of the helicopter's rotors.

Seconds later Perricone's phone rang. He answered it, walked over to the table on the flybridge where Granda sat, and put it on speaker, and he and Granda listened as McKinney barked out orders.

"We're going to have a few of the SUVs try to track the copter from the ground," she said, breathlessly.

"We need you to keep eyes on it for as long as you can and let us know what direction it's headed. I'll keep this line open."

Perricone said they would do their best and Granda jumped up and quickly headed down to the main deck to raise the anchor while Perricone stood up and grabbed a pair of binoculars. As he struggled to hold onto the phone and focus on the helicopter, he heard Granda stumble to the helm and start the boat's two powerful engines.

"I wouldn't swear to it," Perricone said into his phone as he watched the helicopter continue to climb slowly, "but it looks like there are two aboard."

"Duff and Garrison?" McKinney demanded.

Perricone nearly fell over as the pitch of the engines rose and the boat started moving, but managed to regain his balance, cradle the phone between his neck and shoulder and bring the helicopter back into view through the binoculars.

"Hard to tell for sure," he yelled into the phone. "The interior's pretty dark."

"Can you at least tell if it's a man and a woman?" McKinney implored him.

"Not really," was Perricone's reply. "They're both wearing dark clothing and ball caps and I can't make out long hair or a ponytail or anything on the pilot. Hang on a second. They just leveled off and seem to be making a turn to the northwest."

"I can see that!" McKinney shouted. "Okay, just make sure you keep eyes on them and keep this line open."

Granda had the boat at full throttle and while they were probably making twenty-five knots, they were quickly losing ground to the Robinson, which was not only much faster, but had begun heading inland.

"They're turning toward the north, maybe north-east now," Perricone told McKinney." We're going to lose them any minute."

"We've still got them," she told him.

The small blue and white strobe lights that were hidden behind the SUV's grill were flashing brightly and the driver was doing his best to weave through traffic and maintain a decent pace as the Suburban headed north on Pacific Coast Highway, several others in trail.

"We're going to lose them in a minute or so, too!" McKinney shouted. "What's north of here? Shit! Duff keeps his jet at John Wayne Airport in Santa Ana, right, and that's north of here."

Perricone quickly confirmed both points.

"Jesus, you think they're running?" he asked.

Get the fucking tail number of that plane and have every unit the FBI can muster meet us at that airport, Perricone heard a male voice shout in the background of the phone call.

"Gotta go," McKinney said, and ended the call.

Sim and Edan had carefully wrapped bands of black Kevlar rope around the device and it was connected to the helicopter's external lifting hook by a twenty-foot section of the same rope, its length chosen to keep the cargo out of the direct visual field of those gazing at the copter. Spotting that cargo was rendered even less likely by its black, matte finish cotton cover. A keen observer, even one with high-powered binoculars, would be more inclined to believe there was a small, starless section of sky below the copter than any sort of load hanging from beneath it, especially in the hazy L.A.-area sky.

Sim, at the controls, wore jeans, a black turtleneck sweater and a Dodgers ball cap, and she had applied dark make-up to her face. Edan, seated next to her, was dressed and made up similarly. She had also dimmed the panel displays and other lights inside the helicopter as much as possible. Those actions, she thought, and her new lack of long hair, would make it virtually impossible for the watchers to positively identify her as the pilot or Edan as the passenger, which could prove important at some point. She knew that the watchers were likely to assume that they were the ones aboard in any case, but she was also aware that there was a gaping legal distinction between a positive ID by law enforcement and an assumption.

To their enormous relief, Edan's calculations about the device's weight were apparently accurate and ascending with it slung below the helicopter proved no more difficult than flying the craft with three or four passengers aboard, at least once all the slack had gone out of the lift line. Still, Sim had climbed and accelerated somewhat more slowly than usual in deference to her precious cargo, which could become a large pendulum if not treated gingerly.

It was less than thirty miles as the crow flies from Edan's house to Long Beach Airport where the chartered Airbus jet awaited them, but Sim flew a more circuitous route, one that did not follow any of the major highways, to make it more difficult for traffic on the ground to successfully follow them. But they knew the helicopter had headed north and she had little doubt that the watchers would take the bait and assume that it was bound for John Wayne Airport, where they could make a getaway in Edan's jet.

She and Dale Bowdoin had spent a good deal of time communicating that afternoon, arranging for what would play out at John Wayne Airport that night, and she had set things in motion with a text to Dale just before they left Edan's house. Ironically, had she flown a bee line to Long Beach, she would have passed very close to John Wayne Airport, and as she skirted the area, Sim wished she could have been there to witness a hoard of federal law enforcement personnel descend on what they did not realize was the wrong target.

They would, no doubt, speak with airport employees and obtain the FAA flight plan for Edan's Boeing Business Jet. And they would learn that a man and a woman fitting Edan and Sim's descriptions had arrived in a Robinson helicopter at the airport not shortly before they did, that the duo and their luggage had been transferred onto the already-running BBJ and that another pilot had then left in the helicopter. They would also learn that their luggage included something resembling a very large steamer trunk, and that it was concealed by some kind of protective cover.

If the government people had made particularly good time, they might even catch a glimpse of the BBJ's lights as it climbed out over the Pacific.

From the FAA they would learn that there were two passengers and a crew of three on the large jet and that its destination was Shanghai.

Edan had not spoken at all during the flight and Sim had assumed that his mind was far away, focused on the mission to intercept John Foster Dulles, but now he asked how much longer it would be until they landed.

"Just a few more minutes," she told him.

And as she did, she gently banked the helicopter to the left for the last leg of their short flight, then contacted the Long Beach control tower and began an approach toward the airport's bright lights.

Three minutes later, Sim was finalizing a slow descent aimed at providing the gentlest possible landing for the device, despite Edan's reminder of its robustness. Dale Bowdoin and two of his men disconnected the lift line and Sim maneuvered the Robinson R-66 to land nearby, beside the airport's modest air cargo facility and not far from the ACJ319 jet. By the time she had performed her shut-down checklist and she and Edan deplaned, the device had been safely stowed in the jet's cavernous cargo compartment, and the compartment door had been closed.

They left their ball caps in the helicopter and as they walked to the jet each pulled a small Tumi roll-aboard suitcase, which had been stowed in the helo's small luggage compartment, behind them.

"Nice haircut," Bowdoin said from the bottom of the converted airliner's boarding stairs as Sim approached. "You could pass for the best looking Marine in history."

"I'll take that as a compliment," Sim said as she snatched the laptop bag but left her suitcase for Bowdoin to deal with.

He took it, along with Edan's, and started up the stairs. Sim and Edan followed him and Bowdoin's men fell in behind them. Once everyone was on board, Bowdoin closed the boarding door, then led Edan and Sim straight to an eight-seat conference table that separated the main section of luxurious leather seats and sofas from a wood-paneled bulkhead in the aft section of the cabin. As soon as they were seated, one of Bowdoin's people wheeled a service cart with a carafe of coffee, an assortment of soft drinks, china cups and glasses and bags of mixed nuts out to them from the galley.

Sim had dropped her laptop case on the thickly carpeted floor next to her chair and as she leaned over to get the computer out of the case, Bowdoin poured coffee for all three of them. While she was distracted, he emptied the contents of a tiny vial into one of the cups and slid that one across the table to her.

"It's ten-thirty now," he said, glancing at his watch, "the pilots should be here in forty-five minutes and we should be wheels up within a half hour after that."

"Why the delay?" Edan, sipping his coffee, asked.

It was Sim who answered, after taking a sip of hers.

"It's unlikely that the feds will keep searching after they think they missed us at John Wayne," she said, "but you never know. Just in case they do, I didn't want them discovering the departure of another, similar plane too soon after the BBJ left, and getting a hold of its flight plan."

"Got it."

Sim yawned copiously and Bowdoin picked up the thread.

"On the other hand," he told Edan, "we didn't want to be sitting out here for too long. The hour or so delay was a compromise."

"Makes sense," Edan said.

Sim took another sip of coffee, yawned again and then her eyes glazed over and she nearly tumbled out of her chair.

Both Edan and Bowdoin tried to rouse her, but she was clearly either fast asleep or unconscious. Bowdoin winked at Edan, picked her up and carried her over to a door that was set in the center of the wood-paneled bulkhead. Edan opened the door and Bowdoin eased her through it, into a bedroom that was the width of the tapering cabin and roughly twelve feet in length. In it were a queen bed, a small nightstand and an uphol-stered chair. Edan went to the bed and pulled down the duvet cover and blanket and tossed aside some throw pillows, and Bowdoin laid Sim down gently on her back and pulled the covers up to her neck.

"She'll be out for six hours minimum," Bowdoin said, as they left the bedroom, "but I'll give her an injection of something very similar before we land."

They walked past the conference table and went to the galley, fixed drinks and then went back to the table, where they began to go over the final details of the plan they had hatched together in secret, which had nothing at all to do with Suez or John Foster Dulles.

24

DESCRIBING HIS EMOTIONAL state as *livid* hardly did justice to CIA Deputy Director Roger Bates' frame of mind when he realized that they had missed Edan Duff's Boeing Business Jet by only a few minutes and that the plane was apparently headed to China. *Apoplectic* seemed a better descriptor, at least to Mary McKinney, Rip Carver and the other agents who had arrived at John Wayne Airport with or shortly after Bates, so none of them could claim to be truly surprised when the Deputy Director clutched at his left arm and collapsed while they were interviewing employees inside the private jet terminal from which the plane had departed.

A security guard immediately dialed 9-1-1 and a small group gathered around the stricken man while they waited for help to arrive. Emergency Services at the airport responded rapidly but the incident still consumed valuable time, and as the EMTs started to work on Bates, Carver and McKinney stepped away and debated whether to request that the jet be intercepted by Air Force fighters.

"It's been at least twenty, maybe twenty-five minutes now since they took off," McKinney said, glancing at her watch. "For one thing, they've got to be outside U.S. airspace by now or they sure as hell will be before we can manage to get those jets scrambled. And for another, assuming we did intercept them and they refused to turn back, we're really not about to shoot down the next most admired man in the country after the late Steve Jobs, are we? Especially since we wouldn't be able to explain exactly why it was so critical that we do it. And on top of that, we don't know as an absolute certainty what they're going to do in China."

Carver threw his hands in the air.

"We've got to fucking do *something!*" he insisted. "I think we actually do have a pretty damn good idea what they're going to do in China, so this is a potential catastrophe! I'd say let's try to get the Chinese to detain them when they land, but if he's going there to sell them that machine...."

One of the EMTs came over and interrupted to tell them that Bates had been stabilized for the moment and ask whether anyone was going to accompany him to the hospital. Carver pointed out March, the young FBI agent who had driven him around the area, and the EMT jogged over to where the man was standing to speak with him. Carver watched as March then helped load the gurney to which Bates had been strapped into the rescue squad vehicle and joined the EMT in back. As the truck drove away, its lights flashing, McKinney's phone rang and Perricone's name came up on the screen. She sighed, answered it and put the call on speaker.

"We were kind of hoping you'd maybe let us know what the hell was going on," Perricone said, sounding more hurt than angry.

"Sorry, agent," McKinney said. "We're been kind of busy over here. Let's just say we missed them and leave it at that, okay?"

"So we're fucked," Perricone said. "The whole world is fucked."

"Maybe, maybe not," Carver said, leaning in closer to the phone. "There's another possibility."

"And what's that?" Perricone asked.

"Well, pray that I was wrong about what Duff's been building and what he plans to do with it," he said.

25

THE CHARTERED AIRBUS business jet carrying Edan Duff, Sim and Dale Bowdoin and his team landed at Manassas Airport in suburban Virginia, outside Washington, DC, at seven-forty-five on Thursday morning. After braking hard and turning off the longer of the small airport's two runways, it taxied to a remote part of field, where it was met by two white Metro vans painted in Ryder truck rental livery.

Shortly before they landed Bowdoin's alarm had woken him and he had gone to the bedroom to check on Sim and administer an injection of the same strong sedative that he had put in her coffee, back in California. Once he was satisfied that she was breathing normally and that her heartbeat was slow and steady, Bowdoin woke Edan, who had also slept for much of the flight, and assured him again that she would experience no significant ill effects from the drug. He and Edan had then gone over their plan one last time, and after they landed, Edan had gone to see Sim, sitting down on the bed next to her and taking her hand in both of his.

"Forgive me, baby, please forgive me, for doing this to you," he said softly, gently stroking her cheek. "But if you had known what I was planning you would never have allowed it. There was just no other way. I've tried, believe me, but the research guys have concluded that there's just no way to cure your...problem...and that there isn't going to be one."

He wiped a tear from his eye and again took her hand in his.

"More than anything," he went on, "I wish I could go further back than we're planning to go to prevent the torture you suffered through. But there's just too great a chance that others would be gravely hurt or killed if I did. Please forgive me and somehow know that you're my life and that I love you more than anything."

He took one final look at her, her face so beautiful and so calm. Without her long hair to hide it, the pale scar on the side of her head was clearly visible and he leaned in and gently kissed it. Then he walked out of the room, locking the door behind him.

By the time Edan joined Bowdoin down on the tarmac, the device had been unloaded from the plane and safely stowed inside one of the vans. Wordlessly, he slid into the passenger seat of the van holding the device.

One of Bowdoin's men got in the driver's seat while two more rode in back with the device. Bowdoin drove the other van, with two more of his men in back, and led the way off the airport grounds.

Edan's van followed them out onto Clover Hill Road and to Route 66, where they joined the melee that was Washington, DC-area morning rush hour traffic. Things got somewhat worse when they merged onto the Capital Beltway but they were not on it for long, exiting at Route 123 and heading east toward McLean. Edan stared out the side window, his eyes fixed on nothing as they crept along, stopping for a frustrating number of red lights before finally turning right onto Elm Street and then left onto Fleetwood Road. It was a quiet residential neighborhood and they drove on slowly for several blocks before the van in front of them with Bowdoin at the wheel slowed and Edan looked out and saw they were coming up on the high-rise condo-minium building where Sim had owned an apartment before moving to California.

From Fleetwood Road, it presented a façade par-allel to the street, but as they drove on, turning right onto Beverly Road, Edan could see that a section of it angled away from Fleetwood toward the intersection and that the next section angled again and paralleled Beverly, forming the J-shape that Edan had noted on Google Earth aerial shots of the condo tower. He had done extensive research on the complex, going so far as hiring a local reporter to interview current and past employees of the condominium on the pretext of writing a book about significant local buildings, and there was little about it that he did not know.

Thirty or so yards down Beverly Road, Bowdoin steered the first van into the parking lot that curved around the building. Almost immediately, he stopped and then backed up into a space along the grass island that separated the parking area from the street. Edan watched as Bowdoin got out of the van and walked toward the condo's delivery bay, while one of his men moved from the cargo area of the van into the driver's seat, a vantage point from which he would be able to keep the area in sight. The man driving Edan's van, who had stopped to allow Bowdoin to park, continued on slowly for several more yards, stopped, and backed up carefully to within a few yards of where Bowdoin now stood, just outside the delivery entrance.

The delivery bay doors stood open, although a special key would have been needed to use the freight elevator inside. The key had to be obtained from the front desk, but getting a key would not be necessary this morning since the device would remain inside the delivery bay during the entire mission.

Bowdoin tapped on the van's rear doors and one of his men opened them. Edan came around from the passenger side and, with minor assistance from the other two men, he and Bowdoin proceeded to slide the device out, making maximum use of its hydraulic lifting rods to lower it, still clad in its black cover, to the ground. They then pushed it up the concrete path and through the delivery bay doors. Bowdoin's men followed, carrying the vinyl and metal parts that would be assembled into two portable partitions.

The delivery bay was empty and once Edan had positioned the device a few inches from the back wall, across from the freight elevator, Bowdoin's men laid the parts out on the painted concrete floor and began assembling them. They worked quickly and when one partition was finished, they positioned it several feet away from the device, hiding it from view. Edan then removed the cover from the device while the others moved the remaining pieces behind the partition, on the floor next to the device, and proceeded to assemble a second, identical, partition while Edan and Bowdoin stood nearby.

"You'll be gone maybe twenty minutes and I just stand here and make sure no one looks behind this curtain, right, sir?" one of the men asked Bowdoin when they had finished assembling the second partition.

Bowdoin confirmed that it was right and the man, dressed in work clothes, took up a post at one edge of the divider. As he did, Bowdoin gestured for the other man, who was also dressed in work clothes, to wait where he was for a moment. He then went over to speak with Edan.

"We really fuckin' goin' back five years?" Bowdoin, dressed in khaki pants and a blue golf shirt drawled, his voice barely above a whisper.

"September 29, 2010, to be exact," Edan replied in an equally soft tone. "A week before she got home on recovery leave. You sure you're ready?"

"Of course," Bowdoin told him, straightening his back, "anything at all to help our girl. Besides, I don't believe that thing really works anyway."

Edan smiled.

"What did you tell the guy who's coming with us?" Edan asked, glancing over at the man in work clothes who stood nearby, awaiting his next orders.

"Not to ask any questions and to do exactly what I say," Bowdoin replied.

Edan nodded. He wore gray pants and a navy blazer with the logo of a local real estate sales company on its breast pocket, over a blue Oxford shirt. Anyone who might see him and Bowdon in the hallway working to open the door to Sim's apartment, would think he was showing the unit to a prospective buyer.

"I'll go into the device first," Edan told Bowdoin and the other man, "then you guys hand me the partition and come inside."

Bowdoin looked at the six-foot high and ten-foot long array of plastic pipes and thick vinyl panels and told Edan there was no way it was going to fit inside.

"I thought we'd been through all that," Edan said before he stepped through the device's open slat.

"Jesus," Bowdoin whispered.

He picked up one end of the partition and began sliding it toward the slat. The other man reached out to take hold of the other end of it but before he could, the entire partition disappeared into the device. The man stood there, wide-eyed, and Bowdoin took him by the shoulders and walked him right up to the slat.

"Take one step forward," he told the man.

The poor guy's eyes were wide and Bowdoin could feel the tension in his shoulder muscles, but he did as he was told.

Immediately the man disappeared into the device. Bowdoin shook his head slowly, took a deep breath, turned sideways and began to inch through himself. Suddenly, though, he was inside, not thinking he had actually moved in close enough to be there.

"Jesus," he said.

"You can say that again, sir," the other man, standing with his hand on the partition said.

Edan stepped over to the etched circle, touched it and the holographic keyboard appeared on the wall, next to it. Immediately he began making a series of keystrokes.

"Whatever you see, hear or feel," Edan told his two companions as he made his last entries, "assume it's normal."

As soon as he said it, he pressed *Enter* and all three men had the sense of a slight ringing in their ears and a vibration from below their feet. Both sensations steadily grew and the floor's pinkish hue darkened. There were no flashes of light and no disturbing noises, but the sides and roof of the device seemed to disappear entirely. As the men looked around, there were ever-changing snatches of lines, forms and color, but nothing you could lock your eyes onto.

All three felt off balance, too, as if they were standing in a small boat on a rough lake and they needed to concentrate to keep their balance. All of this continued to build for an impossible to discern amount of time. But just as the dizziness, the ringing in their ears and the vibration reached a crescendo, it all stopped, suddenly and totally, the sensations were just not there anymore and it was impossible to tell when they had gone away. And at the same moment or instant, if it could even be called that, the polished-looking walls of the device came back into view, giving off the same dusky cast as when they had first entered the device, and it was just as massively quiet as it had been then.

The man they had left standing outside in the delivery bay, next to the partition, heard nothing, but after a few minutes his curiosity got the best of him and he peered behind it. He blinked several times and his mouth fell wide open after seeing that there was no longer anything there.

Back inside the device, Edan made a number of additional keystrokes and Bowdoin shoved his man toward the slat. As soon as the man was outside, Bowdoin maneuvered the partition out through it. He quickly followed and the two men positioned the partition next to the device in much the same manner as they had the other one. Edan joined them moments later, while Bowdoin was giving orders to the man who would stand guard while they were gone. Then he and Bowdoin walked off toward a locked stairway door and the still-startled third man took up his guard position beside the vinyl divider.

The lock on the stairway door was old and cheap and Bowdoin, using a set of burglar's tools he carried in a small, vinyl pouch in his back pocket, made short work of opening it. He and Edan climbed the stairs, exiting at the fifth floor, and walked down the carpeted hallway until they located the door to Sim's apartment. There was only a single lock on the door but it was of much higher quality than the one on the stairway door and it took Bowdoin nearly five minutes to get it open. While he worked, Edan paced back and forth nearby, keeping an eye on both the stairway door and the elevators, which were further down the hall. An apartment door opened a few doors down from where they stood and both men froze momentarily while a hand reached down and grabbed the folded newspaper that sat on the threshold. When the door closed, they looked at each other and rolled their eyes. Moments later, Bowdoin had the door unlocked and they stepped into what had been Sim's apartment.

The narrow blinds on the windows had been left slightly open and the entryway was lit well enough for Bowdoin and Edan to quickly make their way through the unfamiliar space to the living room and bedroom and find the switches for various lamps and overhead lights and turn them all on.

Bowdoin began his search in the bedroom and very soon he called out to Edan, who was opening kitchen drawers, saying that he had found a weapon. When Edan joined him in the bedroom, Bowdoin was standing in front of a nightstand beside Sim's bed, its narrow drawer open, holding a small, black gun.

"What we've got here is a Kel-Tec P-32 semi-auto," he said, holding the gun up so that Edan could get a better look at it, "which is the gun that the police report mentioned. More than a pea-shooter but not quite a cannon, either. Still, I'm amazed it didn't kill her."

Bowdoin ejected the clip and made sure there was no round in the chamber before handing the gun to Edan, who tucked it into his inside jacket pocket. Bowdoin stuck the clip into his hip pocket.

"Let's make sure there isn't another one around here somewhere before we go," Bowdoin said.

He and Edan spent the next ten minutes conducting a thorough search of every possible hiding place in the apartment, checking each other's work before meeting back in the living room.

"Hang on, boss," Bowdoin said, picking up the remote control that sat on the coffee table and aiming it at the 30-inch Sharp flat screen TV that sat on a small table in front of the windows, "not that I really doubt it now, but I've just got to know for absolutely sure."

When the picture came on, the set was tuned to a movie and Bowdoin quickly began pressing the channel button on the remote until he found CNN. Both men listened intently as Gerri Willis said,

European Union recovery in the second quarter of this year broadened and the outlook for inflation remains moderate, a paper prepared for the bloc's finance ministers said. Rising exports are mainly responsible for the rebound but risks remain from emerging and sovereign debt markets, says the paper, which examined the economy's performance since this past April. It

*also concluded that inflation rates in the EU are
expected to remain moderate for the remainder
of 2010.*

"Ho-ly shit," Bowdoin said softly before turning off the
set.

They made sure that all the lights in the apartment
were turned off, went out into the hallway, locked the
door behind them and walked quickly down the stairs,
exiting into the delivery bay. While the man they had
left downstairs continued to stand watch, Edan walked
around the partition and entered the device. Once he
had, Bowdoin hustled the guard toward the slat and
once he was also inside, began pushing the partition
toward it, as well, and into the device. After standing there for a moment shaking his head, he too then
entered it.

Edan was already making entries on the keyboard
and soon enough all of the same sounds and feelings
they had experienced on their earlier journey began all
over again. Without any real awareness of how much
time had passed, each man was startled as the intense
sensations suddenly ceased and the space inside the
device became dead silent.

The man who had been left behind to stand guard
was chatting with two others who were apparently making a delivery when Edan and his companions stepped

out of the device, bringing the partition along with them. One of its legs scraped noisily along the floor as they did, but no one seemed to care what the commotion was all about. Still, Edan, Bowdoin and the third man waited until they heard the freight elevator door close before stepping out from behind the partition.

Outta here, Bowdoin ordered and both partitions were quickly disassembled and the device was covered and returned to the van that had brought it. Both vans were back on the road minutes later.

It was nearing the end of rush hour and traffic was lighter than before on all but the brief Beltway segment of the drive to Manassas Airport. The Airbus had already taken on fuel and Bowdoin supervised the transfer of the device back into the plane's cargo hold while Edan went to speak with the men who had been left to guard the plane. They assured him that while a few gawkers had approached, surprised at the presence of such a large aircraft on the ramp at the executive airport, there had been no problems and no unusual activity had taken place while Edan had been off with Bowdoin and their other comrades. Edan then ran up the big jet's boarding stairs and headed straight for the bedroom door. As he passed the conference table, he noticed that only two laptops were there, along with only two coffee cups. Bowdoin's kit bag lay nearby and only Edan's suitcase sat on the floor next to one of the sofas.

His hands shook as Edan fumbled with the key to the bedroom door but eventually he got the door unlocked. He threw it open and fixed his eyes on the queen bed. It was a bit rumpled, as if someone had slept in it and then carelessly pulled up the covers, and one of the pillows was askew. The throw pillows lay nearby on the carpeted floor, exactly where he had tossed them. There was a small bathroom in the suite and Edan rushed to it, but it was immediately clear that nothing there had even been touched.

Sim was no longer there.

26

AFTER THE DEBACLE at John Wayne Airport, Roscoe Kemp, the FBI special agent in charge, stepped in and set up a command center in the secure conference room at FBI headquarters in Los Angeles. Mary McKinney of DARPA and Rip Carver of the CIA went straight there from Santa Ana, as did Joe Perricone and Alex Granda, as well as the young agent named March. He had not only ferried Carver around for the past several days, but had actually been the one who originally picked up on the unusual nature of the materiel that Edan Duff had procured, kicking off the whole affair.

Every available agent, as well as personnel borrowed from local law enforcement agencies, had also been enlisted into the quest for Duff, and the team in the conference room had spent the rest of the night directing a small army of those officers, whose only job for the moment was to determine where the elusive billionaire had gone and what he was up to.

Carver's principal contribution to the effort was speaking with his contacts at the U.S. Consulate in Shanghai and requesting their assistance. Specifically, he asked them to confirm the eventual arrival of Duff's aircraft and attempt to determine who might be meeting his flight. And whether or not anyone met the plane at the airport in Shanghai, Carver asked them to find out as much as they could about Duff's actions after his plane landed, which, unfortunately, would be late at night in China.

In addition to informally taking over command from CIA Deputy Director Roger Bates, Kemp assigned himself the job of shepherding an effort to obtain a warrant to search Duff's home, although he was not optimistic about getting it.

"We may be able to help with that," Carver told him.

"Getting a warrant?" Kemp asked, clearly surprised.

"No, getting into his house anyway," Carver replied, "if it comes to that."

By six in the morning, when no useful intelligence had been obtained and exhaustion was beginning to compromise the quality of their efforts, everyone but McKinney and Carver left for home to get a few hours' sleep. After the others had gone, Carver finally thought to call the hospital and check on Roger Bates' condition. He was told that Bates was in serious but stable condition and that there had been relatively little permanent damage to his heart. The nurse also told Carver that she had contacted Bates' wife, who was already on her way to California.

By the time he caught up with McKinney, she was asleep on the couch in Kemp's office, wearing only her panties and bra. Carver admired her body for a moment, locked the office door, stripped down to his boxers and stretched out on the thickly carpeted floor.

He slept fitfully and woke for good at ten. Moving around as quietly as he could, he used the shower in Kemp's large office but stopped short of using the man's shave cream and razor. After he dressed, he woke McKinney. Kemp's assistant was at her desk when Carver unlocked the office door and stepped out into the hallway. He explained more or less what had happened to the surprised woman and asked her to order coffee and some light breakfast foods for the team and have it delivered to the secure conference room. He also suggested she plan on having lunch delivered at around two o'clock.

"I guess an army really does run on its stomach," the woman said brightly as Carver walked away.

By the time breakfast arrived, McKinney had sifted through the few messages that had come in since six and Carver had briefed his superiors in DC about the possible need to send operatives to China. After that, Carver busied himself doing research on his computer and he and McKinney continued monitoring communications. The others started drifting in at eleven and as they did he shared the news that there was no news to share.

"Shanghai's about a twelve or thirteen-hour flight from LA and according to the flight tracking sites I checked, Duff's plane didn't make refueling a stop in Hawaii," he also told them once everyone had returned. "Shanghai is 5,645 miles from LAX and a Boeing Business Jet like Duff's has a range of just about six thousand, so going non-stop might be pushing it unless the wind is right. If they *can* make it non-stop, his plane should be landing shortly, if it hasn't already. If not and they stop someplace just short of Shanghai for fuel, it could be another hour or so. Hopefully, though, I'll be hearing something soon from my contacts there."

"Not that there's much we can actually do once he gets there," Kemp said.

"Well," Carver said, "the CIA can track his movements and potentially intervene if we need to. We've got a team on their way to Hawaii as we speak, where they'll be on standby awaiting further orders. You make any progress on the warrant?"

Kemp grimaced.

"Not yet," he replied. "As you might imagine, it's a complicated matter to explain to a judge."

"Just so you all know," McKinney chimed in, "I asked one of my people from DC to join me out here. If we do get into that house and his lab, I'm going to need some more expertise."

Before Carver had heard from anyone at the U.S. Consulate, flight tracking software confirmed the arrival of Duff's plane in Shanghai. When Carver finally did hear from someone a half hour later, it was to say that the plane had been met by a limo and that a Western couple had deplaned and gotten into the car. That information had been obtained from personnel at the airport. There had been no one available to follow the limo but at least someone at the airport had gotten its tag number. The authorities were looking for it, but for the moment Duff was in the wind.

That news did nothing to raise morale in the conference room but set off a round of questions, mainly aimed at Kemp and Carver, about what other steps might be taken. Instead of helping Kemp field the questions, Carver excused himself and contacted his superiors in DC again with an update. When he returned to the conference room, he told the assemblage that the CIA team would stop only for refueling in Hawaii and then continue on the Shanghai.

Sandwiches and salads were delivered shortly after that and Carver joined the short line of people waiting their turn at the platters of sandwiches and salads. Although she had skipped breakfast and it was now well after two, McKinney was not hungry. She settled for another cup of coffee, but as she was pouring it her iPhone rang and Edan Duff's name came up on the screen.

"Oh my God!" she said, and held out the phone so that the others could see the screen. The room quieted down and when she answered the call, she simply said, "Mr. Duff, I'm surprised to be hearing from you."

"Really?" came Edan's terse reply. "I was expecting you here at my office fifteen minutes ago, Mary. Didn't we have a meeting scheduled for two o'clock today?"

27

EDAN SAT AT a desk in a low-walled corner cubicle on the second floor of his company's main building at its campus in Carlsbad on Thursday afternoon, mulling over events of the last day while waiting for Mary McKinney to arrive. He felt exhausted, despite napping on the flight back from Virginia, and empty, despite now having something of a duality of memories of the past five years.

Or, perhaps, because of it, he suddenly thought.

Edan had done a great deal of research about memory in recent weeks and knew that it could be a strange, sometimes unreliable thing at the best of times. This was not the best of times. His recent excursion had caused his mind to overflow with recollections of the past five years and most were at odds with the others. The trip back to 2010 had not appeared to set off any cataclysmic events, but they had certainly done something of a number on his head.

And, of course, Sim was gone, from his current life at least, although she was so infused in his mind that it was difficult to believe she was, and he figured it would probably take him quite some time to really grapple with it and get things under control enough to separate memories of one reality from the other.

"I hate quantum physics," he said, loud enough for a few people in the area to turn their heads in his direction.

"It's nothing," he said to them. "I was just trying to remember something."

And not go crazy, he almost added, but did not.

The way memory actually works, he had learned, is much more complex than most people believed.

Each element of a memory, he understood, whether created from something you heard or saw, or whether the result of an emotional reaction or some other stimulus, gets encoded in the part of the brain in which that element was originally created. So, in the case of something you saw, it would get encoded in the visual cortex in the occipital lobe. Similarly, learn a new word or phrase in a foreign language and that gets encoded somewhere deep in the left hemisphere, and so on. When you recall a memory, still another part of your brain is called upon to reactivate and bring together all the different elements that went into creating that memory in the first place, which are distributed among all those different areas of the brain in which they had originally been encoded.

Edan had recorded the event when he had gone back that first time to hammer in the nail, complete with date and time stamps, just in case his memory had failed to retain the protruding nail on his bathroom door. It was even possible, he had supposed at the time, that his new memories would, in effect, overwrite the old ones and they would be lost. That supposition had been disproved, though, when he realized that he remembered the protruding nail even after he traveled to the past to pound it in and then returned to the present, where there was no longer a protruding nail.

Unfortunately, he had no encoded memories from 1966, though, so the trip to the Whisky to see the Doors had not put his new belief that encoded memories would always be retained to the test. And while he did have plenty of encoded memories from 2010, the year from which he and Dale Bowdoin had recently returned, and he had traveled to the Washington, DC area several times by then, he and Bowdoin had not visited any of the same places that Edan had visited previously. He had even flown into a different airport this time and traveled different roads, so there was no opportunity to consider whether or not his previous memories might have been rewritten in some way by virtue of the trip.

Still, he believed that he would retain all of his post-September 29, 2010, memories of Sim even though the elements that had created them no longer existed, had no longer taken place, after that date, in the non-quantum world at least. And, for now anyway, freshly returned, he was reasonably sure he had. They were crowding his mind, in fact. He and Sim had never been intimate but they had spent a great deal of time together, and created a great many memories. They all seemed to still be there, as far as he could tell, although they were a bit fuzzier, somehow not as keen, as those from before September 29, 2010. It was almost, but not quite, as if they had happened in a dream. Still, they were vivid enough so that he would not have been terribly surprised if Sim had walked in and simply continued in her role as his head of security instead of Dale Bowdoin, who had filled that role for the past five years.

"Or perhaps I should say, who *also* filled that role for the past five years," Edan said aloud, but this time no one heard him.

He had been aware, when he and Bowdoin had planned the trip to McLean that he might never see Sim again and, in fact, he seemed to have no memories of her other than the *old* ones. It led him to believe that he had not come in contact with her again since they had met at the hospital in Landstuhl, at least in the world that existed after their return from McLean, and the thought saddened him.

So, he was sad but the mission had apparently succeeded. Sim was, presumably, okay, and that thought cheered him somewhat. At the same time, then, it could all be viewed as one big experiment to see whether quantum physics was right, at least about the possibility of a single thing existing in different places at the same time, an experiment that had been successful. Of course, as far as Edan knew, not even the most ardent believers and practitioners in the field truly believed that it applied above the molecular level, and it certainly had not been demonstrated. But now Edan Duff, neither a practitioner nor, previously at least, a true believer, seemed to have proven that belief to be untrue.

On the other hand, it was also true that his memories of Sim that had been formed during the past five years, did seem a bit more dreamlike, a bit more distant and somewhat vaguer than the others. He wished they had crossed paths after McLean. It led him to wonder what her memories were like. It would certainly make for an interesting conversation, if and when he found her. As for the other people who had known one or the other or both of them during the past five years, he suspected that their *old* memories would be even more vague, and possibly a bit confusing.

Perhaps it would be like meeting someone for the first time but thinking you had met them someplace before.

Déjà vu all over again.

On the flight home, Edan had done a Google search and other, more in-depth, online probes looking for Sim. He had entered her full name and enough pre-2010 identifying details to yield a good deal of useful information about what had become of her in the five years since she had, it seemed, begun occupying more than one place at the same time. But all he had been able to get was very basic information and the trail went cold at around the time her parents died, when she was in college. On the other hand, a similar search Edan had done a week earlier had yielded more or less the same results, so he chalked it up to the excellent job the government had apparently done in cleansing her history, and which she had perpetuated, rather than a failure on the world's part to acknowledge the existence of the post-2010 Courtney Jane Garrison.

It had been more or less the same for Dale Bowdoin, as well.

Edan's iPhone buzzed. The screen said it was 4:09 and that he had a text message, which proved to be the security desk at the visitor's entrance advising him that Mary McKinney had finally arrived. He speed-dialed the desk's number.

"Escort her up to the conference room, please," he told the security guard. "I'll be there in a few minutes. Is everything set?"

"Mr. Bowdoin's in his office and said he's ready," the guard replied. "He's just waiting for word from you."

"Good, thanks," Edan said. "Have him where he is until I say otherwise."

"Will do, Mr. D," the guard said, "and by the way, Ms. McKinney's not alone."

Edan was not exactly shocked by the news.

"How many others are there?" he asked.

"Four," the guard told him, "and several more outside in black SUVs."

Edan laughed.

"Why am I not surprised?" Edan said, and ended the call.

He closed his laptop and slid it into its case, slung the case over his shoulder and headed for the men's room. When he was done, he rode a tubelift to the top floor, stopped to get a mug of coffee and walked to the assigned conference room. A uniformed security guard stood outside the door and he held it open as Edan approached.

All five of his visitors stood, more or less in unison, as he walked into the room.

One of them was Sim.

It was all he could do to hold onto his coffee mug and it was a struggle to keep his knees from buckling and his face impassive.

McKinney was the first to walk over to Edan, her hand outstretched. He put his mug down on the table and shook her hand, then put down the computer case.

"I'm so sorry we're so late," McKinney said. "I'm not quite sure how our signals got so mixed up."

"You wanted to get together, so don't ask me," Edan told her, pleasantly enough.

"Well, in any case," McKinney said, blushing slightly, "we're here now and we appreciate your flexibility. So, let me introduce the others. I'm pretty sure you must remember Ms. Garrison," McKinney went on, gesturing at Sim, who arched an eyebrow.

"How could I forget?" he replied. "We got pretty well acquainted at the hospital in Landstuhl, Germany a few years back, although it was under much less than ideal circumstances. I'm very glad to see that you're looking so well," he added, smiling at Sim.

"Edan Duff is the reason I'm walking, among other things," Sim said, surprising Edan by coming over and hugging him.

As she did, she said, *You son-of-a-bitch,* in his ear.

He was both shocked and overjoyed, although he tried hard not to show it. But apparently that did not really work since she then whispered, *So it was true after all.*

"As I said, you're looking wonderful," he managed to say, taking a step back, smiling and slightly nodding his head.

"I hope you don't just mean compared with the last time you saw me," she said, smiling sweetly. "That wouldn't be too difficult."

Edan smiled but said nothing further, although he was unable to take his eyes off her.

He realized that the others must have thought that she was referring to the last time he had seen her in Landstuhl. But Edan was convinced that she meant when she had passed out on the plane after being drugged.

"Actually, I wasn't thinking of any earlier time," Edan said, his eyes remaining locked on her for another moment.

Unlike McKinney, who wore a dress and heels, Sim had on jeans and a white cotton sweater, as well as a more sensible pair of shoes. Her hair was long and pulled back into a ponytail, and she wore little makeup. There were no inch-wide openings in her earlobes, but Edan noticed three gold hoops in her left earlobe and another, smaller one at the top of her ear. He wondered about her tattoos.

"Jane works with me at DARPA," McKinney said, "for nearly five years now. I doubt you know the others," she went on, gesturing to the three men who had also come along with her to the meeting.

Roger Kemp, Rip Carver and Kevin March each took turns introducing themselves and reciting their titles. Only Carver wondered if they had met before, but Edan deflected the inquiry.

He took a seat at the round table and as he did the others also sat down, except for Sim, who went to refill her mug from a carafe on the credenza. Once again, he could not take his eyes off her as she did.

"This was your idea, Mary," Edan said, once Sim had taken her seat. "Why don't you start things off?" he added, notwithstanding that Roger Kemp of the FBI was probably the senior official in the room.

McKinney glanced at Kemp, who nodded, and cleared her throat.

"As I'm fairly certain you know," she began, "the FBI has been keeping an eye on you for some time."

Edan smiled.

"Nice boat, by the way," he said, looking across the table at Kemp and March. "The black Suburbans, not so much. Way too predictable."

March smiled, Kemp did not.

"We'll share why that was the case--" McKinney began.

"And why DARPA and the CIA got involved?" Edan interrupted her to ask.

McKinney glanced across at the other men and cleared her throat.

"Yes, we'll share all that in a little while," McKinney replied. "For now, though, we'd like to talk about the last twenty-four hours or so, if that's all right with you."

Edan looked over at Kemp again before answering. He seemed slightly agitated and Edan was sure the head of the FBI's L.A. field office would have been quite a bit less friendly in his approach than McKinney was being, as would Carver. He continued to hold his tongue, though.

"As I said, Mary, it's your meeting," Edan told her.

McKinney cleared her throat.

"Your personal jet departed John Wayne Airport in Santa Ana last night, bound for Shanghai," she said. "There were two people aboard, a man and a woman. We thought it might have been you and a colleague, but since you're sitting here now, that seems not to have been the case."

"The gentleman who heads our personal electronics division and one of our senior financial analysts were on the plane," Edan said. "We're looking at a joint venture with a large Chinese telecom. Can you tell me why you're so interested in who flew to China on my plane last night?"

"We thought you might've been involved in making a deal with the Chinese," Rip Carver told him.

"I am involved in making a deal with the Chinese," Duff said affably, turning to Carver, "or at least my company is, as I said. I'm not sure why that would be of interest to the CIA, though. I can assure you that we comply with all United States export rules and technology transfer restrictions in every--"

"You have a laser weapon, Mr Duff," Carver snapped.

Edan folded his hands in his lap and let out a breath.

"Yes, I do," he said. "In fact, I was planning to use the, ah, opportunity of this meeting to show it to you, even though it's not quite ready for prime time."

"It was sure as hell ready enough to shoot down a couple of the government's drones!" Carver told him.

"Oh, those were yours?" Edan asked innocently.

Carver looked like he might come across the table and deck Edan, but Edan did not move a muscle.

"Who the hell did you think flew them?" Carver demanded.

"Sorry," Edan said. "I thought they might have been my competitor's. I'm sure you realize they've been out there in the harbor, too, on that Predator yacht, for longer than you folks have been out there, in fact. Now, you still haven't told me what this has to do with the

Chinese. Oh, wait," he said, sitting up straighter in his chair, "don't tell me you thought I was going to talk to the Chinese *government* about the *laser,*" he continued, turning to face McKinney. "Mary, I can't believe you of all people, after all we've done together...."

His words hung in the air for a moment without anyone saying anything further. Sim had a hand over her mouth and Edan was sure it was to hide a smile, not a yawn, but McKinney looked grief-stricken. Carver still looked angry, but embarrassment seemed to be taking over Kemp's face. The younger FBI man, March, got up to get more coffee.

"DARPA's only involved from a technical, consulting point of view," McKinney finally said, looking down at the table.

"We were concerned that you might be considering a deal with the Chinese involving the laser weapon," Carver said. "We're also concerned about what else you might be up to in light of the nature of the materials you acquired some time back."

"You've been looking at what I buy?" Edan asked.

"So, you had no intention of talking with the Chinese, the Chinese government, about that laser, Mr. Duff?" Carver asked, ignoring the question.

"None at all, Mr. Carver," Edan replied indignantly, "and I'm angry and disappointed that *my* government would think I might have had such an intention. In fact," he went on, his anger growing, "now I'm not so sure I want to show you the laser at all, but I am pretty sure my lawyers are going to hear about all this as soon as this meeting is over! I put up with that boat and the damn Suburbans, but now I think I've had enough!"

With that he stood up and Carver and Kemp did, as well. McKinney quickly got up, too, moving closer to Edan and putting a hand gently on his arm.

"I can certainly understand your frustration, Edan," she said. Then, turning toward Carver and Kemp, she added, "On the other hand, these gentlemen were responding to what they perceived to be a valid, potential problem."

"Just doing their jobs, in other words," Edan spat out.

"That's right," Kemp said, his tone more even-keeled than Edan expected.

"I think we may need to try to start over," McKinney said. "Obviously, the Duff companies have provided a number of game-changing technologies to DARPA, to the government, or worked with us on enhancements to our own developments over past few years, and I can assure you that the very last thing we want is to see any kind of erosion of the relationship that we've established. And given the national security aspects of that relationship, I'm sure the FBI and CIA would agree."

Kemp's and Carver's demeanors seemed to change as she spoke, each man softening both his posture and facial expression. It was all Edan could do to remain as impassive as he did, avoid throwing his arms up in the air in victory and yelling either *Gotcha!* or *Fuck all of you FBI and CIA assholes,* or both.

"Why don't we take a short break," McKinney suggested, "and then maybe we can convince Mr. Duff to let us have a look at that laser after all."

28

EDAN STOOD JUST outside the shower stall in his master bathroom, looking at the tattoo that covered most of Sim's back and upper arms, before stepping in to join her on Friday morning.

"I've always loved the tattoo on your back," he said, "although it's a bit different now than it was before."

"Seriously?" she asked, handing him the soap.

"Seriously," he said, massaging it into her shoulders and working down from there. "It was a tad more, I don't know, in your face. And it went further down your arms, almost to the elbows."

"I stopped it where I did so I could wear short sleeves in the lovely DC summers without getting outed," she said.

Edan shrugged.

"Makes sense," he said. "But I actually kind of miss the little gun sight tattoos on your neck and your stretched earlobes."

"I had those, really?" she asked.

"An inch across," he replied.

"I've always kind of wanted to do that but they'd probably kick me out of DARPA if I had them now," she said. "It is conservative Washington, DC, after all. The multiple hoops in my left ear get enough attention."

"I guess it was a slightly different environment out here, when you were working for me," he said, smiling.

"You might say that," she said.

Then Sim's look suddenly turned very serious.

"Until yesterday afternoon," she told him, "I thought so many of my memories were only dreams, or hallucinations or God knows what else. Then, when I called you a son-of-a-bitch and you knew why I said it...."

Edan smiled.

"Is that still what you think?" he asked.

"Yes and no," she replied, "but I think I'm going to need some more time to sort it all out. I mean, it's hard to imagine I actually put a bullet in my brain but in a way it's not. I mean, I really was suicidal when I got back from Germany, so if there had been a gun around...."

"But there wasn't," he said.

They spent a few moments washing each other, neither saying anything.

"Maybe that's why some of my memories always seemed so, so fucked up," she finally said. "The ones from before, from when I was out here working for you. Those were made when my brain was kind of messed up, from the gunshot wound. I mean, it affected more than just my, ah, my love life, right?"

Edan nodded.

"Anyway," she went on, "the other ones, the newer ones I guess you'd call them, weren't. My brain was fine, or at least as fine as it ever was. The truth is, before yesterday, before I knew what really happened, I some-times thought I was going a little bit crazy, maybe more than a little bit, actually."

"And now?" he asked.

Sim smiled.

"Well, since what really happened is even crazier," she replied, "but explains why I've felt that way, I think it's going to be better now. So," she said, shrugging off her serious demeanor, "what other weird shit semi-memories were real?"

"You mean, aside from designing and implementing the security measures when this house was being built, keeping me safe for five years, the covert missions with Bowdoin and all?" he asked smiling.

"Yeah, aside from those," she replied, smiling.

"Well, more recently there was using the laser to shoot down those drones," he told her, "and, oh yeah, you buzzed off all your hair off right before we, ah, before we flew out of here on our last mission."

""I've thought about doing that," she said, "especially when it's a hundred degrees and humid in DC during the summer. But I really did it, all of it, seriously?"

He nodded.

"How did *that* look?"

"Amazing, actually," Edan replied, "fabulous. And between that and your ears and the tattoos, ridiculously hot," he added, smiling as he let the warm water wash over him.

"Hmmm, I might have to try it sometime," Sim said, leaning back and letting the spray from the nozzles on the wall massage her spine.

"You can skip getting a Maori tattoo on your face or taking out your breast implants, though," he said, smiling.

She looked confused.

"Never mind," he said. "We can come back to that later."

Sim started to work shampoo into her still-long hair.

"I think I remember being here before," she said. "It's the most beautiful shower in the universe."

"You've been in this bathroom, so you've seen it," Edan told her, "but I don't think you've been in it before."

A wall of windows formed the outside perimeter of the enormous shower stall, allowing a panoramic view of the Pacific, and she paused to gaze out at the ocean. There were no boats anchored offshore.

"I asked if you wished you could fuck me, didn't I?" she asked, turning to face him. "The other time I was here."

"And I asked if you hated me for saving you," Edan said.

"That was then," she said, coming to him, and within seconds he was hard and she had drawn him inside her.

They barely moved for a minute or more, eyes closed, each taking in the full magnitude of the moment. The intensity of it was almost painful, joy distilled to its purest form and concentrated into such a finite space. It was nearly too much to bear, but they were already learning how to channel the intensity, to somehow break it down, dominate it enough so that it could be savored, as it was apparently meant to be.

It was easier to bear than it had been the first time they had made love, the previous night in Edan's bed. But as they began to move, very slowly at first but soon enough more rapidly, dominance was no longer possible, there was only a wildly spreading, dark fire that erased all thoughts and all memories and left them expended, sprawled out laughing, on the onyx floor.

• • •

Thirty minutes later they were sitting at the table on the terrace behind Edan's house, eating breakfast, Sim facing the ocean.

"You always used to sit with your back to the water," Edan said, biting into an English muffin and washing it down with coffee.

"I can't imagine why," she said. "The view is gorgeous."

When she finally took her eyes off the ocean a few moments later, she absently picked up a spoon and pushed the oatmeal around in her bowl but did not sample it.

"When you went to McLean, to my apartment, when we were supposed to go to London to kill John Foster Dulles," she said softly, turning to face him, "and you took my gun so I wouldn't try to kill myself, you were trying to cure me, weren't you, keep me from blowing away the part of my brain that controls...what we've been doing last night and this morning."

Edan put the muffin down and let out a breath.

"My people told me there would never be a medical cure," he replied. "And it hurt me so much to see you that way...."

She put a finger to his lips.

"You never intended to carry out the Dulles mission, did you?" she asked.

He looked down at his hands before replying.

"It always seemed a little extreme," he said.

Sim laughed.

"And those missions in Afghanistan, Iraq and Syria," she said, "carried out totally on our own, those weren't extreme?"

"There was Ukraine, too," he said.

"You know what I mean," she said. "Those were real, right?"

"Oh, they were real," Edan replied. "You led that team."

Her eyes went wide.

"You're not just fucking with me, right?" she asked. "I didn't think all of *those* memories could possibly have been real. I figured they'd just kind of mixed with my other combat memories, from before I was, before the mortar rounds."

"I would never do that," he replied, leaning over and kissing her.

"Holy shit," she said softly when they parted. "What was I saying?"

"That those missions were extreme, too," he replied.

"Well, they were."

"Okay, fair enough," he said, "but it was all in the present day."

"Which arguably only means that there was more of a chance of getting caught doing something we weren't exactly supposed to be doing," she said.

Edan could not help but smile.

"I hadn't thought of it that way," he said.

"Were you ever actually planning to use the, what the hell did I call it, the *dingus*, for anything useful?" she asked.

Edan smiled again, more broadly this time.

"I did use it for something useful," he said, reaching for her hand.

Sim looked away for a moment and when she turned back to him, there was a tear sliding down her cheek. She quickly wiped it away with her other hand.

"Don't tell me you're planning to give it to the government," she said.

"That's one of the things I wanted to talk with you about," he replied.

"I didn't think you liked them much, the government," she said, "especially now."

He let out a breath.

"For the most part it's a useless waste of resources and energy, watched over by a bunch of morons," he said.

"Don't hold back, tell me what you really think," she said, smiling.

Edan managed a wan smile and slowly shook his head before continuing.

"Show me the last time a real job, one that that truly benefitted the economy, was created by the government, not the private sector," he said. "Despite what some of the assholes in Washington might say, virtu-ally all of the successes the government has had can be traced back to the private sector. The space program, cutting edge aircraft--"

"My legs, among other parts," she interrupted to say, "and let's not forget HDTV."

It stopped him, at least for a minute or so. She waited him out.

"Look," he finally said, "you name it, even DARPA, one of best agencies out there, wouldn't be where it was without private sector help, no offense."

"None taken," she said. "I wound up there by hap-penstance, not design, as you've probably figured out. But I'd argue that the public-private partnership aspect of it is a good thing."

"Okay, but that's only because, for the most part, rational, intelligent people who sometimes have their own good ideas and just need some help implement-ing them are in charge over there," he said. "It's the exception."

She said nothing for a moment.

"I have to ask," she said. "Did you know I worked for DARPA when you, when you did what you did?"

Edan sighed.

"I had no idea where you would be or what you would be doing, or if I would ever see you again," he replied. "As I said, I just didn't want you to have to go through life the way--"

She reached over and pressed a finger to his lips again and he stopped talking.

"Where were we?" she asked.

"That government can be okay if they have private sector help," Edan replied.

"Right," she said softly. "But certain things are best left to them, right? Like war, or maybe avoiding war, or fighting terrorists."

"There aren't a lot of options when it comes to those things," Edan pointed out.

"We apparently stuck our noses in," she pointed out.

"A rare example of a public-private partnership in that area," he said.

"Even though our *partners* had no idea we were involved?" she asked.

"They liked the results," he said. "In any case, wars, fighting terrorists, maybe some other things where there's really no option, are pretty much the limit of where government should be involved."

"How about time travel?" Sim asked.

Edan stared at her.

"I suspect that if I made a list of the reasons why war, or avoiding it, is one of the things that should be left to the government," he said, "I have a feeling it would look a lot like a list of reasons why the device should also be one of the things left to government."

"But?"

Edan got up and stood at the railing, his elbows on top of it, looking out over the ocean. Sim came to join him and put her arm around his waist.

"But?" she said again.

"I'm not sure I can convince myself to trust them enough," he told her. "And if you think about it, the device would probably wind up with the CIA and I *especially* don't trust them."

She tugged at his waist and he turned to face her.

"Do you trust yourself enough to keep it?" she asked. "I mean, you've already taken it upon yourself to sponsor a few little forays into places where you had no business going."

"Another fair point," he said, turning back to face the ocean, "but if I don't give it to the government and I decide I'm not to be trusted with it, either, the only alternative is to destroy it."

"Which would be kind of a shame, don't you think?" she asked.

Edan smiled.

"I could say something about the value of going to see a Doors concert, not to mention what we did in the shower this morning," he said, "but you'd probably give me an argument."

Sim smiled, put her hand on his cheek and pulled him into a kiss.

"In any case," he went on, "the fucking idiots don't even know I have the device, so they'd never know it existed."

Sim looked down at the tile floor for a moment and then up into his eyes again.

"There's something you need to know," she told him, "although I could probably be fired on the spot for telling you."

Edan's look became questioning.

"They know you have it," she said, "or at least they're pretty sure you do."

"How the hell could they--"

"Carver," she said.

"The CIA guy?"

Sim nodded.

"He's brilliant at solving puzzles," she said. "They brought him out here from Langley, put him on that boat and gave him the list of things, your shopping list so to speak, that the FBI had been worried about. He sat out there and subtracted out what he thought you needed for the laser, and with a whole lot of input from a bunch of other really smart people, figured it out."

"I'm impressed," Edan said, "but I'm surprised they believed him."

Sim smiled.

"Even though I wasn't quite sure of what I was really remembering and what I might have dreamed," she told him, "I realized he was right, once I started thinking about it."

"But you didn't--"

"No, of course not," she said, her hands on her waist and her voice rising. "I wasn't even aware that it you were the reason that Mary had come out here until yesterday morning."

"Sorry, I had to ask," he said.

Her expression slowly softened and she let him take hold of her hand when he reached for it.

"I know," she said. "Anyway, Mary told me right before the meeting. That's why they were so hell-bent on stopping you from going to see the Chinese."

"Silly me," Edan said. "I thought they were worried about the laser weapon."

"Oh, believe me, they were worried about that, too," Sim told him.

"But I was never--"

"I know," she said, "and they do, too, now. But they freaked out, imagining something like the dingus getting into enemy hands. And you really did give them the runaround, more than once, which made them even more suspicious.."

"*We* gave them the runaround," Edan said, smiling. "And by the way, how come no one even mentioned the device at the meeting at my office yesterday?"

"They did kind of allude to what else you might have been up to, I think it was Carver who said it," she said, "but after they realized you were never going to the Chinese with the laser and we took that break, they were embarrassed as hell, so they decided to table it for the moment. They realize that's it's incredibly strategic, so once they're sure you're serious about turning over the laser, I have no doubt they'll want to talk about it. And Bowdoin probably convinced them with that demonstration that you talked me into skipping last night," she added, smiling, "so it could be any time now."

Edan suddenly looked as if he had seen a ghost.

"Shit!" he said.

"What?"

But instead of answering, Edan ran inside the house. Sim ran after him, through the kitchen, down a hallway and up a short flight of stairs to another hallway. There was a carved, wood door at the end of it that looked familiar to Sim, and she thought that was where he was headed. But Edan stopped halfway down the hallway in front of another door that she had not noticed at first, although it, too, seemed somehow familiar to her, this one made of steel and painted white. He placed his left index finger against a biometric reader, punched a five-digit code into the keypad beside the door and pushed it open. Sim followed him inside and almost immediately realized why she remembered it. She was about to say something but stopped when she noticed how troubled he looked as he began scanning the dozen or more large-screen monitors that lined one wall of the small, windowless room.

He found what he was looking for almost immediately.

"They're back!" he said. "I should have realized they would be, even if they decided they trust me now."

Two of the screens showed that there were now six black SUVs parked on the shoulder of the Coast Highway, not far from the drive leading to Edan's house. Nothing else on the other screens caught his interest, though, and he sat down in front of a laptop and began typing furiously. As he did, the images on the two screens began running in reverse until the SUVs could be seen leaving, moving backwards on the screens.

"They've been out there since seven this morning," he said, looking at the time stamp on the lower edge of the screens. "Shit. There's got to be more than that going on."

There were three screens that showed views of the sky from different vantage points on the property and Edan stared at each of them, but there were no helicopters or other aircraft in the pictures. When he ran the past few hours in reverse, the sky remained clear.

"Okay, so they're still afraid I might shoot something down," he said absently, "but still…."

Edan turned his attention back to the laptop's keyboard and began typing again. Sim stood behind him and watched as a Google Earth-style image came up on the laptop's small screen. But unlike what the public saw on Google Earth, it quickly became clear that this one was live and in real-time. Sim could see that a few of the people and vehicles on what appeared to be a naval base were moving. Edan made a few more keystrokes and the image on the laptop's screen also came up on one of the much larger monitors on the wall.

"What is that?" Sim asked, moving closer to that screen.

"Naval Air Station Coronado in San Diego," he replied

As she watched the screen, Edan kept typing and seconds later the little movement there was began running in reverse, as the images of the SUVs had. The screen froze when the time stamp read 0700.

"Nothing left there this morning," Edan said, looking perplexed. "Double shit. Wait a minute, hang on."

He began making more key stokes and the image changed to another locale, this one not all that different from the last.

"Okay, what's this one?" Sim asked.

"That," Edan said, "is the submarine base at Point Loma."

He began typing on the keyboard again and a map of southern California appeared on the screen next to the one Sim had been watching. He zoomed in until Sim could see that Point Loma was a peninsula jutting south into the ocean in San Diego, not far from Naval Air Station Coronado.

As Sim's attention went back to the submarine base, a series of images appeared and Sim could make out some movement. After a few seconds, Edan stopped making entries on the laptop's keyboard and one image remained frozen on the screen.

"What you're looking at is a Los Angeles-class fast attack sub," Edan said, "at its berth in port at seven this morning."

"Beautifully lethal looking, isn't it?" Sim said.

Edan ignored the comment, made a few more key-strokes, and what appeared to be the same submarine came up on the screen again, but this time it was no longer in port.

"This was an hour later," he said. "It was off the coast of Encinitas."

Sim glanced over at the map. Encinitas was perhaps twenty miles north of Point Loma.

"And this is an hour after that," Edan went on, as another image of the same boat came up on the screen. "It was just off San Clemente. Motherfuckers!"

"What the...no way!" Sim said. "You're saying it's headed here?"

Edan did not answer but made some more keystrokes and yet another image of the sub came up on the screen.

"Half an hour ago, off Dana Point," he said.

As Sim followed the sub's track on the map, Edan continued making keystrokes and soon the fixed image of the submarine became a video of it slicing through the waves. Moments later, it appeared to slow and enormous plumes of water began shooting high into the air from the sub's bow and stern. Within a minute, its bow and much of the rest of the boat disappeared under the surface, leaving only its towering superstructure in sight. In another minute, even that had gone out of view, leaving only a narrow wake behind it.

In a few more seconds that, too, disappeared.

While Sim stared in silence at the monitor, Edan closed out of the file he had been using and the two monitors resumed their more prosaic functions, which, along with the others, was displaying the entire area around the house. Nothing was moving except the traffic on the Coast Highway. The six black SUVs were still in place on the shoulder.

"As I said, given the lasers, I can understand why there's nothing in the air," Edan said, as he stood up. "And I know the device is strategic, but a fucking nuclear submarine? Give me a break!"

Sim followed as he jogged out of the command center and back through the house, out onto the terrace. As they stood next to each other at the railing, panting and looking out at the harbor, Edan's iPhone rang. The screen said *Blocked number*, but he answered the call anyway.

"This is Rip Carver, Mr. Duff," the voice at the other end said.

Edan quickly put the phone on speaker and mouthed *Carver* to Sim, who nodded.

"How can I help you, Mr. Carver?" Edan asked.

"We'd like to have another meeting with you, Mr. Duff," Carver said. "We're grateful, of course, for your cooperation with respect to the matter we dealt with yesterday, but there's something else we believe you have that's of far greater importance and we'd like to discuss that with you."

"I have no idea what you...."

But as he said it, the sub began to surface before their eyes. Edan stopped talking and he and Sim watched in fascination as its bulbous nose broke the surface of the blue Pacific, no more than a quarter mile offshore. The superstructure appeared seconds later, followed by the rest of the boat. Once the sub was on the surface, two uniformed men walked out onto the superstructure and began looking at Edan's house through binoculars.

"Very impressive," Edan said into the phone, "but don't you think--"

"This time," Carver cut him off to say, "we'll meet at your house. We should be there shortly. Plan on giving us a detailed tour of that lab of yours. And we'll be bringing a much larger group of people, so please reconsider any, ah, defensive actions, you might be considering accordingly."

The line went dead and Edan stood there, staring out at the beautifully lethal submarine, its matte black fuselage reflecting absolutely none of the bright California sunshine.

"Jesus, what now?" Sim asked. "I mean, I'd say let's get Bowdoin and put a little army together, but with that thing out there...."

"I know," he said, his brow tightly knitted. "They've got people up on the road so forget about driving out of here. We could use the helicopter but they'll see us from that sub and this time I have a feeling they're more prepared."

"This time?" Sim asked. "Oh, right."

"Of course," Edan went on, "since Bowdoin's not here, leaving by helicopter also assumes you can still fly one."

"What kind?" Sim asked.

"Robinson R-66."

"Nice bird," she said. "I still belong to a flying club and I fly an R-44 fairly regularly. It's the one with the piston engine instead of the turbine, but they're otherwise pretty similar. I think I could manage a 66 without too much of a problem."

"Would you be surprised if I told you that you've already flown this one, many times?" Edan asked.

"Nothing surprises me anymore," Sim said. "But, as you just said, the people on the sub are going to see us taking off. Who knows what the hell they'd have in store for us."

Edan knitted his brow, but then he suddenly snapped his fingers and grinned.

"That submarine," he said, "it wasn't there an hour ago."

29

THIS TIME SIM remembered and led the way, and she had to wait briefly, panting, in front of the door to Edan's lab as he scrambled down the hallway to catch up.

"Relax," he told her, smiling, as he entered the keypad code and satisfied the biometric devices, then shoved open the door, "we've got all the time in the world."

"Optimist," she said as she followed him into the lab.

They jogged over to the device and stood, catching their breath, staring at it for a moment.

"Okay, what's the plan?" Sim asked.

"Step one," he replied, "we go back an hour, maybe ninety minutes. Step two, we get the device to the helicopter and lift it out of here and over to John Wayne Airport, then get it onto my plane. Step three, we fly to DC where I speak with the President, tell him what's going on here and demand a personal meeting to talk about what should be done with the device."

"I thought you didn't trust him?" Sim said.

"I'm not sure I do, not really," Edan said, "but it's either that or destroy the device right now and I'm not quite ready to do that yet, at least not until we can explore whether there's a chance to make one of those public-private partnerships work here."

Sim thought about it for a moment.

"Okay, that actually makes sense," she said, "but why only ninety minutes? I know it gives us enough time to get out of here without the people on that sub seeing us go, but it won't take Carver and his people long to figure out that we got away and that we did it on your plane. It's about a four-hour flight to DC, so it gives them time to intercept us before we land if they want, and they probably want, the CIA people anyway."

Edan smiled and stroked her cheek.

"Because if we go back further than ninety minutes," he told her, "that will be before we made love this morning and I don't want to chance losing that memory."

"You're a hopeless romantic," she told him, "emphasis on hopeless. There's no way I'm ever going to forget this morning. Besides," she added, smiling, "even if I did, we'd still have last night, and that wasn't so bad, either."

She kissed him long and hard and when they parted he asked if she was sure.

"I'm sure," she said, kissing his nose. "The worst that can happen is that it seems like a dream, right? I can live with that. Besides, you've got a bedroom on that plane of yours, don't you?"

Edan smiled.

"Fine," he said, "we'll make it four hours earlier."

There were several arrays of small flat screens in different parts of the lab that showed the same images as the much larger screens in the house's command center, and Edan glanced up at the nearest one. Four of the six big, black SUVs that had been parked on the shoulder up on Pacific Coast Highway were now pulling into the drive that led down to the house.

"Looks like we're about to have company," Edan said.

"That didn't take long."

"Might be a good idea to disable the countermeasures," Edan said. "After all, we don't want to start a war for no reason, especially since there's still no way in hell they'll be able to get into this lab."

"I think I can remember how to do that," Sim said. "It can be done with a tablet, right?"

"Or my iPhone, in a pinch," he said.

He took the slender phone out of his pocket, pressed the Touch ID sensor button at the bottom and kept his thumb on the button until it read his fingerprint. When the phone unlocked, he tapped an app icon, entered a passcode and handed the phone to Sim.

"It's the same application as on the tablet," he told her.

She opened the app and without really thinking about it, thumbed through the protocols and had the countermeasures disabled moments later. The front doorbell sounded through a speaker mounted next to the monitors shortly after that, as they were taking the cover off the device.

"Good timing," Edan said, as he was about to step inside it.

Sim handed back his iPhone and he suddenly realized that she might not remember going through the slat.

"Just do what I do," he said, tossing the now-folded cover inside.

Sim's eyebrows arched as she watched the cover disappear and her eyes widened as Edan stepped through the too-narrow slat.

"Been here, done this, no big deal, right?" she said aloud.

She walked up to the slat, but as she raised her right foot to take the final step inside, she was suddenly there, standing beside Edan, who was already busy making entries on the holographic keyboard.

"Assume everything is normal unless I say otherwise," he told her as he made a final entry on the keyboard and pressed *Enter*.

As soon as he did, they sensed a ringing in their ears and a subtle vibration beneath their feet. Both sensations steadily grew and the floor's pinkish hue darkened. There was no sound and fury, no noise at all, but the sides and roof of the device seemed to disappear.

Sim looked around but there was little to see other than ever-changing snatches of lines, forms and color. As the ringing in her ears and vibration intensified, she also began to feel dizzy and had the sense of being on a tiny, rolling platform, which required her to concentrate in order to keep her balance. That brought back a clearer memory of having been there before. She tried to count, to figure out how much time was passing, but just as the dizziness, the ringing in her ears and the vibration reached an almost intolerable level, it all stopped, suddenly and totally.

It was impossible to tell when the sensations had ended and the walls of the device had come back into view, giving off the same dusky cast as when they had first entered the device, let alone calculate how much time had passed.

"God, it's quiet when all that, that, *whatever,* ends," is all she could manage to say.

Edan made a few more entries on the keyboard, then picked up the cover and stepped out of the device. Sim immediately followed.

The hands on Edan's Panerai watch had not moved, but when he took his iPhone out of his pocket, it displayed a time four hours earlier than before. He looked up at the array of monitoring screen and saw that the six Suburbans were still parked on the shoulder of Pacific Coast Highway and no vehicles were at the entrance to the house or in the drive.

"Second shortest trip after that first one to hammer in that nail," Edan said, as he began unfolding the cover. "Maybe I should start keeping a logbook, like they do for airplanes. Speaking of which..."

He speed-dialed his chief pilot, let the woman know that they needed to be wheels up in forty-five minutes and to file a flight plan for Dulles International, outside of Washington, DC. Then he called Dale Bowdoin and told him to meet them at John Wayne Airport as soon as possible with as many men as he could round up in that short time. When he ended the call, Edan and Sim put the cover over the device. They spent the next few minutes maneuvering it on its rollers out of the lab, down the hallway and across the terrace at the back of the house, and with the help of its lifting rods down to the helipad.

As expected, the submarine was not yet in the harbor.

When they reached the helicopter, they positioned the device beside it. While Sim climbed in and began familiarizing herself with the layout of the turbine version of the Robinson family of helicopters and going through the pre-flight checklist, Edan got a coil of black Kevlar rope from the craft's small luggage compartment and carefully wrapped several loops around the device, making sure the excess rope was tightly knotted in the top center, leaving a roughly dozen-foot extra length of it dangling free. He then attached that to the helicopter's external lifting hook. When he was satisfied that the connection was secure and that the slack in the rope could be taken up smoothly, he joined Sim inside the craft.

"You going to be okay with this?" he asked, as he fastened his seat belt.

"Piece of cake," she said. "I've already programmed the coordinates for John Wayne into the GPS, everything checks out, we're good to go."

"As soon as we're up," he said, "stay as low as you can and head out over the water. We need to stay below the ridge line so the guys in those SUVs don't see us."

"How long is the slack on the rope?" she asked.

"Maybe twelve feet or so," he said, "just enough to allow you to set it down and maneuver to land on the ground next to it."

"Which means the slack's going to get taken up pretty fast when we lift off," she said, flipping switches. "Thanks for the warning."

Seconds later the whine from the Robinson's single turbine engine began to rise in pitch and the rotor began to rotate above their heads. Edan absently tugged his seat belt tighter. Sim brought up the engine speed, pulled back on the collective lever and pushed down on the left foot pedal and they slowly rose into the air. As soon as the slack had been taken up and the device was off the ground, they headed out over the Pacific, Sim descending slightly as the hillside fell off toward the water. She remained low and over the water, heading northwest, hugging the coastline, until they were nearly at the same latitude as John Wayne Airport. Only then did she initiate a climb. As they slowly gained altitude, she turned the craft toward the east and contacted the airport's control tower. Several minutes later they were back on the ground, thirty yards from where Edan's Boeing Business Jet was parked.

Dale Bowdoin joined them as Sim completed the after landing checklist and he and Edan untied the ropes from the device. Bowdoin's men then wheeled it to the waiting jet.

"Sorry, boss," Bowdoin said as he watched them work, "but I could only get three guys on such short notice. You gonna tell me what's up?"

"As soon as we're in the air," Edan replied. "Now let's get the device loaded and get the hell out of here."

The co-pilot was completing a walk-around inspection of the big Boeing and paused to watch as Bowdoin and his men loaded the device into the jet's cargo hold.

"Good thing 737s sit so low to the ground," the man said as he came over to shut the cargo compartment door once they had finished loading the device. "That thing looks heavy. I guess it must be some new supercomputer or something like that, right, sir?"

"Something like that," Edan replied affably.

"Anyway, looks like we should have some pretty good tailwinds today," the co-pilot went on to say as they all walked around to the boarding stairs. "Computer says four hours flat to Dulles this morning."

"Sounds good," Edan said. "We're on kind of a tight timetable."

30

AT FIVE AM on Friday, while the captain and crew of the nuclear submarine were making ready for an anticipated deployment from Point Loma, Rip Carver had been part of a twenty-man force that descended on Edan Duff's corporate campus in Carlsbad in a Marine MV-22 tilt-rotor aircraft.

The force, comprised of CIA field operatives and analysts, most flown out for the occasion from Langley, was commanded by Carver, whose straightforward mission was to confirm their intel that Edan Duff's device was not housed at the campus. Their best information suggested that the device was kept at the laboratory complex in Duff's house. But before approving an operation that could involve invading the private residence of a high-profile citizen such as Duff, with the even higher legal and privacy rights issues it could engender, the Director had insisted that they be absolutely certain that the device was not elsewhere. And they had concluded that the corporate campus was the only other place it might be.

The arrival of a smaller group of specialized personnel, in a single Chinook helicopter from nearby Camp Pendleton, had preceded the Osprey's landing. Their job was to disable all power and communications hubs for the complex, including back-up generators and alternative energy sources, and to do so before Duff's security personnel could make any outside contacts. Once advised that this had been accomplished and the campus secured, Carver's team in the Osprey came in and the search for Duff's alleged time machine began.

Carver had prepared a computer-generated image of what he thought the machine would probably look like and every member of his team had studied it and carried a copy. As they spread out to begin their search of the buildings on the campus, Carver sat on a sofa in the lobby of one of them. He did not have to wait long until cellphone photos of various suspect pieces of equipment started to come in. As they did, he wondered why a few had even been thought to be the machine and got up and went to view only two of them in person. He rejected both.

The few employees that began arriving at around six were met by members of the Camp Pendleton force, all of whom were dressed in civilian clothing. They were told that a security drill was in progress, were relieved of their cell phones and other personal communication devices and taken to the café in the first building to have been searched and found to be free of the machine.

By six-thirty Carver was satisfied that the machine was not on the premises. But before power was restored to the complex and personal belongings were returned to employees, they and the company's security people were given a short lecture on the need to keep the operation top secret. Terms such as *national security* and lightly veiled threats of military tribunals and Guantanamo were scattered liberally throughout the brief talk.

As Duff's security people and a handful of shaken employees took up their normal duties, Carver phoned Langley to report that they had not found what they were now calling *the trophy*. The CIA Director, in turn, contacted the base commander at Point Loma to authorize the deployment of the sub. Its orders were to proceed northward and to submerge at Dana Point and remain out of sight of Edan Duff's house until told otherwise.

After the operation in Carlsbad, Carver returned to Camp Pendleton with his team and was then driven north to join the personnel in the black SUVs that sat on the shoulder of the Coast Highway near the turnoff to Duff's house. He arrived there shortly before eleven

and it was not long before word came in that the sub
had arrived and was just offshore, submerged, awaiting
further orders.

Carver relayed instructions for the sub commander
to surface. Then he dialed Edan Duff's cell number.

31

WHEN EDAN DUFF'S housekeeper opened the main door to the house at eleven on Friday morning, Rip Carver did not wait to be invited in. He flashed his CIA credentials but no search warrant or any other sort of official document was offered as he pushed past her, followed by the team of CIA and FBI personnel who had been stationed on the shoulder of the Coast Highway in the Suburbans.

Other than shouting *Bloody 'ell* in her thick East London accent as the horde shoved her aside, she made no attempt to stop them or otherwise impede their progress, just as Duff had instructed. Neither Carver nor any of the others asked if Duff was there, but a half dozen of them followed Carver through the house and out to the terrace at the rear while the others fanned out in different directions. Each person carried an iPad mini that had a schematic of the home's layout, as well as Carver's rendering of the device. And each was armed with a Glock nine-millimeter semi-automatic pistol, although the guns remained holstered as the search proceeded.

Carver expected to find Duff, along with Jane Garrison, on the terrace although he was not quite sure why. In any event, the sub was out there, looking quite menacing, in the harbor, but the terrace was deserted.

"Shit!" he hissed.

It was just loud enough that his two companions, who were gazing straight down over the railings, glanced over at him. Carver ignored them, instead staring at the image on his iPad, then after a moment he jogged across the terrace.

"Helipad!" he shouted.

They caught up with him seconds later as he stood staring down the slope at the also empty helipad.

"Get someone at the L.A. air traffic control center!" he barked at one of the men. "I need to know if they worked Duff's helicopter this morning!" He made some entries on the iPad and told the man the tail number of the Robinson R-66. Turning toward the other man, he said, "And you, get a hold of the tower manager at John Wayne Airport! I want to know if Duff's jet is there and if it isn't I want to know where the hell it is!"

While the other two men did as they were told, Carver paced back and forth on the terrace. Every few minutes, one or more of the team members came out-side to tell him that the house appeared to be empty except for the housekeeper. He also got a text from the two experts who had been assigned to get the door to Duff's laboratory open saying they were having no luck and that they were not optimistic.

Keep at it! was Carver's reply.

"L.A. center has no record of working Duff's heli-copter this morning," one of the men shouted to Carver a moment later.

Carver grimaced and looked over at the other man expectantly. The man held up an index finger and pressed his iPhone harder against his ear. "Where the fuck was it headed?" he shouted into the phone. "Dulles International, you're absolutely sure?"

He held the phone away from his ear and looked over at Carver.

"They departed John Wayne at 0735 this morning," he said. "Flight plan says they're headed for Dulles, six on board plus the crew."

"Find out their ETA!" Carver ordered.

It was several more minutes before the man ended the call and reported that the Washington area air traf-fic control center had just cleared Duff's jet to descend from its cruising altitude.

Carver turned away and speed-dialed a number on his iPhone.

"This is Carver," he said into the phone a moment later. "I need to arrange for an F-16 intercept west of DC and an escort to Andrews Air Force Base."

He was placed on hold and was still waiting five minutes later when, instead of the officer he had been speaking with, the CIA Director came on the line. Reflexively he stood up straighter.

"Good morning, sir," he said.

"Stand down, Mr. Carver," the Director told him.

"Excuse me, sir?"

"I said, stand down," the Director repeated. "Duff's plane will continue on to Dulles unescorted. As to what happens after that, I'm afraid I'm just as much in the dark as you are. All I know is that the orders came from the highest level."

32

AS HIS JET began its descent into the Washington area early on Friday afternoon local time, Edan Duff roused from the light sleep he had fallen into after making love with Sim. She was no longer in the bed, beside him, but as he came fully awake he could hear the sound of water running in the shower. By the time he got out of bed and stretched, the water had stopped. Moments later, Sim, wrapped in a large, white towel, stepped out of the bathroom, came to him and kissed him.

"I don't know about you," she said, "but I've kind of got that dreamlike memory thing going on, this time about having sex with you earlier this morning in the shower in your house. But if it really did happen, I doubt it could've been any better than the last two hours were."

Edan sat up, took her into his arms, hugged her tightly and kissed her gently on the neck.

"All I know," he said, "is that it was amazing. And that I'd better shower."

"Wait," she said, taking his arm as he began to walk away, "there's something I forgot to ask you."

"Which is?"

"Do I get to meet the President?" Sim asked.

Edan smiled.

"He asked for you personally," he replied. "Remember, he's got a thing for veterans, especially wounded veterans."

"Even when there's no photo op?" she asked.

"Apparently," Edan replied.

A government-issue beige Impala and a similarly-hued, windowless panel van were waiting on the tarmac as Edan's jet taxied to the ramp outside the Signature Flight Support executive aviation terminal at Dulles International. As soon as the Boeing's engines shut down, two men, dressed in suits, got out of the Impala, and two others, these more casually dressed, exited the driver and front passenger seats of the van.

A Signature line employee rolled a set of portable boarding steps up to the jet just as the cabin door was being opened and two of Dale Bowdoin's men hurried down the steps. One stood at the bottom, looking around, while the other jogged over to the terminal. As he did, the two casually dressed men from the van moved to the plane and up the stairs. At the top, they were met by Bowdoin, who confirmed that they had been briefed on the security protocols that Duff had negotiated. He then searched each of them thoroughly, took their guns, credentials, wallets and cellphones and invited them to have seats in the forward section of the jet's cabin.

When that was done, Bowdoin signaled Edan and Sim to join him at the open cabin door. He then signaled the two suited men, who were now standing next to the Impala. One of them came up the stairs and thoroughly searched Edan and Sim, although none of their possessions were confiscated. The men then escorted the couple down the stairs. One of them held the rear door of the Impala open as Bowdoin watched from the top of the stairway. Once Edan and Sim were seated, the man took his place in the front passenger seat and his partner folded himself into the driver's seat.

Bowdoin ducked back into the jet's cabin and told the two men from the van that he would be taking their guns and other Items wIth hIm.

"The guy at the table over there," he went on, gesturing toward the conference table at the rear of the cabin where a very fit-looking man sat, "is a former Navy Seal. He's armed, as you can see, and he's got orders to kill you if you make any attempt to leave. The pilots have orders to remain in the cockpit until we're back here. It's a reinforced cockpit door, just like the airlines,

by the way. Another one of my guys is inside the terminal. A fuel truck should be pulling up any minute to
refuel this beast. If it looks to my guy in the terminal
or the guy over there at the table like anything unexpected is going down, the pilots will be given orders to
immediately fly the hell out of here. Other than that,
gents, make yourselves comfortable."

Both men made sour faces but said nothing.
Bowdoin tossed their guns and other effects into a
nylon gym bag, slung it over his shoulder and stepped
out onto the boarding steps, where he paused to close
and secure the cabin door before jogging down the
stairs and moving them away from the plane. He and
the man who had been stationed at the bottom of the
stairs walked around to the other side of the jet, opened
the cargo bay door and spent the next several minutes
transferring the device from the plane to the van. Once
it was securely tied down and the van's rear doors were
locked, Bowdoin got into the passenger seat while his
colleague sat down behind the wheel.

The Impala started moving and the van followed
it off the tarmac, then out a manned gate that was
opened at their approach and off the airport grounds
onto the Dulles Access Road. The two vehicles stayed
more or less at the legal speed limit, cruising for about
fifteen minutes before exiting at the Capitol Beltway
and heading north. Edan and Sim in the back seat of

the Impala said little as they drove up the Beltway past Bethesda to the Interstate 270 exit, where they took the exit ramp and continued north. At Frederick, Maryland they followed the signs for Route 15, gazing out at the farmland that lined the road. Eventually the scenery became more wooded and they passed signs for Thurmont and for Catoctin Mountain Park and then turned west onto Route 77, where the road narrowed and the woods thickened.

"If I wasn't following us on Google maps," Sim, looking up from her iPhone, said softly, "I'd have no idea where the hell we were headed. You have noticed there are no signs for it, right? Although I guess that's not totally surprising considering who comes here and that it's technically a high security military installation."

Edan seemed distracted and merely nodded as the name *Camp David* finally came up on the screen. The Impala stopped at two security check points manned by very serious looking Marines who vetted them carefully despite their pre-clearance, before driving on for two more minutes before passing a rustic wooden sign announcing that the place was indeed Camp David.

The car and van stopped in front of the main lodge. Edan and Sim stepped out of the Impala and were met by an attractive young woman in a Navy uniform whose name plaque said **Cross.** She smiled, introduced herself as an ensign and escorted them inside. Bowdoin and his colleague remained seated in the van and the two suited men remained in the Impala.

"Would either of you like to make a trip to the head?" the woman asked as they walked into the lodge. "The President is waiting for you outside so this will be your only opportunity."

Both took her up on the offer and she pointed down a hallway toward the restrooms. When they returned, she led them down another hallway and out a rear door. The President of the United States, Edwin Greavy, stood on a dirt path at the foot of a short wooden stairway, his back to them. He was wearing olive green pants and a blue oxford shirt, its sleeves turned back, and was speaking into a Blackberry. He ended the call moments later, turned around and smiled when he saw them.

"I'll leave you now," Ensign Cross said, turning and walking back into the lodge.

"Good morning, Edan," the President said as Edan and Sim walked down the steps to where he stood. Duff took Greavy's outstretched hand. "So good to see you again," the President continued. "I think the last time we met must have been at that fundraiser at your home in California a couple of years ago."

Edan agreed that it was.

"And this must be Major Garrison," Greavy went on, turning to Sim.

While flattered to have been addressed by her actual former rank, she was not sure if Greavy's smile was genuine. But it was effective, and she beamed at him as she shook his hand.

"It's an honor to meet you, sir," she said.

"I've heard a good deal about you, major," Greavy went on, his gaze fixed on Sim, "and I want to thank you for your service, and for your sacrifices. You're a credit to your nation."

Edan had never seen Sim blush before, but he saw it now.

"And now, if you'll indulge me, major," Greavy said, "I'd like to spend a few minutes alone with Mr. Duff. Ensign Cross will be happy to show you around in the interim."

Before Sim could say anything, the young Navy woman who had escorted them in reappeared at the top of the steps. Edan looked at Sim with a nearly indiscernible look of surprise and then gave the slightest of shrugs.

"Please follow me, ma'am," Ensign Cross said.

"I thought we might take advantage of this beautiful weather and stroll around as we talk," Greavy continued after Sim and Cross walked away. "I've grown very fond of the path that President Reagan and Margaret Thatcher used for their famous talks way back when."

The President set off at a modest pace, keeping to the paved path that bisected the woods, and Edan fell in beside him.

"As you might imagine," Edan said, "I've never been here before. It's beautiful."

"I've grown quite fond of it," Greavy said. "Your unexpected little visit gave me an excuse to come up here and I'm not particularly looking forward to going back to DC tomorrow morning. In any event, let me start off by telling you that there are hardly words to express what you've apparently accomplished in terms of technological prowess, Edan. It's difficult to imagine that you've actually done something that men have only been dreaming, or hypothesizing, about, for generations."

"As so often seems to happen in science," Edan said, "it's not really what I'd originally set out to do. But the research I was doing began leading me down an unexpected path and I guess I just kept going."

"You know, I'm a bit of a sci-fi buff," Greavy told him, "so I'm well aware of the ironies that are sometimes out there when people look at some startling new invention and say something like, *it's right out of science fiction*. After all, it was science fiction writers who first thought up ideas like robots, moon landings, geosynchronous satellite orbits and the internet. But this, this is in a whole other category."

"I've always been a big sci-fi fan myself," Edan said, "particularly the guys like Clarke and Asimov and Heinlein. The funny thing is, as I said before, I didn't set out to build a time travel device. We've been working for a while now on trying to come up with true break-throughs in battery technology, computer memory, materials science and a few other things, which are going to lead to some interesting consumer products and some other things by the way--"

"Like miniaturized laser weapons?" Greavy asked.

Edan smiled.

"Whenever we come up with something really excit-ing," he said, "I tend to start thinking about the span of applications that the technology might have beyond the product categories we're focused on. Hand-held laser weapons are right out of sci-fi, as you know, and coming up with a compact power source with the nec-essary output has been the main stumbling block to making them a reality. Once we had that power source, one thing kind of led to another, especially since we've got a few people around the company whose interest skews in that direction. Once you get immersed in that kind of, ah, call it magical thinking, one thing tends to lead to another."

They walked on in silence for a few moments, the President shaking his head slowly before he finally asked what it was like, going back in time.

"I assume you mean conceptually," Edan said, "not the actual, physical experience."

"That's right," Greavy said, "although I wouldn't mind hearing about the actual experience, either."

"That would be much easier to articulate," Edan said. "I'm not sure I'm the right person to address the conceptual side, except to say that the word *unreal* doesn't even begin to cover what you feel when you discover it actually was *real*."

"Well, along with the technological aspect," Greavy said, "I imagine what you've done has enormously advanced our knowledge about the universe we live in, although I'll leave it to others to sort out the details, let alone the ramifications, of that one."

They walked on in silence again for a few more moments, Edan thrusting his hands deep into the pockets of his gray wool trousers as he described for Greavy the sensations that you experienced inside the device.

"Fascinating, absolutely fascinating," Greavy said. "Of course, you've also created something of a monster, so much so, in fact, that we've given that device of yours the code name *Frankenstein* around here." Edan started to say something but the President put up his hand to stop him. "That machine of yours in many ways might be the most fantastic invention of all time," he continued, "and it could potentially be used as a force for good, of course. But at the same time it's also potentially the most dangerous invention of all time, given the havoc that it could potentially reap."

Edan thought about the uses he had made of the device, especially the mission to prevent Sim's attempted suicide. That was clearly something good, but it was also very personal, nothing that would affect the world at large. Then he thought about his exploration of a mission to kill John Foster Dulles. Although it had been a ruse, the ruse had worked on Sim because the concept had been conceived as a force for good. But it was impossible to know whether the results, in the admittedly unlikely event that it had been implemented, would have been good or bad for the world, despite its good intentions.

"It can be destroyed," Edan said. "In fact I thought long and hard about doing that before I called you."

Greavy stopped walking, turned to face Edan and put a hand on his arm.

"Now *that* would be a tragedy," he said. "And for the record, I never for a moment thought you might be dealing with one of our enemies, although I did have to wonder at one point what the hell you *were* doing."

Edan smiled.

"I suppose that's understandable," he said.

"There is only one of those things, right?" Greavy asked.

Edan had not expected the question and the look of surprise on his face was clear.

"Ah, yes, that's right," Edan confirmed.

"What about the plans?" Greavy asked next. "We'd have to worry just as much about the plans to build it falling into the wrong hands as we would about the device itself."

"There are plans for most of the components," Edan replied, "although how they come together is all in my head. And that's where the breakthrough was, in how they all have to come together, which I'm reasonably confident couldn't be reverse engineered, by the way."

"Or understood well-enough by any of the people who advised or assisted you so that they could potentially recreate what you've done?" Greavy asked.

"For want of a better analogy," he replied, "I ran the process kind of like a high-end drug cartel. No one person has nearly enough information to know what their advice might have been used for, let alone how the whole thing works."

"On the other hand, the CIA's Mr. Carver managed to figure out what you were up to," the President pointed out. "Someone else might be able to do the same thing."

"It's a fair point," Edan said, "and very impressive on his part, by the way. Of course, he would neither be able to operate the device nor figure out how to build it."

"Speaking of which," Greavy said, "I suppose you're the only person in the world who does know how to operate it."

Edan nodded.

"That's right," he said. "And there are no controls in the ordinary sense, just a keyboard."

The President began walking again and again Edan fell in beside him.

"You do realize that all of this puts you at enormous personal risk," Greavy said. "If the device were to fall into the wrong hands the people who had it would need you there with them and would do anything to learn how to operate it. And even if it didn't fall into the wrong hands, if the fact of its existence and who had created it were to get out--"

"It will," Edan interrupted him to say. "That sort of thing always does, sooner or later."

"You're probably right," Greavy told him.

"I was wrong in coming to you, wasn't I?" Edan asked, and this time it was he who stopped walking. "I should have just destroyed the device. You were never really going to approach this the way I suggested, were you? Agreeing to this meeting was just another means to get me, and the device, into the hands of the CIA."

Greavy had also stopped walking and turned to face Edan.

"I don't think you were wrong to come to me," Greavy said. "Your device is something that can only be, let's say, managed, by the government, and frankly I can't imagine any scenario in which a private citizen should be entrusted with it. It's way too risky in any number of ways, from what you might decide to use it for to your ability to protect it, and yourself, from our enemies."

"So you never really considered the idea of a public-private partnership, between my people and a special government agency or unit, did you?" Edan asked.

Greavy let out a breath.

"I told you what I needed to tell you on that phone call, Edan," he said. "I had to make sure that we got the device and this seemed to me like the best way for us to get it with the least fallout, so to speak, and it worked."

Edan rolled his fists into balls and tensed up as if to strike the President. Greavy waived his hand in the air and a half dozen Secret Service agents stepped out of the woods.

"I'm sorry it has to be this way, Edan, truly I am," Greavy said.

"You're going to need me, you know," Edan said.

Greavy smiled.

"Maybe, maybe not," he said. "Remember, we also have one option of simply destroying the device, in which case we obviously wouldn't need you."

"You'd risk the possibility of my building another one?" Edan asked.

"I'm confident we could find a way to, ah, minimize the risk," Greavy replied.

"And if you decided not to destroy it?" Edan asked.

Greavy shrugged.

"We'd very likely want your assistance," Greavy replied, "assuming we couldn't figure out what we need to on our own."

Edan began walking again and this time it was Greavy who fell in beside him.

"But if I were to participate," he said, "wouldn't that essentially put us back at the public-private partnership idea I hoped we'd be discussing?"

"As I said a few minutes ago," Greavy replied, "I can't imagine any scenario in which a private citizen could be entrusted with the device, and by the same token I can't imagine one in which a private citizen would be allowed to wield any sort of power over the use or disposition of the device."

"So I'd have no real say in what it was used for, even though I invented it, I'm the only one who knows its capabilities and I'm the only one who knows how it works?" Edan asked.

"Please don't go down the road of arguing that it's not fair," Greavy said. "As they say, all's fair in love and war and this is very much tantamount to war."

"So I'd teach someone else how to operate it and then you'd kill me, is that it?"

"Come, come, Edan," Greavy said, "There's no need for melodrama."

Edan had not been paying attention to their route and was surprised to see that they were nearly back to the main lodge. They stopped walking and the President turned to face him.

"You were right about one thing," Greavy said. "I'm not the CIA. You're welcome to leave here right now, all of you."

"But the device stays?"

"The device stays."

"What happens then?" Edan asked. "You either destroy it or you get a group of people together and try to figure out how to work it?"

"Unless we need your help later on," Greavy replied, "that's none of your concern."

Edan noticed the young Navy ensign, Cross, step outside and come to the top of the short flight of wooden stairs they had descended from the lodge, and he lowered his voice.

"Just so I'm sure I understand correctly," he said, moving closer to the President, "we can leave now, without the device, and quite possibly never know what became of it, or....?"

Greavy sighed.

"Leaving now is your best alternative, Edan," he said, his tone firm but not unfriendly, "which is an alternative not shared by all of my advisors, I have to say."

Edan noticed movement out of the corner of his eye and when he turned toward the lodge, he saw that Rip Carver had joined Ensign Cross at the top of the stairs.

"The same two gentlemen who drove you here will drive you and your party back to Dulles," Greavy went on. "They'll stay with you until the two agents on your plane are released and they'll all wait there until you've departed. After that you're on your own. As I said, the device will remain here. Now, are you going to leave or not, Edan?"

Edan stared at the President for a moment and without another word, or a handshake, turned and walked up the stairs.

33

THE MOOD ABOARD Edan's jet as it taxied out to the runway at Dulles ninety minutes later was far darker than it had been on the flight to the Washington area, feeding off Edan's clearly angry and frustrated demeanor. Edan and Sim sat next to each other on a leather sofa, her head on his shoulder, and they said nothing as the plane climbed out into a gray late afternoon sky. Dale Bowdoin had joined his men in the seats in the forward part of the cabin and little chatter could be heard from them, either.

It was not until the plane leveled off at its cruising altitude more than twenty minutes later that Edan and Sim moved to the conference table, Dale Bowdoin joining them for a debriefing. Edan made sure than Bowdoin's men each wore noise suppressing headsets before he opened up the conversation.

"Getting out of there when we did was the only opportunity we were going to get to leave at all," Edan told them. "Taking the device with us wasn't an option. And if we hadn't left when we did, I'm pretty sure they would have locked us all up until they decided they wanted me to teach them how to use the device."

"Or locked you up and killed us," Bowdoin said. "Fact is I'm surprised they let us leave at all. I guess it's a good thing you did that fundraiser for him, eh boss?"

Edan managed a half-hearted smile and folded his arms on the table.

"Apparently the decision to let us leave wasn't unanimous," he said. "If certain others had had their way, like our CIA friends, I think we all would have disappeared to some very dark place."

"So what's going to happen now?" Sim asked.

"According to Greavy, there's still a chance they might destroy it," Edan replied, "although I truly believe that isn't going to happen."

"Or?" she said.

"Or," Edan said, "they'll establish a group to take charge of it, but Greavy made it clear that I'll never be part of that group, which is, of course, contra to the direction he seemed to be leaning when I spoke with him on the phone before the meeting."

"So much for the public-private partnership thing," Sim said.

Edan nodded.

"Let's just say that it would be a government only group," he replied.

He then told them what the President had said about how a private citizen could never either being allowed to control or be involved in controlling the future use of the device.

"So they might destroy it and then again they probably won't, but you won't be allowed any say in the matter," Sim said.

"Exactly," Edan agreed, "and we have no way of knowing what they may decide unless and until the President gets back to me about operating the device. And that assumes that they don't find someone or someones, say in DARPA," Edan added, looking at Sim, "who can figure out how to do it, in which case I'll never hear from him again."

"Or they send out some folks to kill you, and maybe us, too," Bowdoin said.

"I don't think we can rule out the possibility," Edan said. "In any case, Greavy did imply that he, or maybe some of his people, think that it should be possible for someone else to figure out how to operate the device."

"They do have some scary-smart people over there, at DARPA," Sim said, "and who knows where else."

"And y'all thought Greavy was goin' to be the good guy in all this," Bowdoin said sarcastically.

"Yeah, sorry about that," Edan told them.

"Hey, you really had no choice, boss," Bowdoin went on. "It was that or let the CIA grab it, and us, and like you said, they were among the ones who were lobbying for not letting us go."

They were quiet for a little while until Sim asked what was next.

But instead of answering, Edan got up and asked if anyone wanted coffee. Sim and Bowdoin said they did and Edan walked to the galley to get it. A few minutes later he returned carrying a small silver platter with three Boeing mugs imprinted with the plane's tail number. He set them down on the conference table and fell heavily into his seat.

"We need to get the device back and destroy it," he said. "I've been naïve. I understand now that even if we *could* trust Greavy, there'd still be the next president and the one after that to worry about, not to mention other people in the government who might try to get control of the device, which might be almost as bad as if it fell into foreign hands."

"You thinkin' like maybe a CIA *coup*?" Bowdoin suggested.

"Something like that," Edan agreed.

"Did Greavy say anything about where they might keep the dingus while they're deciding what to do next?" Sim asked.

"Dingus?" Bowdoin said, looking askance at her.

Sim smiled and explained it.

"Not, really," Edan replied, "just that we had to leave it behind if we wanted to walk out of there."

"You know," Sim said, "one view of the world is that they might leave it right where it is. Not in that van necessarily, but somewhere in Camp David, at least until they decide what to do with it. I mean, moving it around any more than they absolutely have to would be unnecessarily risky. Plus, there's plenty of security out there."

"I agree," Bowdoin said.

"Speaking of security," Sim said, turning to Edan, "did Greavy happen to say how long he was going to be at Camp David?"

"Actually, before we got into the serious stuff, he mentioned that he had to be back in DC tomorrow morning," Edan replied.

"I assume y'all are thinkin' what I'm thinkin'," Bowdoin said, glancing across at Sim. "That security loosens up quite a bit when the President's not there."

"That's exactly what I was thinking," she said.

"Okay, so we assume it's at Camp David and we act quickly," Edan said.

Bowdoin and Sim nodded. Edan stood up.

"I think that's my cue to go watch a movie or something and let the two of you start putting together a plan," he said.

"Does that mean I have a job?" Sim asked, smiling at Edan. "I have a feeling my current employer isn't exactly going to welcome me back with open arms."

"I'm sure we can work something out," Edan said.

It took Sim and Bowdoin only an hour to develop their idea and sketch out a plan, but they waited, drinking coffee and trying to find flaws in it, until the film Edan was watching ended before calling him over to join them. There was a carafe of coffee on the conference table and Bowdoin refilled their mugs before starting to explain what they had in mind.

"There are certain aspects of it that y'all're probably not going to like, boss," Bowdoin began, "but we think it's got a high chance of success, so hopefully you'll bear with us."

Edan listened patiently while Bowdoin took him through each step of the plan. Sim stepped in to add detail from time-to-time but Edan held his questions until they finished, identifying only one small issue that was easily rectified.

"You're right," he said, as they all leaned back in their chairs, "there's at least one aspect of it that I can't say I'm thrilled about."

"I think I can guess what that might be," Sim interjected.

"But despite that," Edan went on, "I think it's outstanding."

"So it's a go?" Bowdoin asked.
Edan took a deep breath.
"Yes, it's a go," he replied.

34

JUST AS EDAN had not shaken hands or exchanged any parting words with the President when their discussion at Camp David ended, he had also put a shoulder into Rip Carver's chest as he walked past the CIA man on his way back into the lodge. Ensign Cross had intervened to make sure that Carver did not escalate the taunt and then followed Edan inside to arrange for his party's return to Dulles Airport.

As soon as Cross and Duff were gone, Carver had taken the opportunity of being alone with the President to request a few minutes of Greavy's time.

"I hope you're not planning some kind of lecture on why I was wrong to let them leave," Greavy said as Carver came down the short flight of wooden steps to join him. "Along with the other reasons we've already discussed, you can tell the Director that I thought that putting some distance between us and

Duff might keep us from going off half-cocked and using that God-damned thing in haste."

"I wasn't planning a lecture or anything of the kind, Mr. President," Carver said. "But now that that ship's sailed, I did want to make a small suggestion, and I don't think it's inconsistent with the point you just made."

"Fine," Greavy said, "let's hear it."

"May I suggest that we get Mary McKinney from DARPA over here, along with whatever genius or geniuses she can dig up," Carver said, "and get them started on figuring out how to work Frankenstein. I'm sure it's not something they can come up with quickly--"

"If at all, if one can believe Duff," the President said.

"If at all," Carver said, "but if we don't try, we'll never know."

"Assuming we don't decide to just destroy the God-damned thing," Greavy added.

"Yes, of course," Carver agreed, "but either way, as you suggested, sir, there's no rush. We have the device so there's nothing Duff can do. And ultimately, assuming we decide not to destroy it, I think you'd agree we'd be better off not remaining beholden to him if we didn't absolutely have to be."

Greavy rubbed his eyes and folded his arms across his chest.

"Fine," he said, "go ahead and call her."

Two hours later, Mary McKinney's Honda Accord pulled into the drive in front of the main lodge. Carver was there to meet her.

"I didn't expect you to be coming alone," he said as he opened the driver's door for her and she stepped out of the car.

"The man I need is a numbers guy from DSO," she said, referring to DARPA's Defense Sciences Office, "and he can't get here until tomorrow morning."

"You think figuring out how that thing works is even possible?" Carver asked as he opened the back door to get her overnight bag.

"Do we have a choice now that Greavy's let Duff get away?" was her reply.

"We could always try to get Duff back here," he suggested.

"Look at how well we've done so far at getting Duff to be where we want him," she said. "He eluded us at his house this morning and he would have gone God knows where instead of coming here if he hadn't thought Greavy might be his salvation."

Carver held his hands out at his sides.

"Hey, he's smart and he's got some pretty good security people," he said. "Not to mention the fact that he had a time travel device. But he doesn't have it any more."

"Maybe not, but I'm sure he'll double down on his personal security now," McKinney said, "It looks like he's got Jane back with him now, too, in addition to Bowdoin. And I have a feeling that I'm not going to be seeing her again any time soon. Anyway, I'd bet Greavy's the only one who might be able to lure him back here, and even that's unlikely now."

Carver shrugged.

"You're forgetting who I work for," he said. "If we have to, anyone can be gotten to."

They went inside the lodge where Ensign Cross was waiting for them along with a handful of men who McKinney assumed were Secret Service agents. Cross introduced herself and then led McKinney and Carver back outside to one of the guest cabins, not far from the one in which Carver had already left his things. Cross unlocked the door, ushered them inside and handed McKinney the key.

"Please let me know if there's anything you need, ma'am," Cross said as she walked out the open door and closed it behind her.

McKinney looked around the rustically furnished room and Carver put her overnight bag down on a folding suitcase rack.

"When can I see it?" McKinney asked Carver as soon as Cross left.

In lieu of an answer, he took her into his arms and kissed her, laying a hand on her generous left breast as he did.

"I was hoping we could have a, ah, private moment, first," he said when they parted.

"I was hoping you might suggest that and if I wasn't as close as I am to a fucking *time machine*," she said, gently pushing him away, "I'd be happy to oblige. But…"

"Unfortunately, I see your point," Carver said. "Oh well. Follow me," he added, walking to the door as she went to get her laptop out of her bag.

There was a small, asphalt-paved parking lot not far from the cabins and McKinney followed Carver through it toward a beige Mercedes Sprinter panel van. As they approached the van, Carver fished a black plastic car key out of his pocket and pressed the unlock button.

"My God, it's in there?" McKinney asked.

"Hiding in plain sight," Carver told her. "Besides…"

He shouted *Guys* and three agents came out from their various hiding places and showed themselves. All of them carried what McKinney thought were AK-47s.

"Ah," she said, as Carver opened the rear doors of the Sprinter.

McKinney stood at the van's rear bumper and stared in while Carver hoisted himself inside and removed the cover from the device. She remained silent and totally still as he folded the cover and put it aside, her eyes locked on the device, her mouth open.

"If my mama was here," Carver said, "she'd probably say something about you closing your mouth unless you were wantin' to catch flies."

McKinney blinked and then turned to look at him.

"You're drawing was amazingly accurate," she told him as he helped her up into the van, adding, "God, it's unbelievably clear," as she stood there and stared at the big glass block for another moment, "although you can't see if there's anything inside it. Holy shit."

"Holy shit, indeed," Carver said.

He pulled the rear doors of the van closed and locked them, then held her laptop as she began examining the device more closely, running her fingertips along its sides and sharp corners and over the top edges. But as she came around to the other long side and neared the entry slat, Carver watched her suddenly disappear into the device.

"Jesus, Mary!" he yelled.

But just as suddenly, she reappeared, looking unharmed, although her face was ashen.

"Oh...my...God," she said softly, standing there, trembling. "How long was I gone?"

"A few seconds maybe," he told her, coming closer and taking her hand. "Why?"

"It could have been a few seconds, I suppose," she said almost dreamily, her gaze miles away, "or it could have been a few hours. There was no sense of it at all. And my God is it *quiet* in there."

"Earth to Mary," he said gently.

"Sorry," she said, her eyes focusing on him. "Okay, let's try that again, but on purpose this time."

They both stood in front of the slat, leaving what they thought was enough distance between it and them to avoid a repeat of what had just happened to McKinney. Eventually, she took a deep breath, said *here goes*, moved slightly closer, and again disappeared inside.

"Jesus," Carver muttered.

He tucked McKinney's laptop under his arm, shrugged and took a step forward. Suddenly he was standing next to McKinney inside the device.

"If that's all this thing did," Carver said, "it would be worth whatever it took to save it from being destroyed."

"But I don't think that's all it does," McKinney said.

Without another word she slipped past Carver and began walking away from him. She continued to walk, taking normal strides, but after a dozen or more steps she was no closer to running into the opposite wall of the device than before she had begun walking. And to Carver, at least, she did not seem nearly as far away from him as twelve steps should have put her.

"That's not possible," he said.

"And yet…"

"This is like the fucking Twilight Zone," Carver said. "Plus, it's like a tomb in here."

"Come with me," McKinney said, and before Carver could say anything she had disappeared out through the slat.

After a moment, he followed her, climbed out of the van and caught up with her halfway back to the guest cabins.

"What are you planning to do?" he asked.

"An experiment," she replied, not slowing down.

She opened the door to her cabin and once inside, began looking around.

"Find a closet," she told Carver, who almost immediately pointed to a door in the short hallway between the bedroom and bathroom.

McKinney opened the door to a large closet part of the space of which was used to store a folding, roll-away bed.

"Excellent, exactly what I was hoping for," she said. "Go get the one from your room and a blanket or two and meet me back at the van."

Carver did as she said but McKinney was not there when he got back to the van. He hoisted the bed in, tossed the blankets in behind it, then climbed in and closed the doors. As he was considering what to do next, McKinney suddenly appeared outside the slat, rubbing her shoulder. The folding bed was nowhere in sight.

"I probably should have waited for you," she said, grimacing slightly. "I think I hurt myself getting the bed in here."

"Don't tell me all that stuff is inside it," he said.

"And there seems to be room for more," McKinney told him, picking up one of the blankets he had brought and re-entering the device.

Carver began moving the folding bed toward the slat, but as soon as one edge of it got close, the entire thing vanished. Without giving it any thought he went and stood at the slat and the next thing he knew was back inside the device, along with McKinney and all of the paraphernalia they had brought along. McKinney had already unfolded one of the beds, extending it to its full length, and as he watched in rapt attention, she opened the other. Objectively, the space inside the device should not have been able to hold even one of the beds, but McKinney had no difficulty opening the second one, nor was there a problem finding exactly where it might be made to fit. It fit anywhere, as McKinney demonstrated by shoving one of the beds toward Carver.

Silently, she then picked up one of the blankets and shook it open to its full size. Again, there was more than enough room to accommodate it.

"This is not possible," Carver said.

"It's called tensile augmentation," she said, "and you're right, it's not possible. I've even seen the math that supposedly proves it's not."

Carver looked around in awe.

"You could probably get a small army in here," he said.

"I'm not sure it would have to be all that small," McKinney told him.

"You know what that means, right?" Carver asked.

"Yes, I think I do," she replied. "If you never even used the time travel aspect of this thing, it would still have enormous strategic potential. The Trojan horse comes to mind right away, for one thing. And who knows what else it may be capable of."

"I think we need to speak with Greavy right away," Carver said. "He needs to know about this before he even thinks about having it destroyed. I mean, we don't even need Duff for this aspect of it."

"I agree," McKinney said, reaching around to unzip her dress, "but I think there's one more experiment we ought to try first."

35

WHEN THE PRESIDENT is in residence at Camp David, no aircraft is permitted to fly within a ten-mile circle around the compound, at any altitude. But when the President is not there, this ten-mile circle is reduced to only three miles.

The three-mile restriction did not pose a serious problem for Sim and Bowdoin who, at four on Sunday morning stood at the open doorway of a Cessna Super Caravan turboprop as it leveled off at thirteen thousand-five hundred feet, roughly ten miles from the compound. The airplane had taken off from Eastern West Virginia Regional Airport, just south of Martinsburg, and headed east. It was flying under visual flight rules and had not filed a flight plan with the FAA, which was entirely legal. On the other hand, its transponder had not been turned on, with the result that local air traffic controllers got only a vague radar signal from the craft on their screens, rather than the very clear and more detailed information a transponder signal would have provided, including the aircraft's altitude. Flying with the transponder off was not entirely legal, but it was unlikely to land the pilot in too much hot water should the offense be discovered.

The plan called for Sim and Bowdoin to parachute in. Once they had done so, the Cessna would continue on its route of flight, albeit at a lower altitude, landing about thirty minutes later at Cecil County Airport in Elkton, Maryland, where it was scheduled to pick up a group of early morning skydivers. The departure airport had been carefully selected so that the plane's route of flight would take it quite close to Camp David on its way to Elkton but would skirt the restricted area by at least a mile or more. Under the circumstances, the flight was expected to attract no undo attention.

Both Sim and Bowdoin wore black jumpsuits, black ski masks under matte black helmets and black gloves and boots. Each had a black canvas pack strapped to their chest, which was filled with the tools they would need for the operation. The chutes on their backs were black nylon ram-air models that would allow them virtually the same level of control as a paraglider once the chute was deployed and the rectangular canopy inflated.

As they got close to Camp David, the Cessna's pilot turned around and gave a thumbs-up to his two jumpers, the signal that they were directly abeam of and exactly four miles from their target, and at the ideal jump speed.

"Good to go?" Bowdoin yelled to Sim.

It was to be a somewhat altered version of a HALO jump, which was one that began at high altitude, involved a sustained period of freefall at terminal velocity and concluded with a chute deployment at a very low altitude. The technique, and the fact that true HALO jumpers carry as little metal as possible, was designed to minimize the chances of being spotted either by hostile personnel on the ground or by radar. A military HALO jump typically began at an altitude of at least twenty thousand feet and more often at thirty thousand feet or more, demanding a much more capable aircraft and a great deal more equipment, much of it aimed at personal survival during the time spent outside at higher altitudes.

Sim and Bowdoin had made such jumps, both in training and in connection with insertions for certain high-risk missions, although it had been somewhat longer since Sim's last such jump. Nevertheless, her answer to Bowdoin's question of whether she was ready was to give a thumb's up, shout *See ya later!* and step out of the plane. Bowdoin smiled and immediately followed her.

They remained in free-fall, aiming for their preselected target, which was a clearing in the woods about three hundred yards from the main lodge, until reaching three thousand feet, then deployed their chutes and used the steering lines to refine their trajectories, They kept their eyes glued to their wrist-mounted GPS receivers and made minor course corrections, maintaining a high rate of speed until they were down to five hundred feet, at which point they slowed for their landing approaches and maneuvered to the landing point.

Their boots touched the ground only seconds apart within ten yards of the selected spot and only a few yards from each other. They jettisoned their chutes and made short work of folding them, then carried them, double-time, to the tree line where they laid them on the ground, gathering a few rocks to hold them down in case a wind came up. Wordlessly, they flipped down the night vision goggles attached to their helmets and each withdrew a lethal-looking, but in fact non-lethal, bean-bag gun from the long, narrow pocket that ran down the right calf of their jumpsuits

The guns were ARMA 100s, black, and they looked like a cross between scaled down shotguns and billy clubs. Each offered only one shot before needing to be reloaded, but the guns were quite accurate at less than ten yards. From that distance, the bean-bag filled plastic cartridge that they fired would knock a man down, causing muscle spasms and a good deal of pain, as well as at least momentary disorientation. Sim and Bowdoin checked their weapons, glanced at their GPS screens and headed off in the direction of the main lodge.

Its built-in tracking system had confirmed that the device was still at Camp David and satellite imagery had indicated that the tan Sprinter van was in a parking lot not far from the lodge. Given the extremely close proximity of the tracker's plotted coordinates to the location of the van, it appeared that the device probably remained inside it. They could only guess why this might be the case since the Camp David compound offered numerous options. Of course, there was sufficient space inside the van to examine and access the device with no difficulty, and leaving it there meant that as few eyes as possible would see it, so perhaps it made a certain kind of sense. Keeping it mobile made some sense, too. In any case, if the device proved not to be in the van, it had to be someplace quite nearby, although likely in someplace less accessible than was the van.

The parking lot was unlit and very little light spilled over from other parts of the compound. But as they approached its perimeter, staying low and as hidden as the sparse shrubs and occasional small tree would allow, their night vision goggles allowed them to clearly see the van among the smattering of cars and SUVs parked there. There were traffic cones blocking out the spaces to each side of the van, so it was clear on all four sides. That would make it more easily accessible, but also provide less cover as they approached.

On the other hand, they did not expect the van to be heavily guarded. After all, beyond the President and Rip Carver, it was likely that no one else knew what was inside it, or its real value. Of course, the Secret Service and CIA mindset would not allow them to leave it completely unprotected, either, no matter how secure the setting or how low the level of knowledge of its significance. As Sim and Bowdoin remained stock-still, gazing out at the parking lot, they could see one man sitting on the van's back bumper drinking coffee from a cardboard cup. An AK-47 sat on the ground at his feet.

Bowdoin pointed toward the back corner of the lot and Sim followed him stealthily along the grass that edged the paved area. There was a black SUV parked in the corner space and as Bowdoin very slowly came around the front of it, he caught sight of two other men and immediately pulled back. Using hand signals, he told Sim how many guards there were and that they were posted in the grass perhaps five yards in from the pavement, one to each side of the van. He then signaled that he would take the two in the grass and she would have to deal with the man seated on the rear bumper, and that they would move on a count of five. He tapped his night vision goggles, as well, suggesting they be left down.

Bowdoin remained motionless, crouched next to the left front fender of the SUV, while Sim moved away slowly along the side of the big vehicle, stopping when she reached its rear bumper. Both readied their weapons and got into position to spring out of their hiding places. When he was ready, Bowdoin turned to her, saw that she was also set, and held his gloved fist in the air. As Sim watched, he raised one finger for each second as he counted to five. The instant all five of Bowdoin's fingers were extended they sprang from cover, Bowdoin running through the grass toward the two men, Sim double-timing across the pavement toward the back of the van.

For his part, Bowdoin got off a shot on the run before either man could raise his weapon. The round hit the first man flat in the stomach and he instantly crumpled to the ground. Bowdoin never slowed and was still running at full speed toward the second one when he lowered his shoulder and executed a perfect open-field tackle, ramming into the man, who dropped to the ground, writhing in pain, and sending his AK-47 flying. Bowdoin easily beat his injured quarry to his feet and tackled the man again just as he tried raising a Glock pistol in Bowdoin's direction. Bowdoin disarmed the man as they hit the dirt, the man clutching his right wrist. It was not until then that Bowdoin heard Sim's muffled shot. It was followed by the sound of the cardboard coffee cup hitting the pavement, along with the man who had been holding it.

Both intruders quickly removed plastic zip ties and auto injector pens from their packs, bound the injured men's wrists and ankles and then hit each in the thigh with a single dose of a strong sedative. Once they were certain the three men were out cold, they cut off the zip ties and put the plastic pieces in their pockets and regrouped in the grass near the front of the van, remaining silent and still, waiting to see if anything resembling the cavalry might be coming.

Edan had prepared a small, electronic device to unlock the Sprinter's doors. Once Sim and Bowdoin were certain that they would have no further company, they flipped up their night vision goggles, unlocked the van and went around to its rear doors. They opened the doors and to their relief saw that the device sat there, covered, exactly where it had been when they left on Friday.

"Excellent," Sim, smiling broadly, said before they climbed into the back of the van, closing the doors softly behind them once they were inside. Then Bowdoin removed the cover from the device and tossed it aside.

"You're on, skinny," he said.

Sim flashed a middle finger at him, then immediately removed her helmet and unlaced and took off her boots. As she undid the straps of her pack, Bowdoin took a lightweight gas mask from his and helped her put it on. Holding it by one of its straps, she then unzipped her pack and checked to see that the two, quart-sized insulated bottles inside it were undamaged before zipping the pack closed again.

"I'll be damned if I could ever see holes in the floor of that thing," Bowdoin said softly, hooking a thumb at the device, "but if Duff says they're there, then I guess they're there."

"You need a strong magnifying glass to see them," Sim said, her voice barely penetrating the mask, "but there are thousands of them. It's kind of like a microscopic honeycomb."

"If you say so," Bowdoin told her. "Ready?"

Sim nodded, eased herself toward the device's entry slat and almost immediately disappeared through it. Once there, she took one of the bottles out of her pack, unscrewed its top and began pouring its contents onto the pale pink floor, starting with the side furthest away from the slat and working slowly back toward it. As she did, noxious looking fumes began to rise out of the floor. At the same time, the pale pink hue began to disappear and the floor began turning opaque as the liquid spread and covered more of it. When the bottle was empty, she screwed the cap back on it, slid it into her pack and got out the second bottle, unscrewing its top and continuing to pour out the caustic contents. As she did, the remainder of the floor began to lose its color and it became dark inside the device.

The second bottle was nearly empty as her backside bumped up against the side wall of the device, touching the edges of the entry slat. But the slat was no longer functional and she did not simply find herself outside the device. She stopped pouring, capped the bottle, put it down on the floor and tossed the pack out through the narrow entryway. Then she turned sideways and slowly eased herself through it, out of the device. Getting down on her knees at the no-longer-magical opening, she reached inside the device, grabbed the bottle and poured its remaining contents on the last, small undamaged portion of the floor.

When it was done, she grabbed her pack, stood up, took off the gas mask and handed it to Bowdoin. She screwed the top back on the bottle and put it into the pack, beside the other empty bottle, then zipped the pack closed.

"So, how's it feel to wipe out the most amazing computer and battery pack ever invented?" Bowdoin asked as Sim stepped into her boots and began to lace them up.

"I'd rather think of it as saving the world from the likes of Edwin Greavy or Rip Carver or God-knows-who else," Sim said, as she donned her helmet.

They put the cover on the device, left the van through the driver's door and made their way back the way they had come, staying low, their night vision goggles once again deployed. Once they reached the spot where they had left their parachutes, they gathered them up and folded them as small as they could, stowing the chutes in nylon bags taken from their packs.

They started walking east, following a route plotted earlier on their GPSs, hiking for almost a half hour before they reached a remote stretch of Route 15. As they crouched in the dark on the shoulder of the country road, Sim sent a text message on the disposable cell phone she carried in her pack. Seconds later they could hear the sound of a car engine being started and soon after that a black Chevrolet Suburban pulled up next to them, its lights off. Sim and Bowdoin got into the back seat and stowed their gear behind them in the luggage area as the driver turned on the headlights and pulled out onto the road.

"So, how'd it go, kids?" Edan Duff asked.

36

RIP CARVER WAS the first to discover that something was amiss, a discovery he made almost as soon as he began his daily run at six-thirty on Sunday morning.

As Carver jogged across the parking lot on his way to the path that marked the start of his two-mile circuit, he was greeted by the sight of the Secret Service agent who had been stationed behind the van lying on the pavement, unmoving, The agent's AK lay on the ground a yard from his body. Next to it was a cardboard coffee cup, brown liquid still pooled on the pavement nearby. Carver crouched down beside the man and checked for breathing and a pulse and there was no doubt that he was alive, but he was unconscious, and no amount of shouting or shaking could rouse him. Carver pulled his iPhone out of the plastic holster clipped to the waist of his running shorts and speed-dialed Ensign Cross' number. Then he dialed the special number for dedicated emergency services in nearby Thurmont, Maryland, telling them he needed paramedics as soon as possible.

As he ended the call, he noticed the spent bean bag round lying on the ground, not far away.

Shit," he muttered, leaving it where it was.

"Two more over here!" Cross, wearing yoga pants and a sports bra, yelled from the other side of the van as Carver ended the call.

He ran to where she knelt, beside one of the two agents who lay on their sides in the grass. She tried to rouse one of the men and Carver rushed to the other's side. Like the agent Carver had discovered behind the van, both men were breathing but unconscious and could not be awakened. It was then that he noticed another spent bean bag round, a few feet away in the grass. He left it where it was and redialed the emergency services number, told them there were actually three men down and then rushed to the back of the van and tried the doors.

They were locked.

"Stay here," he told Cross, "I'm going to go get the keys."

He jogged off to his cabin, returning shortly with a Mercedes key fob. He pressed the unlock button and hauled the rear doors open, his heart pounding. The device was still there and it appeared not to have been moved.

"Nothing missing?" Cross, coming up beside him and staring into the cargo compartment at the covered device, asked.

Carver did not reply but stepped up into the van and shut the doors, leaving Cross to stare at the back of the van. He removed the cover and slowly approached the entry slat, getting what he thought was close enough to get pulled inside, yet nothing happened.

"What the fuck?" he muttered.

He backed a few inches away and then tried again, moving even closer to the slat this time. Again, nothing happened. Tentatively, he reached out and stuck his hand through the narrow opening. When nothing happened, he thrust his entire arm inside. There was no reaction whatsoever from the device. He quickly searched the van, including the passenger compartment, and could find nothing damaged or disturbed, so he went and stood in front of the slat again. He was too big to slide in through the eight-inch wide opening, so he got down on one knee and gingerly stuck his head inside the opening.

When he and McKinney had gone inside the device it had been surprisingly light inside, despite the dimly-lit interior of the van. Now, however, it was dark. He slowly withdrew his head and went back to the passenger compartment where found a flashlight in the glove box. He went and knelt down in front of the slat again, turned on the flashlight and stuck his hand inside, then slowly got his head as far into the gap as he could. He could tell immediately by the lack of color in the floor that whoever had paid them a visit in the night had somehow damaged the device's computer and battery pack. And judging by the slat's behavior and the darkness inside, he was reasonably certain that the damage was serious.

He put down the flashlight and ran his palm slowly over the floor of the device. It was not quite as smooth as it looked, unlike the device's other surfaces, and while he could not really see holes when he picked up and turned on the flashlight, whether he shined the light directly downward or at an angle, he was pretty sure they were there and that the intruders had done their damage by pouring some sort of acid all over the floor.

He got up slowly and took another moment to look around the interior of the van before opening the rear doors and re-joining Cross outside.

"Above my pay grade, I know," she said, "but I suppose I'm allowed to ask if there's anything missing, out of place, whatever?"

"Not that I can tell," he answered absently, shutting and locking the doors. "Wait here for the EMTs. There's something I need to do."

He did not wait for a reply but jogged off again in the direction of the cabins. As he opened the door to his again, he could hear water running in the shower and he hurried to the bathroom.

"Don't freak out, it's me," he shouted, stripping off his shorts and tee shirt and pulling the shower curtain back, and as he stepped into the shower beside Mary McKinney, he added, "We've got a problem."

Ten minutes later, Carver, dressed in khakis and a golf shirt, unshaven and his hair still wet, was back outside. As he walked quickly to the parking lot, he saw that two rescue squad vehicles were now parked there, not far from the van, their lights flashing and their rear doors open. Three more agents had come outside, presumably the ones that the downed agents had relieved at midnight, and they, Carver and Ensign Cross watched as the EMTs examined the three apparently unconscious men. They, too, were unable to wake the men, but after several minutes came over to explain that their vital signs were normal and that they seemed more or less unharmed.

"If I had to guess," the oldest of the EMTs told them, "I'd say they've been drugged, probably with some kind of sedative or anesthetic. Two of them were also hit by what looks like bean bag rounds and have some bruising from it but no serious injuries, it looks like. The other appears to have been in a fight. They're stable so we're going to transport them like this and let the docs figure out how to deal with it."

Carver thanked them and as the three downed agents were loaded into the trucks, asked Cross and the others if there were enough personnel around to organize a grid search of the area.

"There's only a small staff when POTUS isn't here," she replied, "so no way. Why don't you save me some time and call my boss directly and have her authorize getting a bunch of folks out here. Once that's done, I'll handle the details. For now, I've got a checklist of other things that these guys and I need to get done right away."

Cross and the others headed back to her office and Carver dialed the number she had given him, pacing around the parking lot, his iPhone pressed to his ear, as he tried to reach Cross' boss, a commander who was stationed at the Pentagon. To his great surprise, he got through to the woman almost immediately and, while he was speaking with her, Mary McKinney joined him in the now otherwise empty parking lot.

"What's going on?" she whispered in his free ear.

He held up an index finger and when he ended his call two minutes later, turned to her and said, "We had visitors last night, early this morning actually. I have no idea how many or how the hell they got in, but they managed to overpower the three Secret Service ass-holes guarding the van and drug them. I just put them in ambulances."

McKinney's face went white and she turned toward the Sprinter van.

"They didn't take the device?" she asked.

Carver shook his head.

"I may not know exactly how they got in," he told her, "but I'm pretty sure they wouldn't've been able to just drive that thing out of here."

"Thank God!" she said. "But then what the hell were they after?"

"I'm afraid they might have found a different way to keep us, or anyone else, from using the thing," Carver replied. "It looks like the floor might actually be porous, like with a million really tiny holes--"

"Wait, you went inside it?" she asked.

"I'm a bit too big for that now that the functionality's gone," he told her. "It no longer sucks you in. I had to stick my head and arm in to it. Anyway, I'm guessing someone poured something down those holes, probably some kind of solvent or acid. The floor is no longer pink, the entry slat doesn't work and it's dark inside."

"Shit."

"Yeah, shit," he agreed.

McKinney turned and walked quickly to the van. Carver followed, unlocked and opened the back doors and helped her inside, closing the doors behind them. McKinney immediately went and stood in front of the slat, as close as she could get. Nothing happened.

"Here, take this and stick your head in," Carver said, handing her the flashlight. "Better yet, see if you can squeeze into it."

McKinney had dressed quickly in jeans and a tee shirt. She turned sideways, reaching the hand that held the flashlight into the device, then, moving very slowly sideways, leaned her hip inside and slowly turned her body so that her large right breast, then her left, were able to make it through the slat. In another few seconds, her whole body was inside the device.

"You're right, it's dark in here," she said, her voice echoing out through the slat, "not at all like before. And it's not nearly as quiet, either." In another few seconds, she added, "And the tensile augmentation's no longer working, either."

Carver went to the slat, leaned in and stuck his head inside. McKinney was down on her knees, the flashlight beam aimed at the floor, running her hand back and forth over it.

"Clever," she said, "destroy the computer and batteries and you've effectively destroyed the whole thing."

"Yeah, I was afraid of that," Carver said. "So tell me, how's DARPA fixed for guys who can salvage the world's most sophisticated computer after it's apparently had something very damaging poured into it? Oh, and cutting edge battery expertise might be nice, too."

McKinney sighed.

"I suppose anything's possible," she said, "but I wouldn't get my hopes up."

"Believe me, they're not," Carver said.

He withdrew his head and arm and McKinney wriggled out.

"So, what now?" she asked as they stood there, staring at the now-useless device.

Carver folded his arms across his chest and frowned.

"I get to call the President and tell him what's happened."

37

EDAN TOOK OVER the entire Whisky A Go Go on a Saturday night in early May for his wedding to Sim and arranged for The Soft Parade, the best Doors cover band he could find, to perform.

The two hundred or so mostly youthful guests seemed to enjoy the music and the retro theme of the event, but to Edan and Sim it was the ultimate inside joke to be at the Whisky, again, among a throng of young people dressed in late-Sixties attire, listening to a guy who was a dead-ringer for Jim Morrison belt out the band's biggest hits. This time, though, there was an endless supply of high-end champagne and appetizing food prepared by Edan's chef, and there was no need for old money or fake IDs.

They wore the same weathered bell bottomed jeans as they had to 1966 and Sim had on the same off white floral lace-accented blouse with gold trim while Edan wore the same black turtleneck sweater as before, as well as the same uncomfortable shoes and clunky jewelry. Several of the women at the party came up to Sim to ask where she had gotten her handbag, the burgundy leather Bohemian Mexican hippie bag with rigid brown leather handles that she had carried into the Whisky back then, too.

"I think it might be time to go have our own party," Edan whispered to Sim at midnight.

Things were still going strong but her response was to take his hand and lead him quietly out the front door, onto Sunset Boulevard. One of Dale Bowdoin's people followed them at a discreet distance as they walked quickly west down Sunset, slowing their pace as soon as they turned right onto Hilldale Avenue. They strolled through the quiet neighborhood, arms around each others' waists, aware that the tail was there but ignoring it, as they turned left onto Shoreham Drive and then onto Ozeta Terrace. As they walked up the drive toward the modest, old house, Edan suddenly took Sim in his arms and kissed her, hard, passionately. He had done the same thing in 1966 and she had not fought him, but she had not responded, either, she had not been able to then. Now her response was electric and she clung to him with all her might for a long time after the kiss finally ended.

He had arranged for the house to be furnished and they raced each other upstairs to the master bedroom. As they stood, breathing hard, next to the king bed, the contest moved on to one aimed at getting off as much clothing as possible, as quickly as possible. Remarkable as their lovemaking had been ever since they had become reacquainted at the meeting in Edan's office with Mary McKinney and the others, there was an eagerness to it that dazzled them both.

They eventually fell asleep, waking after only a few hours to bright sunlight streaming through the lace curtains. They made love again, this time more slowly but with no less intensity. They showered and dressed afterwards and went downstairs to find a breakfast of scrambled eggs, bacon and hash brown potatoes waiting for them in chafing dishes on the dining room table, beside a basket of breads and muffins and a Nespresso coffeemaker. Edan brewed two cups of coffee while Sim served each of them a hearty helping of breakfast. When they were finished, Edan texted his assistant, saying they would be ready in forty-five minutes and that he should advise Edan's pilots that the plan was to be wheels-up an hour after that.

"Now will you tell me where we're going?" Sim asked as they put the dirty dishes in the sink.

Edan smiled.

"First stop, Barbados," he replied. "It's a long way out in the Caribbean but the plane can make it nonstop. I rented a house on a cliff side that you're not going to believe. If we like it there, we can just stay for a while. If not, we can go island hopping around the Caribbean. I've heard that the Grenadines may be the most beautiful area in the world to sail."

Sim grinned and they went back upstairs to finish getting ready. A few minutes later, their driver came inside and carried their luggage out to a waiting limo.

"Thank you," Sim, draping her arms around his neck, said softly as they were about to leave the house, "for saving my life, more than once."

Edan shrugged.

"Hey, it's what I do," he said, smiling.

Dale Bowdoin was standing next to the car when they opened the front door, and he looked around carefully before motioning for Edan and Sim to walk out to the limo. He held the rear door open and Sim slid inside. Before he joined her, Edan asked Bowdoin how long he thought this *cloak-and-dagger stuff* needed to go on.

"It's been way over a month since Camp David," he added, "and there hasn't been a word out of Greavy or any of his people."

Bowdoin shrugged.

"You know the old saying, boss," he replied, "A President scorned has a long, fuckin' memory."

"I'll be sure to add that one to my dictionary of famous quotes," Edan said, laying a hand on Bowdoin's shoulder.

They waited for a signal from the driver of a silver Range Rover that had been parked at the end of the driveway before Bowdoin, in the front passenger seat of the limo, gave their driver the okay to leave. It was a Sunday, so traffic was only moderately heavy on the 5 and they pulled up to the private jet terminal at John Wayne Airport, the Range Rover right behind them, exactly forty-five minutes later. Edan and Sim followed Bowdoin through the terminal hand-in-hand. Bowdoin ran on ahead, going outside to where Edan's Boeing jet waited. He paused next to the big plane and checked the area, then jogged up the boarding stairs and disappeared into the cabin. Two minutes later he signaled for Edan and Sim to join him and the man who had been driving the Range Rover led them outside and across the ramp to the plane. He waited on the ground while the newlyweds started up the boarding stairs, but Sim stopped a few steps up and turned to face Edan.

"I love you," she said, and Edan realized it was the first time she had said it.

She turned away and started up the stairs again but almost immediately a single, high-caliber shot rang out and echoed all around them. Sim's head was jolted suddenly to the left and she collapsed instantly and lay sprawled out on the stairway, dead before the echo had even subsided.

The man on the tarmac raced up and threw himself on top of Edan and both landed heavily on the steel stairway. Bowdoin was on top of Sim a moment later but there were no more shots and after several minutes, during which Edan tried desperately to reach out and touch his motionless wife, both men stood up.

Edan crawled up to her then, taking her lifeless body into his arms. There was one entry wound and it was not far from the spot where Sim had once tried to end her own life, but this one was heinously larger and had done irreparable damage.

"I love you," Edan said softly.

Epilogue

AFTER SIM'S FUNERAL, Edan closed up the house near Monarch Beach and bought a boat, a very large, very capable one. It was a fifty-five meter, Dutch-built Feadship yacht, less than five years old, which he purchased from a Russian businessman who had recently acquired an even larger, more extravagant boat. Dale Bowdoin had taken delivery of it and overseen its ferrying to a shipyard in Germany. There, in the utmost secrecy that money and threats of physical violence could arrange, much of the guest accommodation deck had been converted into a laboratory of Edan's design. And its name had been changed to Dark Fire.

The Duff Group PR department issued only a single press release after Jane Garrison Duff's death. It recounted in simple terms the personal tragedy that had befallen their founder and said he had forthwith withdrawn from active participation in the business and planned to spend the foreseeable future sailing around the world.

Dale Bowdoin had come along with him on Dark Fire, along with Edan's chef and house staff and an experienced crew vetted by Bowdoin. As the press release had promised, they plied the oceans and seas and bays of Europe, Africa and Asia. But it was not any form of post-trauma healing or solace that Edan pursued during the long voyage. Rather, it was the acquisition of an unusual list of chemicals, materials and specialized equipment, and these he purchased piecemeal from hundreds of suppliers in dozens of cities on the three continents. The costs involved for each transaction were never enough to draw undue scrutiny or trigger regulatory notifications to the authorities, and no supplier was aware of the purchases made from any of the others.

Their itinerary was not designed to take in the sights or follow the most pleasant weather or avail themselves of any of the other bountiful offerings or distractions that the towns and cities they visited could have provided. Rather, it had been crafted solely on the order in which the acquisitions needed to be made so that Edan, locked away in his lab for most of each day, could progress from step to step to step as he methodically implemented the multi-thousand step plan that would ultimately yield version 2.0 of the device.

When it was finished, a year after they started out, Dark Fire docked in Palermo, on Sicily's northwest coast, where neither Edan nor Bowdoin had ever been. Bowdoin rented a van and they transported the new device from the port to an abandoned construction site on the outskirts of the city. There they made their first and only test and it went off without a hitch. Once the device had been safely returned to the boat, they set out for Tenerife in the Canary Islands where all personnel were given extensive paid R&R, the boat was listed for sale and Edan's Boeing jet met them. Edan and Bowdoin transported the new device to Tenerife North Airport and accompanied it on its flight back to Southern California.

The question of where, when and how he would attempt to influence the events that had led to Sim's death had never been far from Edan's mind, just as the possibility of failure had never occurred to him. But he knew that whatever he decided to do, he would once again be tempting the fates, or testing the capacity of the universe to absorb change, or seeking out the limits of quantum physics and the multiverse, however you chose to characterize it.

He never forgot that Sim had said that if they carried out the Suez mission, people who would have died would not die and that therefore people who might not have been born would be born, with heaven knew what results. Of course they had not carried it out and nothing else among the very limited uses that Edan had made of the original device had tested the impact of such a dramatic alteration of the so-called fabric of space-time as he was about to attempt. His plan, if it succeeded, would mean that someone who had already died, in one quantum universe at least, would come back to life, although that characterization of it might not be the correct one. Quantum theory, or at least the *many worlds*, multiverse aspect of it, suggested that Sim would remain dead in the universe in which she had already died and in which Edan now still lived, but that she would not necessarily be dead in another universe.

Edan and Bowdoin had gone back to the morning after the wedding, to a building just off the grounds of John Wayne Airport, which Bowdoin had identi-fied as the sniper's lair. There, before the limo carry-ing Edan and Sim arrived, Bowdoin had surprised and badly wounded the shooter, rendering him unable to take the fatal shot. They used facial recognition soft-ware to identify the wounded man as a former Army Ranger, now a Secret Service agent assigned to protect-ing the President, and sent cellphone photos of him to the President and the CIA Director, along with a brief description of how the evidence would be archived and when and how it would be used against them, if needed.

Edan then programmed the device to return Dale Bowdoin to the present and to self-destruct moments after its arrival, and slipped out just as the vibrations in its floor had begun.

• • •

Halfway down to the beach, she slipped off her flip-flops and striped beach cover-up and stuffed them into her bag, slung the bag over her shoulder and a minute later sauntered onto the sand clad only in a high-cut, one-piece bathing suit, red baseball cap and sunglasses.

The beach in question, Bathsheba, was on Barbados' east coast, its Atlantic side, and she had quickly discovered how different it was from any other island beach she had visited. She walked along the sand passing cacti and giant boulders on one side while foaming lines of giant breakers rushed up to the shoreline on the other. It was rougher than any beach she had ever been to but was strikingly beautiful in its own way.

As she approached the area known as Soup Bowl, dozens of surfers on boards of various colors and styles worked on their technique or practiced their water-borne poses. The one known locally as Tyler Leeds stood out from the rest, even though several of the other men around him in the waves also sported lean, muscular bodies and dirty blond ponytails. Some of them might also have grown up in southern California, like him, and a few might even have won their first surfing championship as teenagers, as he had at sixteen when his name had been Edan Duff.

He had given up surfing soon after, focused as he was on other things, but the rust had fallen off quickly after only a few dozen mornings at Bathsheba. And it was not just his expertise that set him apart. He used an old-school Bing long board shaped in the 1960s by Bing Copeland himself and he lavished as much attention on it as other men might on a rare old sports car.

She sat in the sand and watched him surf for half an hour, until it was clear that he had made his last ride of the day. As he began walking through the shallows toward the beach with his board on his shoulder she got up and jogged over to meet him.

"I never get tired of watching you," she said, looking at him and smiling.

"Must be the electric blue board shorts," he replied, slowing his pace.

"Not exactly," she told him.

He had waited until they arrived in Barbados to tell Sim what had happened and she had slowly come to terms with it during the three months they had been in

Barbados. Although she claimed to remember hearing the rifle shot, to his great relief she had no memories, dream-like or otherwise, that might be attributable to her death. So now it was Edan alone who had the dream-like memories of a time lived, and then lived again.

He stopped walking, laid his board down in the sand and kissed her.

"So, what do you want to do for lunch?" she asked when they parted.

"I'm easy," he said, "your choice."

"Well, I was thinking about the Soup Bowl Café earlier," Sim told him, "although now that I think about it again, I realize that you make a better flying fish sandwich than they do, when I can convince you to cook."

Edan smiled.

"Well, today's your lucky day," he said, smiling.

Sim laughed and kissed him again.

"Every day is my lucky day," she said.

www.ingramcontent.com/pod-product-compliance
Lightning Source LLC
Chambersburg PA
CBHW061322170626
46817CB00001B/270